Readers love
KATE MCMURRAY

The Silence of the Stars

"This is a must read for hopeless romantics…."
—MM Good Book Reviews

"I found *The Silence of the Stars* easy to read, it was sweet and gentle, and flowed well."
—Prism Book Alliance

"I love Kate's writing, it's quiet and thoughtful and she gives her characters so much depth."
—The Tipsy Bibliophile

The Stars that Tremble

"*The Stars That Tremble* has so many lovely elements to its story that it can be appreciated on multiple levels."
—Joyfully Jay

"Kate McMurray picked up my imaginary gauntlet and smacked me with it. This book was fantastic."
—Live Your Life, Buy the Book

By KATE MCMURRAY

Blind Items
Four Corners
Kindling Fire with Snow
Playing Ball (Anthology)
The Stars that Tremble • The Silence of the Stars
A Walk in the Dark
What There Is
When the Planets Align

Published by DREAMSPINNER PRESS
http://www.dreamspinnerpress.com

WHEN THE
PLANETS ALIGN

KATE MCMURRAY

Dreamspinner Press

Published by
DREAMSPINNER PRESS

5032 Capital Circle SW, Suite 2, PMB# 279, Tallahassee, FL 32305-7886 USA
http://www.dreamspinnerpress.com/

When the Planets Align
© 2014 Kate McMurray.

Cover Art
© 2014 Aaron Anderson.
aaronbydesign55@gmail.com
Cover content is for illustrative purposes only and any person depicted on the cover is a model.

ISBN: 978-1-63216-610-4
Digital ISBN: 978-1-63216-611-1
Library of Congress Control Number: 2014952115
First Edition December 2014

Printed in the United States of America
∞
This paper meets the requirements of
ANSI/NISO Z39.48-1992 (Permanence of Paper).

CHAPTER 1

THE LAST leg of the very long trip was the train from Philadelphia to New York City, although Philadelphia had mainly been a means of postponing the inevitable. Simon had certainly wanted to see his old college roommate and the new house on the outskirts of Philly's historic district. And yet, during his two days playing tourist in the City of Brotherly Love, Simon had done nothing but fret about Michael.

Now he sat on a train, unable to read the biography of Thomas Jefferson he'd bought at a gift shop, gazing out the window and watching industrial New Jersey pass by.

How long had it been exactly since he'd last seen Michael? Eight months? A year? Was their friendship really so far gone that this much time could pass without their seeing each other, as if it were nothing?

Simon missed Michael in the depths of his soul. He dreaded seeing Michael again.

It had been a long six years since he'd left New York, and yet it felt like a blink. The move was never really intended to be permanent, but it had felt necessary at the time. He'd been offered a job overseas the same week his life had crashed down around him, and he'd taken it. He spent a year keeping his head down and licking his wounds in Dubai, three years in London, a year in San Francisco, a few months in Chicago. Now his brokerage firm had transferred him to the New York office on Whitehall Street in the Financial District, and though it wasn't quite his dream job, it felt like an opportunity for a fresh start in the city that had always had a pull on him.

He'd always intended to come back.

He thought of Michael, something he couldn't seem to keep himself from doing, despite putting thousands of miles between them, despite the distractions of sex and work and the mundane details of daily life. Though his stomach churned at the idea of this reunion, though he felt the inevitability of it as if it were as natural as the forward march of time, though he was now much older and very different than the boy who had once whiled away lazy afternoons with Michael as if they had all the time in the world, Simon couldn't help but cling to the happy memories. Sometimes they subsumed the turbulent ones, sometimes they caught him off guard during his dark moments, sometimes they convinced him his new life in New York would be all right after all. It was hard to shake the bad memories, though, hard to forgive and forget, hard to pretend Michael hadn't destroyed Simon's life just as surely as Simon had destroyed Michael's.

Yet there was a rubber band around his heart, one that stretched to Michael's heart, and so Simon could walk away, but he'd always be pulled back.

His ears popped as the train chugged into the tunnel under the Hudson River, and everything went dark for a moment as there was some kind of electrical glitch on the train. For that one sweet moment, everything was quiet and still. But as suddenly as it had happened, it ended. The lights came on, the train's AC hummed, and people around him talked excitedly about what they'd do when they arrived in the city.

If he had it all to do over again, Simon wondered, would he have done things differently?

As the train slowed and pulled up to the platform beneath Penn Station, Simon shook his head and decided regrets were futile. He couldn't change the past. All he could do was look forward to the future. To New York. To Michael.

1997

IT WAS one of those friendships that had lasted so long neither could remember how it had begun. Simon's mother seemed to recall an incident in the beginning of their school career that had landed them both in the principal's office, with little remorse expressed on either of their parts. As far as Simon was concerned, however, there had never been a time when he and Michael had not been friends.

Their other friends didn't get it. Michael was loud and opinionated. Simon was quiet and studious. How could they stand to spend time with each other?

It never occurred to Simon not to.

Absolutely no one had been surprised when Michael burst out of the closet at age fourteen. The summer before high school, he'd gotten a crazy, asymmetrical haircut and recruited Simon to help him dye it purple. Michael's parents had been horrified—by the hair, not by Michael's homosexuality, which they seemed mostly unfazed by—but Michael had loved it, touching his hair whenever they walked by a mirror and saying, "It's so me." Simon had also accompanied Michael to the piercing place in the mall, and even though Simon was pretty sure Michael's parents were supposed to have signed something, the bored college girl working that day had pierced both of Michael's ears with no questions asked. Simon had eyed the piercing gun suspiciously, warning Michael his ears were bound to get infected. Michael surprised Simon by actually taking care of the piercings, though, and gloated when, six weeks later, he put in a pair of silver hoops, no infection in sight.

The girls loved Michael. He was harmless, Simon supposed—a friend, a confidant, a shopping buddy. He wasn't a real man, not in the girls' estimation, because real men were sexy and threatening when you were a high school girl. Or so Simon imagined. He certainly found men sexy and threatening.

The girls did not notice Simon.

Which was just as well. Now they were juniors, and he'd taken to practicing saying, "I'm gay too," to his bedroom mirror, intending to tell Michael—and his family—just as soon as he could screw up the courage. That wasn't going so well. It wasn't that he was afraid of Michael's reaction—he was pretty sure Michael already knew—it was that his feelings were complicated. It wasn't like he was in love with Michael or anything, but Michael was his best friend, and he didn't want anything to change between them. They existed in a stasis now where Michael didn't date but was surrounded by a swarm of girls basically all the time, and he would tease Simon about how he should pick off the weak ones for dates, and it was weird, but it was okay.

Honestly, even if Simon had desires, he wasn't willing to act on them. Mostly he wanted to get his schoolwork done so he could get the grades he needed to go to college far away. His only goal was to get the hell out of Iowa.

They were in Simon's bedroom one afternoon, early in the spring of junior year. Michael was considering the lengthy list of girls who had asked him to be their junior prom date while Simon was studying for a trig exam. Michael kept distracting Simon from his studies, but Simon didn't much care; he knew he could pass this exam in his sleep.

Michael had more or less decided which girl he'd be taking, and then he said, "Mom wants me to go to this college fair thing at the VFW hall on Saturday. Come with?"

"Okay. Why is she making you go?"

"I'm supposed to be thinking about where I want to go to college." Michael rolled his eyes.

This seemed sensible to Simon and he didn't understand why Michael was being so blasé about it. "Do you already know where you want to go to college?"

Michael tilted his head. "I figured I'd go wherever you go."

"Really?"

"You're not going to Iowa, are you?"

Simon lived just across Route 6 from the University of Iowa. Most of the people in their neighborhood in Iowa City worked for the university in some capacity, and many graduates of their high school ended up there. Simon couldn't imagine a worse fate. "No. Definitely not."

"Good. Then I'll be happy to go wherever you want to go."

Simon closed his book and put it aside. He swiveled around on his desk chair so he could better see Michael, who was lounging on Simon's bed. "New York City. I want to go to New York City."

Michael grinned. "Then we'll go to New York City." As if it were just that easy. He tilted his head and added, "Any special reason you want to go to New York?"

It wasn't Iowa, for one thing. But Simon had heard New York was a good place for a gay kid who couldn't be himself at home. He'd been checking books on LGBT history out of the library and hiding them under his bed so his mother wouldn't find out; almost all of those books talked about New York, and Simon had been fantasizing intensely about moving for months.

Simon rocked in his chair a little, working out how to say all that to Michael.

Michael sat up and looked at Simon with his brow furrowed in concern. "You okay?"

"Yeah, I…. Michael. I'm… that is, I want to go to New York because, well…."

"Spit it out."

Simon sighed. "I'm gay too, you know."

Michael's eyes went wide with astonishment.

"Are you surprised?" Simon asked, feeling a combination of anxiety and frustration.

"No, not about the gay thing. That was just not what I was expecting you to say." Michael wiped his mouth. "I mean, I knew you're gay, but I wasn't sure you knew."

"I know."

"Good. Come here." Michael patted the space next to him on the bed.

Simon was leery. He grasped the back of the chair, all ready to say, "No, I'll stay here, thanks," but something about the look on Michael's face comforted him, like Michael would give him a hug and tell him it was all right.

They'd been sharing spaces since they'd first learned to write their names—sharing tents on camping trips and bedrooms on family vacations and sofas while playing video games. They'd even slept in the same bed a few times, albeit not since Michael's grand declaration that he preferred men to women. This moment was different from all of those times, electrically charged in a way Simon wasn't comfortable with. His heart rate doubled as he stood up and took a deep breath. His stomach fluttered as he sat next to Michael on the bed, as they both leaned back against Simon's headboard.

It was the same bright blue headboard that had been propped up behind his bed since he was eight years old. It had gold stars painted on it, an art project from when Simon was thirteen. It was childish, foolish, just like the action figures on the bookcase, the stack of video games in the corner, the posters of his favorite cartoon characters on the wall. Everything about his room was carefully curated, placed with the goal of courting no controversy, drawing no attention. It had worked so far with Simon's mother, who had had never deigned to comment on the décor, but Michael, of course, made fun of him whenever he came over. Michael had taken to pinning up magazine pictures of hot male celebrities on his walls—something Simon couldn't see himself doing, well, ever—and kept pointing out that having a poster of a dog playing baseball up in one's bedroom was a very fifth grade thing to do.

Simon was hyperaware of the ephemera in his room and how very childish it all was, down to the baby blue bedspread that was covering up an old set of sheets adorned with race cars. None of it was to his taste, but all of it was intended to convince his mother that he was not having the sorts of sexual feelings that were now racing through his body, drawing him to Michael.

This was about to get strange.

"It's okay, you know," Michael said. "Like, I get it."

He was lately sporting hair the same color blue as the headboard, though his roots were a mess of his natural dark hair, peroxide blond, and fading blue dye. Simon's own blond hair was cut every six weeks at the same barber he'd been going to since he was eight years old.

"I just… I want to get out of this place," Simon said.

"I hear that." Michael smiled. "Have you told your parents? I mean about being gay."

"No. I haven't told anyone. Except for you just now. Obviously."

Michael's smile widened. "That's pretty exciting. I'm happy for you."

Heat flushed Simon's face. "Um. Thanks."

They sat together in silence for a few moments. Years of friendship meant that Michael and Simon were good at comfortable silences, but this one felt frantic and charged. Simon was at a total loss for what to say.

Then Michael said, "Can I try something?"

"What are you—"

Michael kissed Simon. It was the first time Simon had been kissed by anyone, and he wasn't sure how to react at first. Michael's eyes were closed, so Simon closed his own and leaned forward. He pressed back, returning the pressure he felt. Michael's lips were firm and slippery and weird. The sensation was so foreign that Simon wasn't certain he could categorize it as "good," although he didn't dislike it either.

Michael pulled back and grinned. "I have a crazy idea."

Sex was the first thing that popped into Simon's head, along with the sort of horror that could cause him to hyperventilate. "Oh, no. I'm not, like... I mean, my mom is right downstairs...."

"No, Simon." Michael laughed. "Although don't put ideas in my head. I was going to say that maybe you and I should be prom dates."

"What?"

Michael put his hand on the side of Simon's face and caressed Simon's cheek with his thumb. The gesture went a long way toward calming Simon down. He lifted his hand and rested it at Michael's wrist. They'd never touched each other this way before. It wasn't explicitly sexual, but it was more affectionate than anything that had ever happened between them.

Michael said, "You came out of the closet thirty seconds ago, so I know you're still adjusting to things, but think about it. I don't really want to go to my prom with a girl, but since you still hadn't decided if you were gay, I figured that was my best option. But now that you know and you're cool with it, we should go together."

All Simon could do was blink. "I don't... I just don't... I mean, I don't know if I'm ready for that."

Michael ruffled Simon's hair, which he must have known Simon would find annoying. "Think about it, okay?"

"I... okay. I'll think about it."

CHAPTER 2

Present Day

MICHAEL HAD a recurring anxiety dream in which he had to get somewhere by a certain time but couldn't. He'd accidentally get on the subway going uptown instead of downtown, or there would be some kind of accident that got him stuck in traffic, or he'd be trapped on a corner in the rain unable to get a cab.

The afternoon Simon returned to New York was his nightmare come to life. Michael had forgotten to charge his phone and it died. Thirty seconds after he plugged it in, Joan called, but he was too distracted to work out what she was trying to tell him. He couldn't find his keys. Then he couldn't find his left sneaker. Then he tripped over a toy truck and wound up sprawled across the living room floor. By the time he finally got out the door to go meet Simon at Penn Station, he was already ten minutes late.

In all the chaos, at least he didn't have much time to worry about Simon's arrival.

Michael had been wearing Simon down for the last year, explaining that he would always be welcome in New York, that he had a home here, that he belonged here. Simon had been on to him the whole time, pointing out that Joan leaving Michael was the reason Michael wanted Simon back. Michael had denied that vehemently. Simon didn't seem to believe him. Simon came home anyway.

Michael hadn't wanted him to leave to begin with.

He ran down the steps into the subway station at Fourteenth Street, swiped his card in the turnstile, and then got the dreaded "Insufficient Fare" error. He cursed and ran to the machine to put more money on his MetroCard, and then scrambled through the turnstile and down the next set of stairs as a train pulled into the station. He ran for it, but the train doors closed right as he got to them. The conductor stuck his head out the window and stared directly at Michael. Michael flipped him off as the train pulled out of the station.

He stumbled backward and sat on a bench, where he leaned forward and put his head in his hands. Maybe the whole damn universe was conspiring against him getting uptown to Penn Station, postponing this meeting between them. Michael had been looking forward to this for weeks, ever since Simon had called to say he had gotten that job in New York after all. He'd made some noise about getting a hotel room, but Michael had insisted Simon come stay with him. They'd lived together once, after all, so they knew they could peaceably cohabitate.

But could they really? They talked regularly, but it had been so long since Simon and Michael had been in the same city that Michael wasn't sure they were even much more than strangers anymore.

It was a quick trip on the 2 train up to Penn Station. Michael ran off the train the moment he could, down the stairs from the platform to the station, and then got snared in traffic mingling in front of the Long Island Railroad area. Somehow he had to get from one end of Penn Station to another in negative time, because Simon was probably already waiting.

God, Michael wanted to see Simon desperately. He'd been picturing the moment when they were reunited, and in his head, it was always romantic, the two of them falling into a tight embrace, their bodies fitting together the way they always had. In this fantasy, Simon would whisper in Michael's ear about how much he'd missed Michael and how happy he was to be home.

Home. Home was New York, not Iowa. Michael had that much figured out.

As Michael pushed through the loitering crowd like a salmon swimming upstream, he was aware that his fantasies about Simon were unlikely to come to pass, but that didn't stop his heart from speeding up in anticipation of seeing his old friend again. As he approached the designated meeting spot, he slowed down to revel in the moment a little.

As predicted, Simon was already standing under the departures board, looking intently at his phone. Michael smiled. He was sure he'd get an earful about being late, but he didn't care. Simon was home.

1997

THAT MICHAEL loved Simon was a given.

They'd known each other forever. They spent almost all their spare time together. Simon was maybe the only person in the world who really understood Michael. He suspected Simon shared in his frustration with their current lot in life.

Michael was trapped in his role as the sexless companion to the female population of his school, doomed to always be the center of attention as the novelty out gay kid—not that he hadn't asked for that attention, because of course he had, but things hadn't played out the way he'd expected they would. Well, at the end of the day, the issue at hand was that seven different girls had asked him to prom, but he wanted to go with a boy.

When he'd first broached this issue with Simon, Simon had said, "Just because the girls ask doesn't mean you have to say yes."

The problem was that, in small-town Iowa, other gay boys were thin on the ground.

Simon understood that too, and kept saying that Michael would have better luck in college.

Simon was the one person to whom Michael could say anything. He listened. He responded thoughtfully. He told Michael when Michael was being ridiculous. Simon was sweet and caring and so very smart. He was kind of uptight, yeah, but Michael liked that about him. Michael's parents were always saying that Simon was a good influence, that Simon kept Michael's impulsive nature in check. Michael, likewise, wanted to pull Simon out of his shell, wanted to help him cut loose, wanted to help bring him out into the world. Simon was the best guy Michael knew, and he deserved more than books and Iowa.

The kids at school didn't get it. Everyone, Michael's harem of girls in particular, asked him all the time how he could stand to hang out with nerdy, bookish Simon, and Michael always explained that the girls didn't know Simon like Michael did, that Simon seemed standoffish at times but he was actually just really shy, and that Simon studied so much so that he could get into a good school and leave Iowa behind for better things.

So, yeah. Michael loved Simon. That went without saying. But he didn't know he was *in love* with Simon until Simon had muttered, "I'm gay too, you know."

Michael's mom had been reading some book on how to relate to one's gay child, and Michael had been sneaking it out of his parents' room and reading passages every now and then. Most of what he'd learned from the book was that everyone was different—obviously Michael had cornered the market on different, so this was not a startling revelation—but that everyone came to terms with sexuality in their own way and in their own time. Michael had always assumed that Simon was kind of a late bloomer, and he held on to that opinion as Simon waffled about the prom, about kissing, about any physical contact at all. Simon wasn't ready yet, which was cool with Michael.

But, damn, now that everything was out in the open, Michael didn't want to wait.

Still, he went to the prom with a girl named Brynne, who was clearly auditioning to be his new best friend. Or something. He liked her fine but she didn't seem to understand that the fact that he was gay meant they couldn't be boyfriend and girlfriend. Two days after prom, she invited him to be her date to a big graduation party one of the popular seniors was throwing, and then she asked him to dinner, and that was when Michael figured out she was trying to turn him. He let her down gently. She'd cried.

So he was pretty glad when summer finally arrived.

He and Simon planned to drive to Chicago, part of Simon's court-mandated time with his father. Simon resented the hell out of it, an opinion he was not shy about expressing, so he talked Michael into going with him and had for the past three summers. "Having you around is like a buffer," Simon had said when he'd asked Michael to come with him again. "He's on better behavior with company that isn't family. Plus, having you around will keep me from getting bored on days he works long hours."

Michael had plans. There was the three-and-a-half-hour drive to Chicago just to start with—"Road trip!" Michael had giddily declared to much wary eyebrow on Simon's part—but then there would be four weeks in a city that sure beat the hell out of Iowa City and all that time alone with Simon to convince him that the two of them belonged together. Because they totally did and Michael knew this deep in his soul like he knew how to walk and breathe. Simon kept putting him off, though, so he would need some convincing.

The first week of July, they stocked up on chips, snack cakes, and pop and crammed all of their stuff into the ancient mess of steel and vinyl Simon called his car. Simon kept saying it was overkill, that they were only driving for a few hours and the apocalypse was not imminent, but Michael emphasized that this was the first time they would be going across the state of Illinois under their own power—this was the first year that Simon owned a car, one he'd paid for with tips from the classy restaurant where he waited tables three days a week. In previous years, Simon's mother had driven them or they'd taken a bus. Something about driving made Michael feel like they were adults now.

Simon's mother came out and gave him a big hug. He kind of squirmed away when she got all kissy and told him she loved him and she'd miss him. She gave Michael a hug too, and said, "Take care of him, all right? Don't let him spend too much time indoors reading."

"I'm on it," said Michael.

Simon got into the driver's seat and looked at their respective duffel bags and plastic sacks full of junk food perched on the backseat. He turned back around and put his hands on the wheel while Michael got settled.

"It's, like, a four-hour drive, tops," said Simon. "We probably won't even eat any of the food."

Michael reached around and grabbed a bag of chips. He ate a handful and crunched on them loudly. Simon rolled his eyes and put the car in gear.

It was around the end of hour one, as they were driving through a totally flat plain of farmland, that Michael said, "So the thing about the prom."

"Ugh, really?" said Simon. "Do we have to?"

Michael had anticipated this sort of resistance. "Look, all I want to say is that next year, I *will* take a boy with me to prom. If not you, then somebody else."

"Okay."

Nothing. Simon did not react at all. No blinking or grimacing, no hint of a smile, nada.

So Michael pushed forward. "I didn't come out of the closet to date girls."

This time Simon bit his lip and very properly returned his hands to ten and two on the steering wheel. "No. I know."

"I just think, you know, I'm seventeen now. I should be able to date boys."

"I agree."

There was a long pause. Michael watched Simon, who seemed to be thinking things over. He would tilt his head one way or the other and he kept checking his mirrors.

"So, wait, you've never…?" Simon said eventually.

"That summer I went away to camp for two weeks? I kissed a boy named Pete. But that's it. It's not like there's a line of boys to date. I mean, who is even gay at school? That kid Anthony from English class? That guy's ridiculous."

Well, only sort of, in Michael's estimation. He wasn't really attracted to Anthony—the poor guy was skinny and awkward and had a huge nose—but he took a lot of what Michael was trying to do to the next level. Whereas Michael had fun-colored hair and piercings—three in each ear now—Anthony was into fashion and art and theater, things Michael paid attention to but never talked about with anyone. Anthony dressed like a homeless person on acid, yes, but Michael kind of admired that about him. Anthony was a lot braver than Michael would ever be. Of course, the consequences of that were that Anthony had no friends and even Simon steered clear of him.

"I just thought," Simon said, "that maybe you'd, I don't know, met some guy but hadn't told me. You've been out of the closet for so long, I assumed—"

"And made an ass of you and me."

"Well."

"But, no, I haven't ever even really fooled around with a guy. One kiss before I kissed you. That's it. Besides, come on. You're my best friend. You really think I'd keep something like that a secret?"

Simon shrugged. "It's private. I probably would."

"Why, Simon! Have you—"

"No, of course not. I've never even kissed anybody ever. I mean, except for that time you kissed me."

At that, Simon blushed furiously. Michael smiled, feeling a certain satisfaction at that.

"You could kiss me again," Michael said.

"What?"

"I mean, not right now, since you're driving, but this summer, if you wanted to…."

Simon swallowed so hard Michael could see his Adam's apple bob in his throat. "I'll, uh, keep that in mind."

Still, for the first week, nothing much happened. Simon's dad was horrified by the junk-food supply, so it took a lot of sneaking for Michael and Simon to eat their way through it. At least that detracted from the man's horror/amusement over Michael's hair. Simon's dad was also home a lot that first week and wanted to spend a great deal of time with Simon, which both limited Michael and Simon's alone time and left Michael feeling like a fifth wheel.

But by the second week, Simon's father was back to his old ways, working ten-hour days and leaving money on the counter for both boys to buy themselves meals. Simon being Simon, he inspired trust from his father, so Michael decided to see what they could get away with.

It started with taking the El all over the city. They got cheap tickets to a game at Wrigley Field one afternoon. They went to see the dinosaurs at the Field Museum the next. And then one day, Michael said, "Trust me," and he dragged Simon onto the Red Line, but instead of going all the way to Wrigley, they got out at a stop in Lakeview.

"Hey, what are we—" Simon started to say as they walked down the sidewalk toward Michael's intended destination. Michael just took his hand and told him to shut up.

They didn't get carded, which Michael had been mildly worried about.

He didn't want to drink, though. He merely wanted to see it.

Simon sat across from Michael at a little table off to the side. He looked around and said, "This is a gay bar."

"Yup." Michael smiled. "We're in Boystown."

Simon put a hand over his mouth, but Michael heard him mutter, "Holy shit," before he did.

"Hey, be cool," Michael said. "We're only going to order pop and look around, okay? I don't want to get in trouble. I just want to see what it's like."

Simon nodded and ordered a Coke when the waiter came by. Michael did as well, plus a plate of fries. The waiter—who was wearing very short cutoffs and a tight T-shirt that displayed a thin strip of his bare belly—scribbled down their order and then said, "I'm not supposed to serve you, but I'll let you stay as long as you don't ask for tequila. Got it?"

"Yup," said Michael with a smile.

The waiter narrowed his eyes. "I mean, I get it. I was your age once too. Just don't get me in trouble. Capisce?"

"Got it!" said Michael with a salute.

The waiter rolled his eyes and left. Simon sat there with wide eyes, looking around, gawking at Michael.

"You're gay, Simon. This is, like, your Mecca."

"I know, but…." Simon squirmed in his seat. "I don't think I'm ready for all this yet. Can't I just… finish high school first?"

But Michael had moved beyond the high-school foolishness. He was ready for the big world. He wanted Simon by his side for that, of course, but he was starting to doubt his ability to continue to be patient.

Naturally, having the real experience would have to wait a while—they could get into a gay bar in the middle of the day if they didn't order alcohol, but Michael knew they'd need fake IDs to do more. How to acquire one was beyond Michael's knowledge and budget. So he was willing to let it be, to spend the summer with Simon, but soon, he vowed. Soon they'd have the world at their fingertips and they would conquer it together.

IT WASN'T pressure. Simon never felt pressured. He'd heard everything Michael said, saw the way Michael pushed against the borders of what he could do as a seventeen-year-old kid from Iowa, and he'd felt resistance. There was a part of him that envied Michael's bravery, who kind of wanted to dye his hair pink and get a fake ID and have sex, but there was a part of him that was deathly afraid of those things too.

That Michael was still a virgin was a relief in some ways. It was encouraging, comforting; it made Simon feel okay about himself.

It made it okay to try things on his own terms.

Since Simon's father had no idea about Simon, Michael and Simon were sharing the guest room, a tastefully designed space put together by Simon's father's interior-designer ex-girlfriend. It had a full-size bed but also a daybed near the window. Michael and Simon switched off who slept where each week. But then in the third week, when Simon was on the daybed again, awake in the middle of the night, miserable, and a little sore from trying to fit his six-foot frame on a short mattress, he made a decision.

He got out of the daybed. He stood next to the full bed and looked down at Michael, who was definitely asleep, his body contorted into a weird position and his mouth hanging open. Not the most attractive of poses, granted, but it was Michael, and he was right there.

Simon sat on the bed.

Michael woke up with a start, jerking to the side and then lying on his back and looking up at Simon. "Huh?"

"Move over."

Without responding, Michael moved over on the bed, creating a Simon-sized space. Simon slid into the space and under the covers with Michael. And then he just lay there, because he had no idea what to do next.

"Um. Hi," said Michael.

"Hi. I can't sleep."

"Okay." Michael yawned.

It wasn't really about Michael. Well, it was, because there was no one on earth that Simon trusted even a little bit as much as he trusted Michael. But, really, this was about curiosity and pent-up frustration, and like with Michael and the gay bar, he wanted to see what it was like.

"Can I?" Simon asked.

Michael yawned again and said, "Can you what?"

Simon kissed Michael.

Probably he was being too analytical. Sex ed in school had been a joke and certainly didn't cover what happened when two boys got together. Simon had been reading books—romance novels snuck from his mother's bookshelves, mostly—so his rudimentary understanding of sex was based on a lot of purple prose and flowery narrative. Still, he expected for his mind to be blown when he kissed Michael, when he was ready for it. And the kiss was nice, he liked kissing Michael and all, but there were no fireworks or waves crashing or whatever the hell else.

Michael pulled away slightly and grinned. Simon could barely make out his face in the dark, but the sliver of moonlight coming through the window did bounce off his teeth.

"Are you serious?" Michael asked.

"I think so."

Michael pulled away farther and propped himself up on one elbow. "Oh, no, my friend. I want you to be serious. I want you to be sure. If we fool around with each other, I need to know that you are totally into it. I don't want to do something you don't like and have you hate me later."

"I'm here, aren't I?"

"That's not an answer."

Simon definitely wanted this. But he wasn't sure how he'd feel on the other side. "I'm sure."

Michael lunged for him. They kissed again, this time with Michael threading his fingers through Simon's hair and adding pressure, and Michael sliding his body forward so that the two of them touched from chest to knees. This time, Simon could smell Michael, could feel the heat radiating off his body. He could also feel Michael's erection, the sensation of which made his heart race. This time when they kissed, everything felt like so much more, like flames and fireworks and everything, and all Simon could do was lean into it and grab on to Michael for dear life.

Michael pulled away slightly and gave Simon a stern look.

"Wow," Simon managed.

Michael's face cooled to a smirk. "So that was okay."

"Again," Simon said. "More." He leaned toward Michael.

Michael laughed. He put his arms around Simon and pulled him close. The two of them lay together in a sort-of hug for a good minute.

"Oh, Simon. This is for real? You feel ready for this?"

"Yeah, I do." Simon meant it.

They didn't take it too far that first time, just touching and groping until both of them came in their pajama pants. But things escalated as the rest of the week played out. Each night, they took it a little farther. They shed more clothes, they touched more places, and on the last night, Simon stood before Michael completely naked and open to whatever would come next.

It wasn't all the way, at least not in what Simon assumed was the conventional sense. Simon was too nervous to go there. But he knew he would never be the same after that summer.

CHAPTER 3

Present Day

SIMON STOOD under the departures board in Penn Station, pretending to look up something on his phone but really seething because Michael had not shown up to meet him, because of course he hadn't, because it would be a cold day in hell before Michael ever actually showed up for something on time. Penn Station was also crowded and noisy and much more disgusting than Simon had remembered. College-age kids were napping on overstuffed duffel bags flung haphazardly on the concourse, a whole troop of Boy Scouts was standing over by the ticket machines, and businessmen in rumpled suits gazed hopefully at the departures board to see if the track for their train had been posted. A pair of cops did a lap around the concourse periodically to tell the sleeping kids that they couldn't sit on the floor, and the kids would dutifully stand up until the cops disappeared, at which point they were back on the floor and dozing. The odor of fried food permeated everything, and Simon could feel little grease particles sticking to his clothes and his skin. A homeless man had asked him for change twice.

He'd been waiting in that spot for twenty minutes. He was going to kill Michael.

He did take a moment to work out what was really bothering him. Michael was certainly a symptom, but being back in the city—encountering the déjà vu familiarity of Penn Station and all its gray greasiness—was seriously bothering him. It didn't fit. The city was like a pair of pants that was tight in the waist but had too long an inseam. This wasn't Simon anymore. This wasn't his home.

The man of the hour finally showed up right when Simon was seriously thinking about giving up. He looked tired and rumpled and, well, a lot older than he had the last time Simon had seen him. Had it really been that long?

Michael grinned sheepishly. "Sorry I'm late. It's... been a day." He ran a shaky hand through his hair and looked harried, like he'd run from the bulls at Pamplona to get here.

Simon tried to let go of his anger as he nodded, though it was hard. Michael lived fifteen minutes away by subway, tops, which meant that he hadn't even left his apartment until after it was time to pick Simon up, but Michael's inability to manage time was not news to Simon. Yet, given Michael's expression, Simon found he wondered what happened. Maybe Michael had seen something awful on the subway or gotten stuck there or maybe he'd gotten some bad news.

Except... no. Michael had lost the right to Simon's sympathy a long time ago. The days when Simon dropped everything to smooth Michael's ruffled feathers were long over. It wasn't Simon's job anymore. Not his place. He wasn't that man any longer.

Or so he told himself.

"I probably could have found your place on my own," Simon said. "I used to live here, you know."

"Yeah, but I wanted to pick you up." Michael held up his hands. "It's been a while."

And because it had been a long time, Simon stepped forward and pulled Michael into a tight hug. Michael hugged him back. There was no hips-apart stance, no manly back pat, only the tight embrace of two old friends who had once loved each other fiercely but had not seen each other in a very long time.

"God, I missed you," Michael said near Simon's ear.

"People are going to stare at us."

"I don't care."

Simon pulled away reluctantly and grabbed his suitcase. "Well. We should get going. Cab or subway?"

"I was going to take the subway, but that suitcase looks heavy. Are all of your worldly possessions in there?"

"Most of them. The rest is in storage in Iowa City until I find a place."

Something dark clouded over Michael's features. He frowned, but then he wiped his face and offered up a weak smile. "You can stay with me as long as you need to, you know."

"I know. But not forever. You don't want a brother type in your hair all the time."

Michael raised an eyebrow. "You are not my brother." He headed toward the escalator out of the station. "Let's get a cab."

1997

MICHAEL HAD a vision.

It often took him a long time to fall asleep at night, so he'd while away the time thinking about the future. Oh, sure, he'd jack off—sometimes while thinking about Simon, sometimes while thinking of actors or the guys in the men's magazines he'd been shoplifting from the convenience store near his house—but then, as he drifted off to sleep, he'd think about the future.

Probably they wouldn't stay in Iowa. Simon didn't want to, for one thing. Michael wasn't opposed to staying, necessarily, but he didn't think the Iowa City suburbs had much to offer except sprawl and all the same people and issues he'd grown up with.

But he imagined him and Simon owning a house. They'd sleep together in a big bed, like a married couple. They'd have a couple of dogs and eventually adopt children. Michael's lesbian cousin had gone to a sperm bank to have a baby, something Michael's mom didn't think Michael was old enough to understand, but he did. He understood he would not be having biological children of his own, at least not through traditional methods. But that didn't mean he couldn't picture a happy future with a full house.

In fact, once he got past the idea of staying in Iowa, the possibilities seemed endless.

Sometimes, when imagining the future, he thought about the month he'd spent at summer camp right after he turned sixteen. A boy named Pete had flirted with him, and though Michael had his sights set on Simon by then, Pete was there and Simon wasn't. Late one night, after their big kiss, Michael confessed that he wanted to grow up and have a family.

"Guys like us don't get to have families," Pete had said.

Those words had haunted Michael ever since.

He lay awake one night a couple of weeks after he and Simon had returned from Chicago, and he thought about what Pete had said. On the one hand, that first night Simon had climbed into bed with him had been one of the greatest of his life, if not *the* greatest. Since they'd returned, they'd continued to fool around when they could get each other alone. So things were progressing apace.

But he worried about life outside of Iowa.

Because the thing was, in Iowa, they were safe. Or, at least, Michael knew what to expect. There weren't many other gay people, granted, at least none that Michael knew. There was a rumor around school that the former drama teacher, who had died right before Michael and Simon's freshman year, had been gay, but it was also rumored that he'd died of AIDS and not cancer. Michael didn't know if any of that was true. If it was true, it was a reminder of what else was out there: outside of their little town, there were other gay men. Michael found that both exciting and terrifying. Because on the one hand, he was sick of being a novelty act. On the other, would that mean more temptation? Would it mean men who could get between him and Simon? Could it mean he'd become one of the guys who didn't get to have a family? Could it mean disease?

Michael didn't know.

Simon wanted to go to New York, which Michael was on board with, though he had reservations. New York was many times bigger than Iowa City, bigger than Chicago, even. There were a lot of people there, a lot of places to get lost. Would he and Simon stay together if they went there? Would they even stay friends?

He'd go wherever Simon went, he knew that much. He'd follow Simon to the ends of the earth. Michael knew in his soul that they belonged together, and he was determined to prove it to Simon, who, despite recent events, still seemed not quite sure. There was the nagging worry, though, that their relationship might not withstand whatever was out there. Michael worried he and Simon wouldn't be able to make the family Michael could so vividly see them having together.

Still, he remained optimistic. If he could only figure out how to persuade Simon that they belonged together, they'd be unstoppable.

SIMON CAME out to his mother on a cool September evening. He had spent the afternoon at Michael's, making out on the sofa in the basement. It wasn't too crazy—no under the clothes stuff, just as much kissing and groping as they thought they could get away with given that Michael's mother was upstairs.

It wasn't a thing. Simon didn't want it to be a boyfriend thing, even though that seemed to be what Michael wanted. He wanted an outlet, maybe. He was a little grossed out with himself for needing it, but now that he'd tasted Michael, that he knew something tangible about sex, he couldn't quite get enough.

Lately, Michael had been pestering him to come out. So far, Michael was still the only person on earth who knew Simon was gay—except, Simon supposed, for that waiter at the gay bar in Chicago—and Simon understood what Michael was saying and all, but he still didn't understand why it was so urgent. It wasn't like they were a couple. They were best friends who, granted, made out whenever they could get away with it, but they definitely were not boyfriends.

Michael kept saying that if Simon came out, his life at school would change. Simon disagreed. He was invisible now as it was; he couldn't imagine that telling everyone he was gay would do anything but bring unwanted attention. Michael seemed to think that the only reason he had people, albeit mostly girls, around him all the time was his homosexuality, but Simon knew better. Simon knew Michael was friendly and charming and, well, really cute. More than cute. Hot?

Handsome? It was strange to think of his best friend in those terms, their time spent naked together notwithstanding.

Simon promised to think about it. But first, he would try climbing the mountain of coming out to his mother, who at least deserved to know, unlike the people Simon went to school with.

When he got home that day, he found her in the kitchen making dinner.

"Table or couch?" she asked.

They had of late taken to eating without talking to each other, looking at the TV instead of interacting.

"Table. I want to talk to you about something, if that's okay."

She looked over at him, a somewhat alarmed expression on her face. "Is everything all right?"

"Yeah. Everything's fine."

She narrowed her eyes but nodded. "Then make yourself useful and set the table."

She had made some kind of noodle casserole, which brought to mind TV shows from the fifties. Simon doubted this was an issue any of those shows had tackled, though.

After they'd taken a few bites, Simon's mother said, "So what did you want to talk to me about?"

"I... um, I mean." Simon took a deep breath. He'd just blurted it out to Michael and that had gone all right. His stomach churned now, his heart raced, and he was probably sweating like crazy. He had no idea how his mother would react, if she'd freak out or kick him out of the house or hug him or what. He'd never heard her say anything explicitly homophobic, but he hadn't heard her embrace homosexuality, either. The only gay person Simon was aware she knew was Michael. She seemed to like Michael okay.

"Sweetie," his mother said. She reached over and rubbed his arm. "You can tell me."

So he took another deep breath and said, "I'm gay, Mom."

An eerie silence descended on the room. Simon's mother sat perfectly still, but then, so did Simon.

"Really?" she said eventually.

Not a judgment. Not an endorsement, either.

"Yes, really."

"Because I know how much you like Michael."

The implication there was that Simon was gay to be like Michael. "That's not why. I mean, I'm not gay because Michael is gay. I'm gay because I was born gay."

That was probably the most times Simon had ever said "gay" in one breath. He felt a streak of something running through him, a bit of rebellion, maybe, the desire to throw off the trappings of his perfectionist self. He wanted to run outside and mess up his hair and wear the kinds of crazy clothes Michael wore and shout, "Gay, gay, gay!" at anyone who would listen.

But instead, he sat there perfectly still and waited.

"Well, okay," his mother said. "You're sure?"

"I'm sure, Mom."

"Are you and Michael, you know, boyfriends?"

"No. It's not like that with us."

Simon's mother grimaced. It wasn't the reaction he was hoping for, but it also wasn't as bad as he feared.

"Okay," she said. "Okay. Well, I guess I'm not too surprised. But, ah, maybe don't tell your father yet. Unless you already have?"

"No. Michael and now you are the only ones who know."

"Maybe we should keep it that way for a while. I don't... things could get bad for you at school, couldn't they?"

"Mom, I—"

"I mean, it's okay, I still love you. Okay, Simon? I will always love you. But I don't want anything bad to happen to you."

Simon felt dissatisfied with that. He finished his meal and then asked to be excused. His mother made him promise to do the dishes, which he said he'd do later. In the meantime, he retreated to his room, grabbing the cordless phone on the way. He called Michael.

"I told my mother," he said.

"Congratulations! How did she take it?"

Simon appreciated that he didn't have to explain what he'd told his mother. "She's... well, she's kind of weird about it."

"I would expect no less."

Simon laughed despite himself. "She thinks I should keep it quiet at school."

"That's crazy. I'm telling you, our school is pretty accepting."

"Is it, though?"

A long silence ensued. "Better than lying," Michael said. "It's better than pretending to be something you aren't. You should own your true self. I mean, school's almost over. What do you have to lose?"

What indeed?

AFTER MANY months of Michael pressing his suit, Simon finally relented and agreed to go to prom. "As friends," he insisted. This was good enough for Michael, who had *plans*. The prom was to be at a hotel in Iowa City, and Michael had been saving his allowance money for months to pay for a room there. He planned to set the stage for more romance than Simon had ever seen, with flowers and candles and wine pilfered from his parents' liquor cabinet. Friends, schmiends. Michael would prove to Simon once and for all that they should be partners. But first, they would dance together for everyone at school to see.

His mind buzzed as he went to Mr. Lucas's classroom after school to purchase a pair of tickets. Simon had given Michael his half in advance, even though Michael offered to pay for the ticket. "It's not a date," Simon had said.

Whatever. It *was* a date. Simon just needed to see that Michael could be everything he wanted in a man, that they belonged together. This was obvious to Michael.

He strolled into Mr. Lucas's room and said, "I'm buying prom tickets."

"All right." Mr. Lucas pulled open a drawer in his desk and extracted a tin money box and a large envelope. He pulled two tickets and a sign-up sheet out of the envelope. "Are you bringing another IHHS student?"

"Yup."

Mr. Lucas nodded and scrawled Michael's name in the first column of the sign-up sheet. "What's her name?"

"Simon Newell."

Mr. Lucas froze for a moment and then slowly lifted his head to look at Michael. "You... what?"

"I'm bringing Simon as my date."

"But you can't...." Mr. Lucas frowned.

Michael could see him hedging about what to say. He had wondered if this might be the reaction, if the lack of a precedent meant that there was an unspoken rule that prom dates had to be opposite-sex pairs. After all, tickets were only available in pairs, so no one could go stag, which struck Michael as an outdated rule, but if that was how this was going to go....

Mr. Lucas drew a line through Michael's name. "You should reconsider."

"Why?" asked Michael. "Everyone in this school knows I'm gay. Why can't I bring a boy? It's not fair to make me bring a girl. That's discrimination."

"No, it's school policy."

"What policy? I didn't see anything on the prom invitation that said I couldn't bring a male date."

Mr. Lucas started putting his things away. "I'm sorry. If you insist, you can take it up with Principal Naughton or the school board, but I can't sell a ticket to you if you're bringing Simon."

"I *will* bring it up with the school board!"

But that got him nowhere. The high school principal proved to be a bigot who flat-out told Michael that it was forbidden because he would not bear witness to boys dancing with each other at prom, even though Michael pointed out that girls danced together at school dances all the time. Simon helped Michael write a letter to the town Board of Ed, but that plea fell on deaf ears there, as well. The Board agreed to a hearing, so Michael made an impassioned speech in person, but the board voted five-to-two against Michael.

Michael was devastated.

Six weeks before prom and two weeks before the deadline to buy tickets, Michael and Simon sat in the mall food court, discussing what to do. Michael prayed Simon wouldn't say, "I told you so."

"Maybe we could pretend to bring other dates but really go with each other," Simon suggested as he ate a french fry.

"What do you mean?"

"You bring Brynne or one of your friends, I find a female date, we make it clear that we just want to go as friends, and then we spend time with each other. It'll be kind of the same."

"It won't, but I see your point." Michael was irritated. Spending time with each other at prom while there with other dates didn't make a statement. It wasn't romantic.

Things were further complicated when Brynne wanted to go to an after-party hosted by a restaurant downtown instead of allowing Michael his alone time with Simon.

And when Simon's date, a mousey girl named Angela, monopolized all of his time at the dance, Michael saw all of his plans evaporate. There would be no romantic night in the hotel. There would be no dancing together in front of the whole student body. His opportunity to show Simon how much he loved him was slipping through his fingers.

Late in the night, just before the end of the dance, Simon approached him where he stood in a corner of the ballroom. Simon said, "You're upset."

"Upset" was too mild a word. Michael was so devastated, he would have cried if he didn't think that would make things worse. "This is not how my senior prom was supposed to go."

Simon glanced around him. Then he shrugged and leaned forward. Before Michael knew what was happening, Simon was kissing him. It was short, but sweet and intense. When Simon pulled away, he smiled.

"I know you wanted romance," Simon said.

"What brought all this on?" Michael asked. "I had to twist your arm pretty hard to talk you into being my date to begin with."

"I just… I don't know. I wanted you to be happy. I know this didn't go as planned, but you wanted to be with a boy at prom, so here I am."

"I wanted to be with *you*."

A flash of uncertainty, a little bit of a frown, moved over Simon's face, but then he smiled again. "Someday, Michael. Someday." Then he walked away.

No one had seen them. Michael was pretty sure of that. So much for the grand gesture. Simon had kissed him at the prom, and it had been nice, but he'd done it when Michael was wallowing in self-pity in a dark corner where no one could see them. Simon had only done what was safe, not what was risky or right. The disappointment was like a knife to the heart. Michael sighed heavily and left the ballroom.

CHAPTER 4

Present Day

IN THE cab, Michael stole a moment to look Simon over. Aside from the hug, Simon had been cold and closed-off during this whole little reunion. Why Michael had expected more was elusive now.

The cabby hit a pothole, jostling them in a way that seemed to push them further into their respective sides of the bench seat in the back of the cab. Simon fiddled with the little TV set built into the driver's seat rather than talk to Michael.

"Are we really so estranged?" Michael asked.

Simon shot him a sidelong glance before hitting the "Off" button on the TV. "No, you're right. I'm sorry."

"I mean, Jesus, Simon. We've been friends for most of our lives. I know things have happened so now there's a lot of nonsense between us, but I'm not a fucking stranger. Stop treating me like one."

Simon sighed and leaned back. He lifted a hand and rubbed his forehead near his hairline. "It's not just you. I'm feeling... out of sorts. It's weird being back in New York."

"You've only been back, what, half an hour?"

The cab sped down Eighth Avenue, through Chelsea and past some of the bars they'd once gone to. Simon gestured at one as they zoomed past it. "Some of this is the same, but some of it looks different. That place on Seventeenth. Wasn't that a gay bar?"

"Still is. It got bought out a couple of years ago, and the new owners decided the city needed a gay *sports* bar. I've been a couple of times. They have really good fries."

"There was a place in Chicago like that. In Boystown. I only went once."

"Did you go out much in Boystown?"

"No, not really. I was working too much. I'm hoping the hours in the New York office are less intense."

"Yeah, geez. It would suck to get you back only to never see you."

Simon nodded. "Is that Thai place we used to eat at all the time still there?"

"Yeah, we just passed it. Your old gym is still on the corner there too. It's still basically a meat market, by the way. So, see? The city isn't so different."

"I can't figure out if that's good or bad."

So that was how this was going to go. Simon was back, but held himself two feet away. They were sitting now with as much space between them as the cab would allow, with Simon's briefcase on the seat between them like a wall. Heaven forbid they should touch or, worse, express a real emotion.

Michael sighed and looked out the window.

"Lord only knows what you must think of me now," Michael said. "Was I ever anything more than that flighty boy who was in love with you?"

Finally, Simon turned. His face remained neutral for a minute, but then his forehead creased and his eyes went wide. "God. Of course not. You know you're so much more than that for me. We were best friends once. More than that, even."

"But not anymore."

"What do you want me to say?" Simon shook his head. "No. No, I'm not having this conversation in the back of a cab."

"I'm not asking you for anything except friendship. I want us to be friends again. I thought, with you moving back here, we could at least try. But if things are really so far gone…."

"No, they're… that's not it. I mean, yes. We're still friends. We have always been and we will always be friends. You have to… give me some time to adjust to being back here. We can't just magically pick up where we left off. Too much has happened, and not only between us. I had a whole different life when I was away."

"I know."

Simon huffed and looked out the window. The cab pulled up in front of Michael's building. Simon grabbed his briefcase and reached for the door handle, but before he got out of the cab, he turned back to Michael. "I will try. I want for everything that happened to be water under the bridge. If I could go back and change things I did or things I said, I would. If I could let go of how I felt that first time I saw you with Joan, I would do that too. I'm… I'm not quite there yet, but I'm willing to try. Okay? I will try to make things right with us, in whatever form that takes."

Michael nodded and Simon got out of the cab. Michael paid the driver while trying to convince himself that this was good, that Simon putting in an effort was a step in the right direction, because this tension between them would surely kill Michael.

After Michael and the driver wrestled Simon's gargantuan suitcase out of the truck, Michael led Simon into his building. He said, "I'll try too."

A small smile passed over Simon's face. It was the first time he'd come anywhere near an expression of happiness since the moment they'd met at Penn Station. "I don't believe it will be easy."

Michael reached over and touched Simon's arm. "Nothing worth doing is ever easy."

2008

LATE IN the night, Michael was jolted awake by Joan rolling over in bed. He reached for her, putting a hand on her hip to keep her from crushing him as she moved. She woke up with a gasp and looked over at him.

"What?" she asked.

"I don't know. You were flailing in your sleep."

"Nightmare," she muttered.

"You okay?"

"Yeah. I've already forgotten what it was about. Sorry for waking you up."

"It's fine."

But nothing was fine. As was often the case when Michael was having trouble sleeping, he thought of everything that had happened recently, turning events over in his head until he thought he'd go crazy with it. His best friend was halfway across the world, and Michael felt like his left arm had been cut off. And now that this thought had entered his mind, he knew he definitely wouldn't be going back to sleep.

And it wasn't like he didn't have the very reason Simon had left now curling against him. Joan reached over and put her hand on his chest. Michael sighed heavily.

"You're thinking about Simon again, aren't you?"

"It's wrong, him being gone. This city is wrong. It's not New York without Simon."

"I know, sweetie." She stretched and sat up. She looked down at him and said, "But you and Simon, by your own admission, had been growing apart."

Michael groaned. Joan was the last person he wanted to talk about Simon with. He'd been honest with her, but this was tough. It was tough to realize that the universe had presented him with the man he'd loved his whole life, with whom everything lately had felt fraught and difficult, and a beautiful woman, a woman with whom everything was easy, who got him better than Simon did sometimes. He'd chosen the easy thing, the thing that made him happy, the thing that was not so complicated. Or so he thought at the time. Late in the night now he wondered if he'd made the right choice.

"I know you miss him," Joan said, "but you have to let him go for a while. Let him blow off steam. Let him travel. Let him find himself. If your friendship is as strong as you always say it is, then he'll come back and things will be all right between the two of you."

Michael nodded. She was right, of course. "This city is hard without him." Hell, life was hard without talking to Simon every day.

But Michael knew they'd fucked up and hurt each other and he had to give them space to recover.

"On the other hand," Joan said, "you could view this as entering the next phase of your life. I know it's hard to move on, but, you know, nothing worth doing is ever easy."

Michael chewed on that so long that Joan lay back down and started to drift back to sleep. Her words echoed in his head. Would whatever happened next relieve any of this anguish? Would it be worth it in the long run? Would Simon come home and make this city feel whole again?

1998

NEW YORK was everything Simon could have hoped for and more.

A month in the city had shown him noise and light and bustle. There was grime and art and beauty and decay. There was always something to do, something to see, and something to hear. Just walking to his classes each day took him past more people than he imagined lived in all of Iowa City. Michael complained about the sounds and the dirt, but Simon loved it.

The day he saw two men holding hands in Washington Square Park as he cut across it to go to class was the day Simon decided this was where he belonged. Just that day, he'd gotten scones with a cute boy from his English class, and though probably nothing would happen there, at least the West Village had cute boys with soft hair to gaze at dreamily. After breakfast, he'd taken the subway uptown to see an exhibit at MoMA for a class assignment. Then he'd taken the train back down to the Village and grabbed lunch at a dinky little deli off Waverly Place that had the best roast beef sandwiches he'd ever eaten, and then he'd cut across the park. And lo, there was a gay couple, two men who looked like they were in their midtwenties, smiling at each other as if nothing else existed in the world. Simon wanted that, felt an ache in his chest yearning for it. Or maybe that was just his libido, since one of the guys was seriously hot.

He hadn't let himself look before. He'd seen plenty of hot guys in the past. He'd even had crushes on classmates. But he hadn't let himself just indulge in the act of looking, afraid to get caught. Here, though, in New York City, men could hold hands and look at each other and be together. Merely bearing witness to that had awoken something in Simon, and now he wanted it all: he wanted to meet new men, to get naked with them, to hold hands, to have sex, to find the pockets of the city where gay men congregated to be a part of them, a part of the whole culture of this place. He wanted to touch all of it.

For the first time in his life, Simon felt like he was really living.

MICHAEL OFTEN had plans but they rarely came to fruition. He followed Simon to New York for college but wound up in different dorms freshman year. Simon got into the business school at NYU and Michael pursued something nebulous in liberal arts—he ultimately chose English as his major because he liked to read but was at loose ends for what he really wanted to do with his life.

Still, he never gave up on Simon. In the middle of their second semester, he took Simon out on a proper date, although he soon came to realize that he was the only one who knew they were on a date. Simon kept trying to pay for his share, he mentioned boys in his classes he thought were cute, and at the end of the night, he said, "I have to go study."

Michael lost it. They were walking back to their respective dorms through Washington Square Park, near the fountain, before their paths diverged. The streetlights cast an orange haze over them. Michael lost his temper, his patience, his mind.

"Don't you get it, Simon?"

Simon narrowed his eyes. "Get what?"

"This was a date. I'm trying to show you romance. I'm trying to make moves on you. You're supposed to come back with me to my dorm—my roommate's out of town, by the way—and then we will have totally awesome sex and you will spend the night with me and… romance."

"Is that what this was? A date?"

Michael groaned. "Yes! Yes. You and me, we come from the same place, we've been friends our whole lives. No one knows me like you do and vice versa. We're supposed to be together. We're supposed to have this epic love story. I don't know why you don't get that, but it's obvious to me."

Simon tilted his head. He looked thoughtful, like he was solving a math problem in his head. "We're only eighteen."

"What has that got to do with anything?"

"How can you know who you're supposed to be with at eighteen?"

Michael was astonished. How could Simon not know? Michael had known for years, it seemed. "I just know."

"Well, I *don't* know. I love you, I do, but the whole reason I came to New York to begin with was to experience life. Experience other people. When I... when we commit to each other, it will be for life. But I'm not ready for that yet. Not when I've got this whole city in front of me." Simon spread his arms and spun around in a circle, gesturing to the whole of New York.

When we commit to each other, it will be for life.

"So what you're saying," Michael said, "is that you want to be with me, but not right now."

Simon looked up toward the moon. Michael followed his gaze. The moon seemed less bright here than it did back home.

Simon said, "I think... yes. That's true. Can we maybe... I think we would both, you know, do well to see other people."

"That's what you think."

"I don't know, Michael. I'm not ready for a lifetime commitment."

"You want to *fuck* other people." The words came out angry, bitter. Michael practically spat them.

"I... well, yes. That's a crude way to put it, but yes. You got to be the gay guy in high school. I didn't."

"Because you wouldn't come out."

"Because I'm not you. We're very different, you know. And now that I'm here, I feel like the possibilities are endless in a way they weren't back home. I can do anything here, be anyone. I just... I want room to fly. Do you get that?"

"You're still the only man I've ever been with."

Simon shook his head. "It doesn't have to be that way."

Michael's heart shattered. Right there, in the middle of Washington Square Park, with only the orange streetlights and the moon showing them the way, his heart broke into a million pieces. "I... fine. If that's how you want it. You can have all the goddamn room you want." He stormed away from Simon.

"Michael! Michael, wait! That's not what I—"

"I get it, Simon. Good night!"

He stomped all the way back to his dorm room.

THERE WAS a redheaded boy named Keith who lived on Simon's floor. From where Simon sat, he was perfect: thick hair, defined muscles, a pleasant face. Simon put more energy than was probably healthy into concocting fantasies where they were stranded on a desert island together—or in which the showers at the gym down the block were crowded and they had to share—and it made Simon happy as far as it went. Keith did have one character flaw, however: he was straight as an arrow.

Simon confided his crush to his roommate Eric, also straight, who would look at Keith with a raised eyebrow and say, "That guy? Really?"

But it was safe and, after Michael had blown up at him, it was all he could manage.

He did regret hurting Michael—and he knew that was what had happened—but he didn't see their relationship the same way Michael did. Simon did love Michael, he hadn't lied about that, but he knew that if they started dating for real instead of the occasional hookup, as had been going on for the last year or more, it would be for life, and that was too much. Every time Simon thought about being with Michael and only Michael for the rest of his life, he started to panic. Simon wanted to see what was out there. He wanted to live his life. He wanted to shake off Iowa and experience New York. And Michael had lately felt like a chain pulling him back into his past.

But here! Here he could sit in the lounge of his dorm building with Eric and comment on Keith as if it were no big deal, which it wasn't. He could sneak into bars and go to shows and museums and cheap concerts. He joined clubs and met other gay students and made friends. And he studied; he studied a hell of a lot, thinking he might want to go into accounting. He took his studies seriously.

When Michael blew him off, though, he missed his old friend fiercely.

That surprised him. Through the entire first semester of college, Michael felt like a relic of Simon's old life, a reminder of everything he was running away from. More than anything, Simon had wanted to get away from Iowa. During his first weeks in New York, he had almost regretted that Michael had insisted on coming with him to college. They both could have used some space to learn new things, get to know new people.

But Michael hadn't talked to Simon in three weeks, and Simon felt that like part of his heart was missing.

What the hell was that about?

Simon came back to his dorm one afternoon and ran into Keith in the lobby. He managed to keep from swooning and offered Keith a smile and a little wave.

"How's it going, Simon?" Keith asked.

"Okay. Glad the semester's almost done."

"Me too, man. Me too. Hey, my girlfriend is hosting a party at her place Saturday. You want to come?"

"Sure." That was the first rule of college social life, Simon thought. Say yes as much as possible.

"Awesome. Her brother's visiting. He's gay too. Maybe you two will hit it off." Keith made a little gesture with his hands, like his two index fingers were meeting each other for the first time. Simon thought it unspeakably adorable. Then Keith waved and took off.

That was something, Simon thought as he rode the elevator up to his room. He'd never have Keith, that was clear, but maybe he'd meet someone. He'd fallen in with a few other gay guys on campus, but none of them really did much for him sexually. Not like Keith did.

Not like Michael did.

Surprised by that thought, Simon dismissed it as he got off the elevator. When he got to his room, Eric was there, lounging on the bed, headphones clipped on his ears. "Voice mail for you," he said loudly.

Simon dumped his stuff on his bed and reached for the phone.

The message was from Michael, and it was simple. "Simon. It's Michael. Can I see you today? I want to talk to you about something. Maybe come by after dinner. Like, eightish? Uh, thanks. Bye."

It was weird, hearing Michael's voice after a couple of weeks without any contact. Michael had always had a soft voice, though he'd dropped the weird lisp he'd cultivated in high school and now just talked like Simon imagined he was meant to talk. Simon liked Michael's real voice; he found it soothing. So it was nice to hear the voice mail. And Michael wanted to talk? Maybe they could be friends again.

Simon had dinner with Eric and then trekked over to Michael's dorm. He felt optimistic. Maybe, he thought as he walked, he didn't really need to shed all of his past. Maybe he hadn't realized what an important part Michael played in his life until Michael instituted the radio silence. But now he wanted to talk. Maybe they could compromise. Maybe they could figure out how to be friends.

When Simon got to Michael's, he ran into a girl from his macroeconomics class, who let him into the building and waved him past security, no questions asked. He spared a thought for the appalling lack of security on this urban campus, but then he focused on his goal and went up to Michael's room. When Michael opened the door, he said, "I'm surprised you actually came."

Simon shrugged. "I guess I missed you."

"Yeah?"

"Yeah." And he had. Michael looked exactly the same as he always had, but that familiarity was startling. It felt wrong. Something had changed between them, hadn't it? Shouldn't Michael look different? Something?

"That's good," Michael said. "I mean, us missing each other kind of sucks. That's kind of what I wanted to talk to you about."

Michael's roommate didn't seem to be around. He rarely was; earlier that semester he had more or less moved into his girlfriend's dorm room.

"So I know we got hosed on the housing situation this year," Michael began. "But I was thinking. If we do the lottery, we could team up, get a room together next year. What do you think?"

Simon wasn't sure what to make of that. He wanted to ask Michael what his intentions were—if he still had romantic designs on Simon or what. Probably he did, in which case living together seemed like a spectacularly bad idea.

"I don't know."

"It could be really fun."

Simon sat on Michael's bed. "Can I… can we speak honestly? Without the other person getting pissed off."

Michael sat beside him. "All right." He looked at Simon warily.

"I'm sorry for being blunt the last time we saw each other, but I needed you to understand. I don't feel like I'm ready for a relationship. I know that's what you want."

Michael frowned.

"Can I just… have more time? I need more time. Maybe in a year or two, I'll be ready to have a real relationship with you."

"Simon, I—"

"I'm sorry."

"No, that wasn't what I was going to say. I mean, I get it. You're not ready. Thank you for being honest."

There was a "but" in his voice.

"I missed you, you know," said Simon. "But it's weird. You didn't talk to me at all for three weeks. You wouldn't answer my calls, you wouldn't respond to my e-mails. But now you think we should move in together?"

"I see how it sounds." Michael squirmed a little. "I didn't mean to be, like, manipulative. I thought it would be cool, us bunking together. Like old times. But I forgot that you want nothing to do with old times."

Simon let out an exasperated huff. "It's not like that."

"What's it like, then?"

Simon stood. "It was all so easy for you. You woke up one morning and waltzed into school and you were like, 'Hi! I'm gay!' and everyone loved you. People barely ever paid attention to me. Well, unless it was to harass me. Do you know what happened after prom? Some asshole stuck a note in my locker that said 'I saw you kissing Mike Reeves at prom, faggot.'"

"You never told me that."

"Because it wasn't important. We graduated three weeks later and it was over. But the point is that everyone loves you because you're *you*, but I was this plain, forgettable nerd and no one cared. I couldn't be like you in high school. That's not how I'm made."

"It wasn't always a picnic for me, either, you know."

"I know, but... I need you to understand. I wanted to come to New York because... I mean, I wanted to get out of Iowa so much, but I didn't pick New York randomly. I kept reading about this city and I thought I could be myself here. And I am. I really like it. I'm not that same invisible kid anymore."

"I'm... glad?"

Simon wasn't sure Michael understood what he was saying, or even if Simon was explaining himself clearly.

"Do you hate it here?" Simon asked.

"No. New York is awesome. I kind of don't ever want to go home."

"I... okay."

Michael stood and walked over to Simon. "I get that you think I'm manipulating you into being with me by proposing that we move in together."

"I don't think that," Simon said, although he did.

Michael was suddenly very close, which was a little alarming. It shouldn't have been, but it was. Simon took a step back.

"I just thought...." Michael said. "I mean, I don't really know a lot of other gay guys, and things with my roommate are so weird, I thought it would be easier. That was all I meant. I totally heard you when you yelled at me."

"I didn't yell."

"You don't want to be with me. I get it." Michael shrugged.

But that wasn't what Simon meant at all. It was like a punch to the gut to watch Michael shrug it off too. "That's not what I.... Did you even listen?"

"Why does it even matter? You say maybe someday. What the hell is the point of that? If we're meant to be together, we should just be together."

"But I'm not ready!"

"What is there to be ready for? Things are like they've always been between us. We just put a different label on it. Instead of friends, we become boyfriends. Except… you want to fuck other people."

Simon sighed. That part was kind of true. The idea of committing to one man for the rest of his life, before he even turned nineteen, gave him hives. "I just… want to see."

Michael grimaced. "So you're telling me we shouldn't live together?"

"I just don't think it's a good idea."

Michael stomped away and threw his hands in the air. "Fine. Go fuck other guys. See if I care."

Simon knew full well Michael did care, and that he was barely keeping a lid on his tantrum. "I'm not saying these things to piss you off."

"Could have fooled me. You know, I haven't been with anyone since we moved here. I could have, plenty of times, but I didn't, because I thought that we—"

"I haven't been with anyone, either."

"Why the fuck not, if that's what you want so much? Why not fuck all the guys at NYU? Why not stroll on through the park and pick up whatever homeless guy wants to give you a blow job? That'll surely take care of whatever urges you have."

"That's kind of insulting." Simon spoke quietly.

"I know! That's the whole fucking point. You stand here, cool as a cucumber, and tell me that you can't be with me because you want to, like, sow your wild oats or whatever, and I have to just stand here and fucking take it like a sucker, but, really, you should just come out with it. Just tell me you're not attracted to me. You don't like me in that way. Or just kick me in the balls, while you're at it. That would hurt a hell of a lot fucking less."

"But that would be a lie."

"So you do want to be with me?"

This whole conversation was starting to give Simon a headache. He couldn't figure out how to articulate what he meant, or at least couldn't say it directly without twisting his knife further into Michael's chest. "I don't know. It's not that I'm not attracted to you. I think maybe someday you and me could…. Just not right now. I'm not in the right place for—"

Michael was on Simon in a flash, cutting off his words with a fierce kiss. He sucked Simon's lip between his teeth and bit gently. He put his hands through Simon's hair. Simon was surprised at first, but responded in kind, the adrenaline surge rushing through his body as he grasped onto Michael's waist.

Because the thing of it was, it wasn't only adrenaline. It was desire too. In an instant, he was hard and wanting, and he grabbed at Michael, groped him, really, and Michael groped him right back. They pushed and pulled at each other, bit and moaned, until they toppled onto Michael's bed together.

"This wasn't what I meant to happen," Simon said, though suddenly he wanted it.

"Me neither," said Michael, though Simon didn't believe him.

"Doesn't change anything."

"I get that. Want to do it anyway?"

"God, yes."

It didn't take long to start getting naked, for Simon to be on top of Michael grinding their hips together, for them to be kissing and groping in desperation. It felt good to be back in Michael's arms, good to press against each other. It was familiar. It was *right*, the way their bodies fit together.

They ripped each other's clothes off, tossing garments everywhere. There was a familiarity to Michael's body as Simon unwrapped it, but that didn't make him any less sexy, any less arousing. Simon ran his hands up Michael's bare chest, and then bowed to suck on a nipple. Michael hissed below him and thrust his hands into Simon's hair. Simon cupped his hand over Michael's cock and rubbed it through the fabric of his underwear. Michael was hard and he thrust his hips up to meet Simon's touch. Simon slid his hand into Michael's briefs and wrapped it around Michael's cock. Michael groaned and clutched at Simon's shoulders. Simon pressed his own cock against Michael's thigh, rubbing and seeking friction enough to sate his own mounting arousal. But he needed Michael naked and he needed to be naked and pressed against him. He peeled off Michael's briefs and stripped off the last of his own clothes, and then he straddled Michael's hips.

They kissed, snaking tongues into each other's mouths, grabbing at whatever they could reach, moaning and thrusting against each other.

Michael arched up beneath Simon and said, "I want…." But then he stopped, panting, and clutched Simon's shoulders.

"What do you want?"

"I want you inside me."

Simon pulled back in surprise. They'd never done that before. It was an act that featured heavily in all the porn he'd seen recently, and he was certainly curious, but the actual mechanics of it were a little daunting.

"There's lube in the shoebox under the bed," said Michael.

"Do we need condoms?" Simon asked, mostly as a stalling technique.

"Got some of those too. It's up to you. I mean, if neither of us has ever been with anyone else…."

Simon's heart rate kicked up to an unnaturally high speed. He leaned over the side of the bed and felt around for the shoebox. When he found it, he pulled it out. And there it all was. A well-thumbed issue of *Playgirl*, a bottle of lube, a handful of condoms—different brands, making Simon think these had been taken from Health Services or the RA down the hall—and a very large purple dildo that Simon was trying not to see. He knew he'd wandered past some point of no return, that he now shared a strange intimacy with Michael, that he was privy to Michael's inner life and sexuality in a way he never quite had been before. Making out to pass the time was entirely different from *this*.

Simon grabbed the lube and a condom and crawled back on top of Michael. He was at a loss for a moment. "I'm not entirely sure what to do."

Michael reached up and ran a hand through Simon's hair. "In the past, we've always just… gone with our instincts. I think we can do that here."

"But what about—"

"I showered before you came over. Squeaky clean down there."

Simon's heart pounded. The idea popped into his head that maybe Michael had plans to make use of that purple dildo. Michael certainly seemed to have a better handle on this act than Simon did.

They were really going to do this, weren't they? Somehow, Michael had thought of everything. But Simon was still unsure. "I don't want to hurt you."

"Then I'll help."

Michael wriggled out from beneath Simon and took the lube. Simon took the condom and tore off the wrapper. Nerves had caused his erection to flag. He held the little rubber circle in his hand and then looked at Michael.

The look on Michael's face was pure sex. His eyelids were low, his lips were parted, and he cocked his head in a confident way, as if he knew exactly what he was doing. He curled his body a little as he poured lube on his fingers. Then he pressed a finger against his own hole. Simon sat back a little and watched for a moment as Michael touched himself, stretched himself, and then dropped his head back in ecstasy. Michael was so sexy, looked so completely debauched, that Simon was aroused again. He stroked himself as he watched Michael prepare his body, until he had to reach over and touch Michael.

He'd only put a condom on twice before, mostly as practice. The first time, he'd concentrated so hard that he'd lost his erection. He worried that would happen this time, but every time he looked over at Michael and thought about what they were about to do, heat surged through his body. He was overjoyed when he successfully rolled on the condom. He took the lube from Michael and poured some on his cock.

"Come here," Michael said.

Simon climbed between Michael's legs and held himself up with straight arms. Michael kissed him, nipping at his lips and running his hands down Simon's back.

"I want you," Michael said.

"Are you ready for me?"

"Yeah. Definitely."

Simon guided himself to Michael's body. Michael sucked in a breath as Simon encountered resistance. "Okay?" Simon asked.

"Yeah." Michael let out a breath and shifted his hips. "Yeah, keep going."

Michael shut his eyes. His erection waned. But he kept pushing toward Simon, encouraging him to keep going, and Simon felt the moment when Michael's body gave way. Michael grabbed Simon's shoulders and groaned softly. "More," he whispered.

Simon took that as his cue. He pressed in slowly, and already the sensation was almost too much. It was hot and tight and squeezed the head of his cock, and Simon thought he would lose it right there, but he closed his eyes and pressed forward slowly, as much as Michael would let him.

"Is this okay?" Simon asked, breathless.

Michael winced, but said, "Yeah. Push in more."

So Simon slowly thrust his hips forward. Then he was inside Michael.

This was miraculous. The two of them had always felt bound together in a way, but this was so much a symbol of that too. They literally fit together, their bodies connected in the most intimate of ways, and it felt almost like this was how they belonged together.

Then Michael whispered, "Move."

So Simon did, pulling out and then thrusting his hips forward. They both groaned. Michael's body was a revelation. It squeezed and caressed Simon's cock in all the right ways, making Simon hotter and crazier with each movement.

"Does this feel good?" Simon asked as he moved slowly.

"Yeah. It feels amazing. What about for you?"

"Best thing I ever felt." Simon picked up the pace experimentally, thrusting in and out faster and… oh. Jesus. He was going to come embarrassingly fast. "I'm not going to last long."

"Come inside me," Michael said as he reached for his own cock, which seemed to be coming back to life. He wrapped a hand around it and started stroking. "I want you to come inside me."

That would be easy, because this was exquisite. Simon had never felt anything like it. No hand or mouth could duplicate the sensation of moving in and out of Michael's body. He bowed his head and kissed Michael, because if Michael felt half of this, he needed to be kissed. Then *pow!* The orgasm hit him like a slap to the back of the head. He grabbed on to Michael, dug his fingers into Michael's flesh, and then he thrust one last time before coming hard into the condom.

Michael was right behind him, stroking himself to orgasm, coming right as Simon was floating back down to earth. Michael's body clamped down on Simon's softening cock, pushing him out, but that was okay because watching Michael come was maybe the hottest thing Simon had ever borne witness to.

Afterward, they lay next to each other on the bed.

"So… that happened," Simon said.

"You know, all of our firsts have been with each other."

"No. You kissed some guy at camp first."

Michael laughed. "All of the important firsts have been with each other. All of our sexual firsts. That's how it should be, don't you think?"

Simon thought about it. Certainly he trusted Michael more than any other guy he'd ever met, and even if things had been a little weird between them lately, Michael made a fair point. "Yeah," Simon said.

"Well, I don't know what's going to happen from now on, but… if I sleep with a hundred other guys in my life, I'll still always remember my first time with you."

"Yeah. Me too."

Michael rolled onto his side and kissed Simon's cheek. "Well. Thank you. For all of it."

Simon nodded as a way to say "You're welcome," because that seemed like such a weird thing to say after sex. "Thank you too."

Michael cuddled up next to Simon. "Stay here. Just for tonight. Okay?"

"Okay."

They talked for a little while, until both were sleepy. Simon must have fallen asleep, at any rate, because the next thing he was conscious of was the ceiling of Michael's dorm room as the sun came up. Michael was turned away from him, facing the wall and snoring softly. So Simon slipped out of bed. He'd given Michael that night, but he realized that was all he had right then. Today, tomorrow, those were for Simon to live for himself. He slipped out of the room and walked out of the building, into the sunlight, into the future.

CHAPTER 5

Present Day

MICHAEL LIVED in an apartment on West Twelfth Street off Seventh Ave, at the north end of the West Village. The building was so familiar that Simon wondered if it wasn't the same apartment Michael had been living in during one of Simon's less pleasant visits to the city, but it was clear once they were inside that it wasn't. It was much smaller, for example, than the old place. It was more cluttered without Joan's influence. It reminded Simon of the apartment he and Michael had once shared. There was an open box of cereal on the kitchen counter, a pile of unopened mail on the coffee table, and the whole place smelled a little musty.

"So you cleaned for me," Simon said.

"I am sorry it is not up to your specifications, Captain Clean," Michael said, taking Simon's suitcase and wheeling it into the bedroom. "These are hard economic times and I had to let the maid go."

Michael had never in his life had a maid. "It's fine," said Simon. And temporary.

"If you want, you can take the bedroom and I'll sleep on the couch."

"I don't want to put you out."

Michael cocked his head. "Really, Simon. We've known each other how many years and you're being all polite? No, I insist. It's fine, the couch folds out. I sleep on it all the time when the weather gets hot and the crappy AC in the bedroom can't handle it."

"If you're sure."

"I'm sure." Michael gave Simon a playful shove into the room.

The bed was made at least. The dressers had been cleared of most detritus aside from a few small-framed photos atop the taller one. One photo was of Michael's parents. One was of Michael with an arm casually thrown around Joan. One was of a toddler boy that Simon didn't recognize. And the last was a photo of Michael and Simon as teenagers, standing awkwardly next to each other in their prom tuxes. The photo had been taken by Simon's mother before their dates had shown up, but Michael had later joked that the photo showed who their real dates to the prom had been.

Which was true. Simon had barely seen Angela once he'd caught sight of Michael in a tux.

"You hungry?" Michael asked as he walked into the room.

"I could eat."

"Great. Put your stuff down. There's a good bagel place on Sixth. I'll buy you lunch."

There'd once been a bakery on Bleecker owned by a woman whom Simon had gotten to know. He had gone there for lunch between college classes sometimes, and the woman would slip him a couple of extra cookies with his sandwich. That was the New York Simon remembered, not the assembly line at the crowded bagel place, with the guys behind the counter barking orders at each other and motioning the slow-moving tourists to keep moving.

"I hope this is worth it," Simon said as he shelled out an absurd amount of money for a bagel with cream cheese and a can of soda.

"Best bagels in the neighborhood."

"That's an interesting qualifier."

"I'm not saying best bagels in the city. There's a better place on the Lower East Side. But this is close to home."

They sat on a bench outside the bagel place. Simon glanced at his watch. He'd been back in New York just over an hour. He already wanted to run away screaming.

"It's not the same," Simon said, meaning the city.

"I know," Michael said, but he could have meant anything.

THERE WAS a spring in the sofa bed that must have come uncoiled or something, because it stabbed Michael in the back every time he moved. He wondered if perhaps this was his penance for persuading Simon to come home even though Simon hadn't seemed ready.

Simon had spent most of the afternoon lamenting how much the city had changed, not only in the six years he'd been away, but since they'd been in college. Michael had tried to argue that the changes were for the better; sure, everything was more expensive now, but the city was so much cleaner and safer, and it wasn't like Simon couldn't afford to live here with his fancy finance job.

Simon himself had hardly changed at all. His bright blond hair looked a little dustier, maybe, but he was still in good shape, he still had the same perpetually flushed pale skin, he still wore glasses with dark frames. Not that it had even been that long since they'd seen each other, only eight months, maybe, but having Simon back in New York for the long term made it feel like Simon had never left.

Michael reflected, as he squirmed across the mattress to get away from the spring, that a lot *had* changed since Simon had left. Joan was currently enjoying the quiet, open air of the Catskills with Trevor, for one thing.

And with that thought, Michael was awake and knew he would not be sleeping for the rest of the night.

His stomach churned as he got out of bed and walked into the kitchen, where he poured a glass of water and fished through the cabinets for crackers or some other bland snack food.

What was it that he wanted here? He wanted Simon back. He'd take Simon's presence in his life again, though he wanted his friendship and craved his love. But there was damage to repair.

Michael had hurt Simon and he knew that, even though he had often pretended he didn't understand why his taking up with Joan had cut Simon so badly. But he and Simon had been at odds back in those days, and Simon could never understand about Joan. Michael didn't understand what had happened with Joan either most of the time.

She was one in a million, no doubt about that.

She and Trevor had a nice spread up there in the Catskills, which Michael could say with authority since he'd seen it, both on occasions he'd been invited and ones he hadn't. The last time he'd said, "I could sue," without really meaning it, which probably hadn't been the way to go and had only served to piss Joan off more.

Regrets. Michael had a lot of them.

He couldn't seem to undo the damage to his relationship with Joan without digging himself in further, but Simon's presence in his apartment told him maybe he could repair his relationship with Simon, which was what he intended to do. And maybe that wouldn't solve anything, and maybe it would make them both as miserable as they'd been when Simon moved to Dubai, but Michael wouldn't be able to live with himself if he didn't give it a shot.

And by "it" he meant the whole thing.

Aren't you gay?

That was what Simon had said when Michael had come to him with the news that he'd hooked up with Joan, and for whatever reason, those words still rung through Michael's head. Simon had been stunned. Michael knew that. He knew, also, that Simon probably would not have felt as thrilled about Joan as Michael had felt at the time. He'd hurt Simon deeply. He knew all of that.

So, fine. Michael had been a lousy friend, but all that had been years ago and he'd changed a lot since.

He supposed the problem was proving that.

The bedroom door opened and a tousled Simon emerged. "I thought I heard you get up."

"Couldn't sleep," Michael said.

"Sorry to hear that. I just wanted a glass of water. Do you mind if I…?" He gestured toward the cabinets.

Michael got a glass down and handed it to Simon. "I want you to know, for whatever it's worth, that things… everything is different now."

Simon shot him a sidelong glance. "How so?"

"A lot of shit went down while you were gone."

"I know, but—"

"There's a lot you don't know. A lot I didn't tell you."

"Like what?"

Michael spared a thought for Trevor and then said, "Like I don't want to get into it at three o'clock in the morning, but just... I didn't want you to think that you would be moving back here and putting up with me and my old bullshit. It's not like it was."

"All right."

Michael smirked. "I have all new bullshit now."

Simon laughed. "Yeah. I'll bet you do. You still can't read a clock to save your life, though. It's actually almost six."

Michael looked at the microwave clock. "I'll be damned."

"Look, I'm sure a lot has changed. I told you when I agreed to stay here that I was willing to see how things played out, didn't I? I do genuinely value your friendship, regardless of what else happened."

"Really?"

Simon looked at the floor. "We did love each other once for good reasons."

"But we don't anymore?"

Simon looked up and met Michael's eyes. "Well, first, you couldn't keep your dick in your pants if someone paid you. I don't know how I was supposed to react to that. And then there was the problem of us never quite being in the same place at the same time. But, eh, none of it matters now."

"But it does matter," Michael said. "All of it matters. You were the most important part of my life once."

"So what the hell happened?"

What *had* happened? New York had happened.

"If I had it to do over—"

"Forget it," said Simon. "I don't want your apologies. I want to start fresh. All right?"

"Yeah. All right. But you should know—"

"No. Don't tell me. Keep some secrets for now. We'll sort all this out later. I'm going to go back to bed."

2004

MICHAEL WAS like a Chihuahua, hopping around the apartment and giddy with excitement. "This is perfect. Isn't it, Simon? Perfect!"

Simon took another walk through the empty rooms, not loving the paint job—the walls were all kind of a faded, cloudy blue—but finding the space adequate. Two bedrooms, a decent-sized living room, a tiny kitchen—which was okay, since neither Michael nor Simon cooked much—and they had the makings of a reasonable living space. It was certainly better than the place Simon had until three months ago been sharing with his ex-boyfriend, Reed, who had the nerve to call Simon a "cold, calculating robot" before giving him the boot. So he'd been bunking at Michael's, sleeping on the couch until he could summon the motivation to find his own place. Then one day Michael had said, "You know, my lease is up next month. Let's get a bigger place together."

Simon stood in the doorway of one of the bedrooms and tried to mentally furnish it. He didn't own much stuff. He'd moved in with Reed two weeks after graduating from NYU, and nearly all of the stuff in their "shared" apartment had been purchased by Reed or his parents, leaving Simon with not much more than a few suitcases and a box of miscellany currently residing in Michael's living room.

But it wasn't like Simon didn't have money to burn now that he was single again. Reed had taken care of him, so he'd just been squirreling it away. He'd had the good fortune to land a job at an international bank, and though he sometimes felt like he worked for the evil empire, it was hard to say no to those paychecks.

So he could certainly afford his own place, but the prospect of living alone was daunting. He was happy enough to share with Michael—Michael, who had apparently given up on his romantic pursuit of Simon, because he hadn't tried anything or said anything in the three months they'd been crowded into the same space. Michael hadn't actually tried much of anything with Simon in a few years, not since Simon hooked up with Reed. Not only that, but Michael was currently seeing a guy who lived in the East Village somewhere, whom Simon had only met once and instantly disliked.

Anyway, it seemed like a good idea, and the apartment was in the West Village, very close to the Christopher Street stop on the subway, and so convenient to Simon's office just off Wall Street. The place was a little pricey, but split with Michael, it was a bargain. It really was pretty ideal.

"We'll take it!" Michael declared.

"Whoa, hey," said Simon.

Michael threw an arm around Simon and gave his chest a gentle pat. To the landlord, he said, "Sorry. My friend here is a practical sort. He doesn't like making snap decisions."

"No, I mean… it's a good place," said Simon. "I just thought we should talk about it before we agree to take it."

"Do you want to live here?" Michael asked.

"I… yeah."

"Great! Talk done. We'll take it."

THEY MOVED in two weeks later. Moving for Simon mostly involved buying new everything. He found the whole process exhausting, but he was happy enough with the results once it was all delivered and set up.

He stood in the door of his bedroom and took a photo with his phone.

Michael walked over and peered inside the room. "You are pathologically neat."

"We moved in hours ago. All I've had time to do is set everything up."

"Me too. I've already lost my blue sneakers. You haven't seen them, have you?"

"Under the sofa."

Michael turned around and said, "Oh! Thanks." He resumed peering into Simon's bedroom. "Seriously, though. I forgot what a freak you are."

That made Simon suddenly self-conscious. He wanted to shake up the bedspread to make it look a little messier. Of course, then he'd have to straighten it. He sighed. "I'm not... you don't think I'm cold, do you?"

"What?"

"It's robotic, the way I've cleaned this room."

Michael took a step back and looked at Simon with his eyebrows askew. Then understanding seemed to dawn and he smiled. "This is about that nonsense Reed told you when he dumped you."

"He's right, isn't he?" This had been something nagging at Simon for a long time. He should have felt something more for Reed than affection. He liked Reed, certainly, liked spending time with him and enjoyed the hell out of sex, but he never felt the passion he'd expected to come with love. And any couple that had been together as long as Simon and Reed had been must have been in love. So where was the fire Simon had been expecting to feel? "I'm an unfeeling robot."

"No, he's not right. Reed is a dick and you're well rid of him."

"But—"

"No. I know for a fact that you have a big heart and you care about things and people, and Reed deserves to get kicked in the balls for making you feel otherwise."

"How can you know that?"

"Because I know *you*. I have known you your whole fucking life, practically. You're a little weird, sure, but if Reed chose to interpret that as cold, well, his loss."

That soothed Simon somewhat. He turned back to his room. This was the first bedroom he'd had to himself since he'd left for college.

"I... thank you," Simon said quietly.

Before he knew what was happening, he'd been pulled into a hug. He let out a breath and went with it, putting his arms around Michael and leaning his head on Michael's shoulder, letting go of some of the pain he'd been holding on to since Reed had dumped him. This was probably the first time he and Michael had really touched in years, Simon realized, and it was a comfort.

Before it got carried away, Simon pulled away gently and said, "Why did you hug me?"

Michael smiled and shrugged. "You looked like you needed it."

"I think I did."

"And that's how I know you're not a robot."

Simon couldn't help but smile at that. So he hugged Michael again.

"I know things have happened," Simon said.

"Oh, no. Don't apologize. All of it is water under the bridge."

"No, I... I just wanted to say, lots of shit has happened between us, but you're a good friend. You've always been a good friend to me."

"I'm not always sure that's true."

Simon looked at Michael, really looked at him, and saw fatigue and a bit of pain. "You're always honest with me. You always want what's best for me. You took me in when I was down. What more could I want from a friend?"

"Well, but I had... romantic feelings for you for such a long time. I was kind of a brat for a while there."

"But you were always honest about it."

"I guess so."

Simon looked back toward his room. It was all new stuff, but it was set up to his specifications. It felt like it was his. Standing there, next to Michael, it felt like home.

Michael swayed back and forth a little and shoved his hands in his pockets. "I'm supposed to meet Carl for a thing tonight."

Simon knew that by "a thing," Michael meant sex. "Okay."

"I can cancel on him if you need me."

"No. I'm good, actually."

Michael nodded. He got up on his tiptoes and kissed Simon on the forehead. "I'll text you if I'm not coming home. Love you."

"Love you too."

When Michael disappeared out the door and off to his date or whatever with Carl, Simon realized how true those words were.

"SO I'M thinking about going to art school," Michael said as he chipped at the varnish on the bar with his thumbnail.

Carl raised his eyebrows. "Why?"

"Well, for one thing, I hate teaching." Despite the crappy, post-9/11 economy, Michael had managed to secure a job teaching English at a private school in the Village. He'd been really jazzed at first, but trying to get overprivileged twelve-year-olds interested in the classics was an exercise in futility.

"But art school?"

"For something practical, like design. I used to draw, you know."

"I didn't know." Carl laughed. "What a stereotypical thing to do. Another fag at art school."

"Hey, now. I do not mock your choices. What is up with this orange scarf? No heterosexual man would wear a thing like that."

"Good thing I'm not heterosexual," Carl said, flinging the scarf around his shoulders.

Michael contemplated whether to order another beer or to talk Carl into taking him home. He was mildly disgusted with himself, because he didn't even like Carl that much. Yeah, he was hot and had a huge cock that he definitely knew how to use, but as a person, he had some qualities that were less than desirable, including a bizarre internalized homophobic streak. But things had been starting to get a little weird with Simon, which was why Michael hadn't canceled. Michael fingered the piercings in his left ear, something else Carl had made it known he didn't especially approve of. Hell, the board of the school where he taught hadn't approved either, and Michael had gotten a haircut and had to take the hoops out of his ears during the day. He wondered what Carl would have thought of him if they'd met when he'd still had blue hair.

He was over Simon, wasn't he? He'd long since gotten over his conviction that they'd end up together—Simon moving in with Reed had pretty effectively put a nail in that coffin—and he'd followed Simon's advice and gone off to experience the city and its men. Carl was just another in a long line of men Michael had partaken of. He was sure there would be many more.

But something about that look on Simon's face when he wondered if he was robotic had really gotten to Michael. Like, reached through his chest and squeezed his heart.

And yet Simon did not want Michael. Michael was fully aware of this fact and had been when he'd proposed they get a place together—with separate bedrooms, of course. He'd thought he was ready to deal with Simon as an adult, a fully actualized person who would probably bring dates home and have sex on that immaculate new bed.

Of course, it was not a coincidence that the bedrooms were on opposite ends of the apartment.

Because shit. *Shit.* Michael still wanted Simon, had wanted to hold him even longer than he had that afternoon. He wanted to take Simon's pain away, to convince him that he was real and warm and passionate and not at all the things Reed had accused him of. Because Michael knew better. Because Michael loved Simon and knew Simon loved him in return, and not in merely the token way they'd taken to tossing the words at each other.

But Simon didn't want him. Not in that way.

Carl lifted his hand in signal to the bartender. Michael reached over and put his hand over Carl's. "We should go," Michael said.

"Yeah?"

"Yeah. I want you to fuck my brains out."

Carl leered. "I believe that can be arranged."

2010

"MIKE, WE need to talk."

Nothing good ever came after those words.

Michael was in the kitchen, washing dishes and generally playing the part of good domestic partner, something he knew he'd been slacking on lately. He was putting in a conscious effort to be a good partner to Joan, especially lately, as it felt like the seams were showing in their relationship.

"What is it?" he asked her, a bit afraid. He'd been bracing himself for what he suspected was inevitable: Joan finally getting fed up and leaving him. They'd been arguing a lot lately, and, well, Michael's will to fight for his relationship was waning. It wasn't just that he missed being with men, though that was certainly a factor in whatever was going on between them. But, really, that was small potatoes. The bigger issue was that the magic of the initial euphoria of being together had worn off, and once the novelty of their coupling had lost its luster, there just wasn't much left between them. The relationship was too unbalanced; they were both too flighty and idealistic, Michael supposed, and didn't have an anchor between them to weigh them down to earth when they needed it.

Simon had always been Michael's anchor.

He pushed that thought aside, because Simon was not here now, but Joan was, standing before him, in the kitchen of the apartment they shared, and she'd said they needed to talk.

She bit her lip. Her hands were behind her back and she rocked on her heels. Michael sensed this was bad news.

She stepped closer to Michael and whipped her hands forward. She was holding a piece of white plastic. Everything went in slow motion then. Michael lifted his own hands to take whatever it was from her. He stared at it for a long moment, not believing what he was seeing. It was a pregnancy test.

It was positive.

"Holy shit," he said.

CHAPTER 6

Present Day

SIMON STARTED the new job on his third day in New York, and one of his first acts in the new office was to call a real estate broker.

Renting seemed the safer option, since he was already contemplating talking his boss into transferring him anywhere that wasn't New York, though at this point he'd settle for an apartment that wasn't Michael's.

Things had changed since he'd left New York. Well, that was obvious, wasn't it? His regular haunts had come and gone in his absence, the culture of the Village seemed to have shifted, and there was a shiny newness to parts of the city that hadn't been there when he'd left. But more than that, Simon wasn't the same man, couldn't have been after all he'd seen and done during his years away. Michael wasn't quite his old self either; he seemed sadder, for one thing, though that sadness was hidden under a lot of bravado. This was a man who professed not to care about anything but whose face was a mess of changing emotions as Simon had watched him do his weekly phone call with his son the night before. Trevor was coming up on his fourth birthday, if Simon's math was right, but had apparently needed a lot of prompting from Michael to be able to talk. And the agony on Michael's face had not been from enduring a phone call with a toddler but instead was from frustration of not being able to be there for his son. When he'd put the phone down, he'd said, "Trevor barely even knows who I am." Then he'd gone into the bathroom and shut the door.

Not being able to see his son was clearly deeply affecting Michael. Simon couldn't recall ever seeing him look so defeated.

Perhaps, Simon reasoned, he should give his old friend the benefit of the doubt; he should believe Michael when Michael insisted he'd changed. But it was hard to get all those old memories to fade. That time Simon had walked in on Michael getting a blow job, for example. And every time he'd seen Michael and Joan together was burned in his brain like a high-resolution photograph. The way his relationship with Michael had fallen apart, the betrayal of Michael falling for Joan—all of it was there in Simon's mind, and he couldn't change the past, couldn't make those old images stop stabbing him. And, oh, wasn't it just like Michael to assume Simon would come crawling back after Joan left?

He should have cut ties, but it had felt disloyal, and anyway, he hadn't really wanted to. Michael was too integral a part of his life.

Simon, it seemed, still had plenty of feelings.

Maybe Michael had changed. But maybe Simon could give him the benefit of the doubt while living in a different apartment.

Three days of Michael getting in Simon's hair later and he was standing in the kitchen of a two-bedroom place in SoHo with really ugly linoleum floors. The broker was extolling the virtues of the neighborhood—it didn't matter how many times Simon interrupted to explain that he had lived in New York for almost ten years before his defection overseas, she still spoke to him as if he were just off the boat—but Simon couldn't see himself in this place. It was too stark, too spare, and that blue linoleum floor was really an eyesore.

"There's got to be something in my price range with wood floors," he said. "Or carpeting, even. I'd take carpeting over this."

The broker grimaced. "I've got a place in TriBeCa, but it's a little above your range."

Simon looked at the floor again. Baby blue, that linoleum was; it was a crime against good taste. "We can look further uptown. I don't need to live walking distance to my office."

"There are simply not a lot of vacancies right now," said the broker. "You know the vacancy rate is less than 1 percent, right? I have a dozen rentals right now. That's it."

"Really?"

"I've got one place in Chelsea that meets all your criteria."

Simon sensed there was a catch, but he said, "Great. Show me that! Why are we wasting time here? Have you seen how ugly these floors are?"

The broker crossed her arms over her chest. "It's not available for another month. The owners won't let anyone see it until the twenty-eighth."

The twenty-eighth was a little over two weeks away. "Crap."

"You've got a place to stay, right? If you can hold out a little longer, there should be a few openings next month that are more in line with what you're looking for. Unless you want to buy." She looked at him hopefully.

"Too much of a commitment. Also a shitty investment. You should know better."

She shrugged, although Simon suspected she knew as well as he did that New York was the one market in the country where it was actually more economical to rent instead of buy.

Basically, the broker was telling Simon that his options were to stay with Michael for another month—or longer, probably—or to take this place with its horrific flooring. Did he really want to compromise this much, living in a place he really didn't like, to get away from Michael?

"All right. Well. Call me when that other place is available, I guess."

RESIGNED TO the fact that he'd be in Michael's apartment for a few more weeks, Simon decided to take a walk on Saturday afternoon. Partly, he wanted to escape Michael, who had been hovering all day, making sure Simon was okay, offering him food, asking if he was too warm or too cold. But partly, he wanted to take a look at what the city had become in his absence.

The city had changed, as all things did with the passage of time. The West Village was as different now from what Simon remembered as he and Michael were. He walked down Seventh Avenue, then walked east on Twelfth Street, then walked down Sixth, past the Jefferson Market Library. He turned down Eighth Street, and the shops and restaurants there were still populated by NYU students from what he could tell, even if the shops themselves were different.

As he walked, he catalogued what he saw, what he remembered. The geography was the same, as was the architecture, the basic structure of the neighborhood. But the surface was different. The bars he'd once hung out in were now fine dining restaurants. The shops where he'd bought most of his wardrobe when he'd been in his twenties—clothes he still owned, though they were in his mother's storage unit in Iowa City—had become chain stores. The indie coffee shop that had kept him pumped full of caffeine when he was in college was now a cupcake bakery. The dingy diner where he'd eaten many a late-night meal was now a fancy Thai place.

Michael had often said that, even though they'd spent the first eighteen years of their lives in the Iowa City suburbs, New York City felt more like home than Iowa ever had. Simon agreed, especially now. Even with the shiny new façade, so much of the Village was still familiar. He crossed Fifth and saw the little shop that sold wigs and shoes to drag queens. He walked past the shoe store that was still, apparently, blasting hit rock songs from the nineties out of its speakers. He passed the sandwich shop where he and Michael had spent many hours studying; through the window, he could almost see them huddled down together at their regular table in the corner. He kept walking, arriving at Astor Place, crossing over it to St. Marks. What had once been the coolest part of the neighborhood was now full of frozen yogurt places and looked like a sanitized version of its old self, but the funky clothing store where Michael had picked out club clothes for Simon was still there. The cheap noodle place where Simon and Michael had gone when Reed had dumped Simon was there, and Simon paused to stare at the outside table they'd sat at while Simon had cried about the end of his relationship. He remembered, even, that Michael had worn a hot pink T-shirt, something Simon had opinions about but hadn't voiced because he was too distraught about being homeless.

When he got to First Ave, he decided to head back. He walked up to Ninth Street and turned back west. And he thought, well, maybe the neighborhood wasn't so different. Because he passed a dozen apartment buildings he'd definitely been in. Here, littered all over Greenwich Village, were the scattered remains of Simon's love life: the buildings where he'd gone to parties, the apartments of his ex-boyfriends. There was the guy he'd dated for a few months in 2005 who lived near McSorley's. There was the building he'd been in only once when he'd fucked that guy whose name he couldn't remember. He remembered being pressed against the brick of the building next to the Ethiopian restaurant as he and another guy kissed hard, a prelude to a crazy night of sex and marijuana and being alive.

This was his home, that was certain. Every inch of it was imprinted in his memory. And everywhere, there was Michael. These old buildings he walked past, well, Simon knew his former loves had probably moved by now. But Michael was still here. It was Michael whose hand he'd held experimentally when they were college freshmen, just to see what it would be like to hold a man's hand in public. It was with Michael that he ate blintzes and pierogies at Veselka late at night after drinking themselves silly at the bars on St. Marks. He'd been with Michael that time he'd discovered the organic pet food store and talked about getting a cat, although they never did. He walked past the cafe with the garden out back where he and Michael had talked each other down from various crises over the years.

Simon wanted to weep with the familiarity of it all. Here he was, almost thirty-four and still somehow reveling in the relics of his past, this old neighborhood, his home.

He'd resolved not to take Michael back, but he'd taken the job in New York, hadn't he? The transfer to the New York office hadn't been forced upon him. He could have said no, and if that had backfired, he could have gotten another job. He was good at what he did, and other companies would clamor to have him. But when his boss had approached him with this promotion and transfer, he'd taken it, because coming back to New York felt inevitable.

Coming back to Michael felt inevitable.

Simon had been away long enough. He'd been ready to come back. Yes, he was still hurt and sore, still angry about Michael and Joan, but perhaps it was time to focus on the present. Now the Village had a sheen on it that it hadn't had ten years ago. It was cleaner, brighter, had more chain stores and more money. Now Simon had loved and lost and traveled the world; he had few regrets to show for it. Now Michael was nursing his own hurts and pains. Now Michael was a father.

Michael had bailed on what could have been a great relationship with Simon to be with a woman, a relationship he'd called "easy." It was true that Simon and Michael's relationship was always complicated, had always had so much history behind it. It was full of memories, like this neighborhood. Simon had wondered about that often, what it would be like to fall for a woman. He supposed it would have been easier in a way; maybe if Simon had, his relationship with his father wouldn't be strained. If Simon had been attracted to women, maybe he'd be a married father by now. Maybe his life would be easier.

But no. Simon wouldn't change himself for anything. He loved that he was gay. It had taken some time to get there, but he loved it. He loved men, loved being with men, loved being a part of this whole culture of people. Just as he loved the part of himself that was a dorky banker who was good with numbers, the part that had to wear glasses because his vision was so terrible he couldn't wear contacts, the part that liked things just so, he loved the gay part of himself and was proud of it. No one could take that from him.

He still had feelings for Michael. That was impossible to deny. It wasn't only that Michael was his oldest and best friend, though that was a lot of it. But, no, he still had sexual feelings. He still thought Michael was as sexy as he had been when they were younger, despite the melancholy that hung over him these days. There was a part of him that could still see them together at some point in the future, if the goddamn planets ever aligned and they could figure out how to be together.

As he walked home, Simon held his head high, determined to look to the future. This place was always going to be imprinted with his memories, but maybe he could make some new ones.

2007

IT HAD not been a great week for Michael.

He'd been dating a man named Christopher for a few weeks. Christopher was an otter type with a brilliant, toothy smile and a wicked sense of humor, both of which Michael appreciated. He wasn't sure he saw the relationship going anywhere, but he was having fun. Until, that is, Christopher's latest STI test came up positive for the clap. Michael was dead certain he didn't have anything, and he and Christopher had only had sex once, anyway, but Christopher disagreed and then completely lost his temper. He became so angry and violent that he punched Michael several times. The peculiar thing was that all of the punches, and hence all of the subsequent bruising, landed on parts of Michael's body usually covered by clothing. Michael clued in pretty quickly that Christopher was kind of an old hat in the boyfriend-punching business, so Michael said good-bye and ran out.

The bruises fucking hurt, though, as did the price of the antibiotics his doctor insisted he take for just getting near the clap, and the whole situation was both painful and humiliating.

It made him leery of men. It wasn't the first time he'd gotten hit over the course of a relationship, although it rarely was hard enough to actually leave bruises. There was a particularly angry-looking purple blob on Michael's side that he was very careful to keep hidden from Simon. He had taken to wearing a robe on trips to and from the shower instead of prancing around in a towel.

"Oh, did you finally learn modesty?" Simon had asked. Which, *ha-ha*.

But it was better than having to explain all this to Simon, who would either judge him harshly or rush out to vanquish Christopher. Not knowing which reaction he wanted less, Michael had opted to stay silent.

The situation was getting to him, though. The drama left him feeling hollow and lonely and anxious. His STI test came back negative for everything, which was good, at least. But the night he ran into

Christopher at his favorite bar had caused him to spend a good five minutes hyperventilating in the bathroom, after which time Roberto, whom Michael had hooked up with a couple of times but whom he found kind of annoying, tried to pick him up again, and Michael sort of lost his shit.

He went home to an, of course, empty apartment. That whole week went that way. No sign of Simon until very late at night, usually. It had been like this more or less since Simon had gotten promoted, and he was putting in zany hours and then hitting up some low-rent Irish pub in the Financial District with his coworkers when he needed to blow off steam. Michael didn't think Simon was sleeping with anybody these days, but he supposed he could have been wrong about that because it wasn't like they even really talked much anymore.

The next night, he met up with Roberto for dinner. Roberto proceeded to then ask, "When are you getting a real job?" as if teaching drawing and painting classes while he finished his MFA did not count as a job. He was picking up some design freelance work here and there, too, but he was still honing his design skills. He was pretty sure that was what he wanted to do after he graduated from Parsons, but explaining to Roberto that he had to finish his degree to get a goddamn "real job" was mostly futile.

The night after that, Michael stayed in. He felt like he was losing his mind. Since there was no Simon to speak to, Michael finally picked up the phone and called home. He was desperate for someone to comfort him.

"You know, a lot of this is your own doing," Michael's father said after Michael gave him the abridged version of the week's events.

"Wait, what? I broke up with a guy because he punched me, but that's my fault somehow?"

"Oh, sweetie," Michael's mother broke in. "He only means you need to be smarter about some of the choices you're making."

"Mom, I broke up with a guy who hit me. How did I make the wrong choice there?"

She made tsking sounds. "Really, Michael, you should be smarter about who you date. Maybe you shouldn't date at all for a while. You know how I feel about this behavior."

Michael rolled his eyes, grateful that they couldn't see him. "What you want is for me to meet a nice boy and have a chaste relationship. Or, even better, you want me to bring home a nice girl."

"It would make things easier," said his mother.

Michael prided himself on the fact that he never lied about who he was or what he wanted. He'd told his parents within weeks of realizing he was gay. He'd felt like they'd had that kind of relationship. He'd been a naïve fourteen-year-old at the time. He supposed he was still kind of naïve for always answering the, "Are you seeing someone?" question with something glib like, "Oh, I've been seeing a guy named Carl, but I don't know if it's going to go anywhere." He didn't understand until quite recently that, "We'll love you no matter what" actually meant, "We'll love you but still judge you" to his parents.

As he hung up the phone, Michael felt like things couldn't get any worse, so that was when Simon came home, of course.

One look and Simon said, "Hey, is everything okay?"

"Fine," Michael said, trying to wipe his eyes surreptitiously.

Of course, Simon saw through that. "It's not. What is it? What can I do?"

Simon was part of the problem, Michael realized. He'd been waiting around all week for Simon to come home and say these words and make it better, but why? They were friends, nothing more, and Simon lived in his own little world and nothing that Michael wanted would ever work out in his favor. Simon hadn't been there for him in a long time, nor was he required to be. All of it made Michael sad.

"I just… I need some space right now." Michael retreated to his room.

SIMON CAME home Friday night and found Michael passed out on the sofa with a book open on his chest. Rather than wake Michael up, Simon picked up the book and looked it over. He was mildly amused to see it was a romance novel with an overwrought cover featuring a woman with long red hair clutching onto a shirtless Fabio type. His chuckling must have caused Michael to stir.

"You read this shit?" Simon said.

Michael snatched the book back. "I found it in a box someone on Morton Street left out on their curb. It's pretty good, actually. See, the dude is this Scottish laird and the woman is an aristocratic woman from London who needs—"

"I don't need to know."

"You're no fun." Michael wriggled himself up to a sitting position.

"What are you even doing home? I thought you were going to Fire Island for the weekend with your flavor of the week. What's his name?"

"Roberto, and no. I called it off."

"Really? Why?"

"I'm tired, I don't know. Wasn't feeling it. Roberto told me I should go fuck myself, so I guess that's over."

"Oh, sorry."

Michael rubbed his eyes. "Don't be. I didn't wreck any of your plans, did I? Were you expecting to have the apartment to yourself this weekend to hold an orgy?"

Simon scoffed. "Hardly. Well, I was going to invite this guy Joel over. I told you about him, right?"

"The cute barista from Think Coffee? Yeah, yeah."

"I hadn't gotten around to calling him yet, though."

Michael nodded. "You want to rent some tawdry movie and then get frozen yogurt from that new place on Sixth?"

"Sure, okay."

"I mean, don't cancel your plans on my account. You want to seduce the guy who makes your lattes, that's cool with me. But maybe tonight, we could—"

"Michael. I'm in. Let's do it."

They walked to the little indie video store a few blocks away. Michael seemed to be in the mood for something schmoopy and kept picking up romantic comedies. Simon wanted something brainier. They compromised on some indie movie the store clerk recommended.

They got frozen yogurt from the new place. Michael made fun of Simon for getting plain yogurt with just a couple of strawberries on it, so Simon made fun of Michael for negating the nutritional value of yogurt by piling his high with cookies and candy. They both laughed as they walked back to the apartment.

The movie ended up being a bit schmoopy after all. It was a drama about five friends in New York who were all about to turn thirty, and the acting wasn't great—Simon reasoned that was why none of these actors were famous—and worse, the token gay friend was always shown sleeping with a new guy. The four other characters found love by the end of the movie, but not the gay character, who said, "Maybe this isn't the right time for me. But at least I have you guys!"

When it was over, Simon muttered, "Angels or sluts."

"Huh?"

He turned toward Michael. "In all of these movies, the gay character is always a perfect, saintly, celibate angel, or he's a total slut. How many extras did they have to hire to show walking out of Drake's bedroom?"

Michael smirked. "So you don't think this was an accurate portrayal of gay life?"

Simon shrugged. "Hey, maybe some guys live their lives that way, and that's cool if it makes them happy, but it's not the *only* way gay men live."

"Yeah, I didn't like Drake either. But I would bone the actor who played Cliff in a hot minute."

Simon laughed. "Maybe you don't like Drake because he's just like you."

Michael rolled his eyes and threw a pillow at Simon. That only made Simon laugh harder as he caught the pillow.

"Seriously, though, you don't think I'm a slut, do you?" asked Michael.

The truth was that Simon had lately taken to watching the parade of men Michael dated with something like awe. Part of him was disgusted and part of him was a little jealous that Michael could get all those guys into bed with him.

Or he was jealous, period.

"I don't think you're a slut. At least, not in a bad way." Simon smiled, attempting to be reassuring.

"Good. Because I was only taking your advice."

"What advice was that?"

Michael reached over and lightly ran a hand along the edge of Simon's hair. Then he withdrew it and said, "You remember that night in Washington Square Park? I all but declared my love for you, but you told me you weren't ready for forever yet, and I got really mad, but I still heard you. You said you moved to New York for a reason, that you wanted to experience everything before you settled down. So that's all I'm doing."

Simon had taken to wondering lately if Michael still had those old feelings, if he still loved Simon in that way. It seemed not. "You think you'll ever settle down?" Simon asked.

"Maybe. If I found the right guy."

Simon was not the right guy, was the implication.

Why that made him so sad, he wasn't sure.

Well, no, that was a lie. He'd been lying to himself for weeks that he didn't want Michael romantically, but the truth was that he did. He'd recently gotten a promotion and could easily afford a much nicer apartment closer to his office, but the thought of leaving Michael filled him with dread. He was slowly coming to terms with the fact that, though they were not currently romantically or sexually involved and had not been for years, Simon enjoyed the easy companionship between them. But lately—really only since the promotion, which made him feel like a real adult—he'd been wanting more.

"Hey, now. Hey. What's going on behind those thick glasses?" Michael asked.

"Nothing."

"Right. And plain yogurt tastes good. Come on, Simon. Tell me."

"I… nothing. It's really not a big deal. I was just thinking about the big promotion and what that'll mean. I'm already working longer hours. I have less time for dating. And I think I'm kind of over the scene, you know? Not that I was ever really in it, but…."

Michael raised his eyebrows. "You mean you're done trying to experience everything."

"No, of course not. But I want to experience different things now. I want to travel. I want to fall in love. I want to do well at my job and get other promotions."

Michael nodded. He laughed quietly. "It's funny, don't you think, that you and I are never quite in the same place?"

Simon sort of understood what Michael was saying, but he leaned back on the couch and said, "What do you mean?"

"I want a committed relationship, but you don't want to commit. I decide to live life to the fullest, you want to settle down. I want fun and sex and New York, but you want to travel. I think maybe for five minutes when we were seventeen, we both wanted the same things at the same time, but never again since."

"I'm sorry," Simon said, though he wasn't sure what he was apologizing for.

"Don't apologize. That's just life. It's never quite the right time for us."

"Do you think it ever will be?"

There was hope and fear and everything in the question. Because suddenly, that was what Simon wanted. He wanted him and Michael together, in love and committed, married, maybe, and he wanted it fiercely, like he hadn't wanted anything in a long time. He wanted them both naked and pressed together on the couch instead of sitting a foot apart. He wanted Michael to look at him the way he hadn't in years.

Shit. He'd fucked it up. He'd told Michael ten years ago that he wasn't ready, that he didn't love Michael in that way, but now he did, now he wanted everything Michael had wanted for them. But Michael had already moved on. As he should have, because Simon was a wishy-washy prick who was never quite sure what he wanted.

Now he knew. Dammit.

"Someday," Michael said.

"Maybe what I want is to be in one of those relationships like the straight couples have," Simon said, gesturing toward the TV, "but in the end, I'm like Drake. I haven't had a long-term relationship since Reed. I fuck and run most of the time."

"So don't run next time."

"Easy for you to say." Simon took a deep breath and tried to get his thoughts in order. "I don't know. Lately sex has felt like trying on a jacket that doesn't fit quite right. Nothing fits quite right."

Michael nodded. "Yeah, I know how that goes. You and me, though. We always fit."

That couldn't be denied. There had been a time, a year or so in college, when Simon would go to Michael for sex regularly because it was comforting. Michael had always welcomed him. But that hadn't happened since before Simon dated Reed. Simon wondered if they'd still be as good in bed together as they had once been.

Still, that memory should have been a sign. Michael had been there all along, waiting for Simon, but Simon couldn't figure out he had feelings for Michael—real, romantic feelings—until it was too late. He felt like an idiot.

"It's not too late," Michael said quietly.

"How can you still want anything to do with me?" Simon asked. "I've been such an asshole to you."

"You haven't."

"I have. You offer me love and I push it away. That's been the dynamic of our friendship for ten years. You're right to move on. You're right to experience everything, to be with as many men as you want, to live your goddamn life the way you want to without me."

"Simon."

"I was wrong. All along, I was wrong. I thought there was something bigger for me out there, some other person or place or... I don't even know. I thought that there was this great big world waiting for me, but the one thing I really needed was in front of me the whole time. And now it's too late."

"It's not."

"No?"

Michael kissed Simon. He cupped his hand behind Simon's head and leaned into it, pressing hard, pulling harder. He licked against Simon's lips, so Simon opened up to let him in. Simon opened his whole heart, his mind, his spirit, and let Michael in, let them be together. Finally.

Michael backed away. "I'm always going to love you. Always. Even when we're not together. Even when we each do boneheaded things. This may not be the right time for us, but it's not too late. It will never be too late."

Simon reached over and grabbed Michael's hands. He twined their fingers together. "So if I told you I wanted you right now, you'd be with me."

"Now, yes. Tomorrow, I don't know. Things are complicated."

Not the answer Simon had been looking for. "Next year? Five years from now?"

"I'll still love you. But I can't…." He looked away.

"You can't what?"

Michael stuck out his lower jaw for a moment and then wiped his face with his hand. "I can't promise you forever until I know you can promise it to me."

"You don't trust me?"

"It's not that. Just. All the times you came to me and I thought *this time. This time will be the time he stays.* But you never do. And now you're saying all the right things. You want me. You love me, probably, though you haven't said. But I can't put my heart out there to get stomped on again."

"I won't. Not this time."

"You say that. But how can I know it's true? How can you? You may change your mind tomorrow, and then what?"

Michael looked up and his eyes were red. Simon hated that he'd done that, that he'd caused Michael this pain. He intended to make up for it this time. He'd be better than he ever had before.

Because the promotion was like the first step in his adult life, and having a real, solid relationship with Michael should have been the second. They'd be together, make a family together, give each other everything they had been holding back.

"Let me prove it," Simon said.

Michael shook his head sadly. "Tonight. I can give you tonight. But that's all I have."

That was something, so Simon leaned over and kissed Michael, putting his hands on Michael's shoulders to pull him closer.

Part of him wanted to keep arguing, wanted to continue making the case that he was serious this time, because in Simon's heart and mind, he was. He meant it. He wanted Michael by his side for good.

But the time for words had passed, so he decided to make his case with his body.

He disentangled himself from Michael and stood. Michael's gaze followed up the length of Simon's body, so Simon knew he had Michael's attention. He knew this time that he couldn't wait for Michael; he had to be the one to put himself out there. He unbuttoned his shirt and peeled it away, and then pulled off his undershirt. As Simon reached for his belt, Michael stared at him, all rapt attention, as if he had no idea what was going to happen next, as if it weren't obvious. So Simon undid his belt and slid it off. He unbuttoned his pants and dropped them. He stepped out of his underwear. And he stood there, completely naked, exposed, hard, and ready for Michael.

Michael stood slowly. He put his arms around Simon and kissed him, pressing their bodies together. Michael's clothes were rough everywhere they touched Simon's bare skin. But Simon knew this had to be on Michael's terms. He knew that he was putting himself out there for Michael to take, that he wanted to give himself wholly to Michael for Michael to love him or take him or incinerate him or reject him.

He wanted Michael naked but he waited. Michael kissed Simon, slid their lips together slowly, ran his hands over Simon's naked body.

Michael whispered, "In high school, when you thought no one was noticing you, I was noticing you. You have always been so much sexier, so much more amazing than you realized." Michael slipped Simon's glasses off and put them on the coffee table. "I used to fantasize about us together. Back then, I mean. I knew what you looked like naked. I knew you had pale skin and pink nipples and hardly any body hair. I wanted it. I wanted all of you for so long."

"I'm sorry."

"No, don't… I'm trying to tell you, I always thought you were the sexiest, and if you ever felt otherwise, never feel that again. Maybe no one else in high school noticed how hot you were, but I did. I do. So even if I can't be with you tomorrow, please know it's not because I don't want you. I do. I always have."

"Then why—"

"I don't want to talk anymore."

Michael took a step back and pulled off his T-shirt. He shucked the track pants he'd been wearing, along with his briefs. He seemed hairier than the last time Simon had seen him naked, with dark hair dusting the broad planes of his chest and collecting near his cock. He was different, but he was also so very much the same. He still had the scar on his belly that he'd gotten as a seven-year-old when he fell off a jungle gym. He still had the tattoo of a four-leaf clover on his hip that he'd gotten one drunken night in college, and he still had all the piercings in his ears. He was still essentially Michael, a man now and not the kid Simon had grown up with—a sweet but complicated man, a deeply troubled man. And Simon was also a man now, one who finally knew what he wanted, a man who knew to take what was right in front of him while he still could.

"My room," Simon said.

Michael nodded. He grabbed Simon's hand and led the way. There was no sarcastic comment about the neatness of the room, which Simon had half expected. It was just Michael, dragging Simon to the bed but then letting go. He lay down on his back and spread his legs.

Jesus.

Simon took a deep breath and took lube and a condom from his bedside table drawer. He remembered the first time they had done this, way back in college, all the first times Simon had done anything, and all of them were with Michael. In between, there had been Reed and a host of other men in whom Simon had thought he could find what he needed; all of them had come up short.

In the end, Michael was everything. Simon wished he had known that all along.

He didn't need Michael to show him what to do this time. He knew from practice and experience. He knew from figuring out with other men what he liked, what worked. He'd developed tricks and moves, he'd figured out how to let instinct take over, he knew exactly what to do with Michael's body now that it was laid out before him.

He stroked Michael's cock, and the texture of it against his palm warmed something in him. Simon loved men, loved how they looked and tasted, loved low male voices and thick body hair and the scrape of stubble against his cheek. He'd been fantasizing about all of it since the day he'd figured out how to jack himself off. Then Michael came out and made all of it okay. Simon's shame at being different had been lifted because Michael was like him too. Michael had made feeling the way he did okay. And Michael was here with him now, so very much a man, possessing all of the qualities Simon craved in a primal way.

Simon poured lube on his fingers, on Michael, and he prepared Michael's body with practiced ease. Michael groaned and thrust, wordlessly begging for more. Simon gave it to him. Simon wanted to give Michael everything.

Simon was hot and hard, his body's baser nature taking over from his mind, and he crawled between Michael's legs. He dipped his head and kissed Michael softly.

"I do love you, you know," Simon said.

"I know," said Michael.

But that was where they left things. Verbally, anyway. Simon pressed forward, entering Michael's body, and it was like every time he'd done it before—hot, familiar, tight, arousing—and completely different too. It meant something different this time. Simon wasn't entirely sure what, but he did know that as he began to thrust in and out of Michael, he felt overwhelmed by a warm emotion, not quite joy, but definitely not sadness. *It's love*, he thought. *I love Michael and have for a long time.*

Michael put his arms around Simon and groaned. They kissed as Simon moved, and Michael wrapped his legs around Simon's hips, as they pressed and pushed and thrust against each other. Their rhythms seemed to match, moving together in the ways that brought the other the most pleasure. Simon felt himself sinking into Michael's flesh and lost a bit of himself there, wanting to make this good for Michael, wanting to prove to Michael that they should be together like this always.

He got a hand between them and started stroking Michael's cock. Michael hissed and sighed and clutched at Simon, pulling Simon's hair, digging his nails into Simon's shoulder. Simon wanted to watch Michael come apart, so he kept stroking, even when Michael said it was too much, even when Michael said he was about to come. Simon stroked faster, harder. Simon wanted everything as he drove his own hips forward, and it was all sweet, hot pleasure where their bodies connected. Then Michael arched his back and thrust his hips forward and he was coming across his own chest in long ribbons. Simon watched in awe as it happened, as he felt Michael's body close in around him, as the pure sexual energy of Michael's movements and expressions triggered Simon's own orgasm. So Simon held on for dear life, grasping at Michael and pumping his hips forward until that orgasm flooded his system, made him stop seeing, made him only feel Michael around him. He came inside Michael while grasping at him and calling his name, as if "Michael" were the only word he'd ever needed to know. He sighed and whispered it over and over. "Michael, Michael."

A little while later, they lay together in Simon's bed, Simon resting his head on Michael's chest, Simon still feeling half out of his mind. Michael stroked his hair.

Simon wanted to talk about what had just happened, about how surely that must have changed things between them. He lifted his head and said, "Do you think—"

But Michael shook his head and pulled Simon back down on top of himself. "Shh," he said. "Just sleep."

MICHAEL WOKE up in the middle of the night, probably because he was in Simon's bed and not his own. Simon was splayed out next to him, sleeping the way he had since time immemorial, with a hand under his head and his mouth slightly agape.

God. This was everything Michael had ever wanted. He'd actually begged off the Fire Island trip because he'd wanted to spend time at home without all the nonsense. The pace of his life had gotten out of hand, and he found it hectic and unsatisfying. He didn't need three days crammed into Roberto's rented beach house with six other dudes. He needed home. He needed Simon.

And tonight, Simon had said all the things Michael wanted to hear, and that was unsatisfying too.

Did Simon really mean it or was he affected by the movie or by his own longing or by the nonsense he'd been spouting lately about how, now that they were in their late twenties, it was time to fucking grow up already? How could Michael trust this when he'd trusted so many times in the past and then been rejected? Simon had asked to prove himself, so fine. Michael would give him the weekend. But after that, he was done offering up his heart for Simon to stab, because he was tired of the bullshit between them.

But, oh, to glimpse what could be. They'd made love that night—that was the best way to describe it—and Michael had been over the moon about it, until Simon fell asleep and Michael started thinking.

He sat up and looked down at Simon's sleeping form for a moment. He loved Simon, so much that his heart ached with it, but he couldn't keep doing this.

He got out of bed. Simon stirred and Michael thought at first that he'd escape, but right as he got to the door, Simon said, "Where are you going?"

"Back to my own room."

"No, stay."

Michael thought about it. He looked at the bed, at the impression in the mattress and mangled sheets he'd left behind. "No, I better not."

"Please, Michael."

Michael knew he was a sucker as he walked back to the bed. He tentatively climbed in. Simon spooned up behind him and put an arm around his waist.

"You don't need to leave," Simon mumbled against the top of Michael's spine.

"No, I probably do," Michael said, but it was too late because Simon was already back asleep.

CHAPTER 7

Present Day

MICHAEL HAD decided that the occasion of Simon moving back to New York was an opportunity for a clean slate. They'd both done things that were really hurtful to each other, and Simon, in particular, was still wounded. He kept shooting Michael these forlorn glances, and Michael had overheard him on the phone with a real estate broker at least three times in the last week, so it was clear he was aiming to move out.

For the last couple of years, Michael had been working at an advertising agency, designing print ads for toothpaste and mouthwash, mostly. Not glamorous, but it paid the bills and challenged him creatively. The Midtown East offices made the commute home to the West Village a little arduous, but it wasn't bad in the scheme of things. Michael couldn't imagine moving out of the Village; he'd never lived anywhere else in the city. Well, he and Joan had shared a tiny two-bedroom on West Twelfth that was really on the border of the Meatpacking District, but Michael thought that counted as part of the Village.

So he put up with the trip downtown from work that required him to change trains a couple of times, and he came home to find Simon sitting on his couch, flipping channels on the TV. He settled on the news.

Michael dumped his stuff on a side table and plopped down next to Simon on the couch. "How was your day?" Michael asked.

"Fine. I'm still adjusting to being back in a New York office. To the pace of things. In some ways, it's like I never left, but in other ways, it feels like I've been gone for twenty years."

"I imagine the whole city is like that."

"Yeah, it is, kind of. It's almost like culture shock. Some days, Dubai feels like it was less of an adjustment. I mean, I—"

Michael's phone rang and interrupted Simon. He pulled it out of his pocket. The caller ID said "Joan." "Hang on. Let me get this. Hello?"

"Daddy!"

"Hey, kiddo." A strange surge of joy went through Michael. Man, he missed Trevor. He worked hard to tell himself he didn't, that Trevor was better off because Michael had no business being a father, but while he still thought it was basically true that Trevor was better off with his mother, that didn't stop the palpable ache he felt when he thought about Trevor, all the way up there in the Catskills.

"Daddy, I have five red trucks. Five! One, two, three, four, five!"

"That's great!" God, now he was counting? He'd become much more verbal all of a sudden in the last six months, and though Joan complained that he didn't shut up, Michael couldn't get enough of Trevor talking. "Where's Mommy? Is she there with you?"

"Uh-huh. I wanted to tell you that I had red trucks, so she said I could call. Can you come visit?"

"I can't right now. I'm all the way in New York City."

"I know, but I want to see you."

Michael wanted to cry. He closed his eyes and said, "I want to see you too. I miss you a whole lot. You know that, right?"

"I miss you too, Daddy. I asked Mommy if we could come see you, but she said we can't. But I want to show you my trucks."

"I'll come see your trucks as soon as I can, okay?" Michael had been renting a car to drive up to Joan's house once every three months or so, and sometimes they came down to the city. It was getting so expensive that Michael was thinking about buying a car just for this purpose—Lord knew he had no use for one in the city—though he hadn't gotten around to that yet.

It had been a while since he'd been up there, though, closer to four months now. He'd gotten distracted by Simon moving back, but that was a poor excuse.

"Can I talk to Mommy?" Michael asked.

"Okay. Come see me, Daddy."

"I will soon. I love you."

"I love you." Trevor giggled.

There was a shuffle while Trevor handed the phone to Joan. Michael heard muffled voices. Then he felt something odd. He opened his eyes and saw that Simon had taken his hand and was holding it tightly.

Michael just about broke right then.

"Hi, Mike," said Joan, sounding happy enough. Lately a lot of their conversations had been tinged with bitterness, though Michael wasn't entirely sure why. He knew he hadn't been the best father, so he figured he'd earned some of her ire, but he sensed something else was going on that she wasn't telling him.

"How are you?" he asked.

"Hanging in there."

Michael figured they'd just make dumb small talk, so he chatted for a minute while working out when he could next leave the city.

But then Joan was saying, "You're a little overdue."

Michael sighed. "I know. Things have been hectic. But you could come here anytime. You know that. I'll pay for the hotel this time, if you want."

"I can't really travel right now. It's a health thing. I need to stay close to my doctor until the treatment is over."

"Health thing?"

"It's not really any of your business, you know."

"Hey, you brought it up. Just tell me if it's serious."

"I don't feel great, but my doctor thinks I'll be fine in a few weeks."

"So not a simple case of the sniffles? Because if it's serious, I can take Trevor for a couple of days. Maybe I can drive up this weekend, and—"

"No, Kelly's here." Kelly was the part-time nanny Joan had hired when she moved upstate. Michael liked her fine and trusted her to take care of Trevor, but she wasn't Trevor's *parent*.

"I could come up this weekend anyway."

"No, don't. This weekend's not so great. We've got a playdate scheduled on Saturday and a birthday party Sunday, so he'll be pretty busy."

Maybe it was cowardly to bow out so easily, but he squeezed Simon's hand and said, "Okay. But if you change your mind, Simon's here, so it wouldn't be just me."

"How is that going?"

Michael didn't like the subject change, but he said, "Well. Better than I expected, honestly. Not much to report, but—"

"Maybe no news is good news."

"For now, yeah. How are you doing, really?"

Joan breathed heavily for a moment and then said, "I'm all right. A little worn out. But Trevor's making friends with some of the other kids at the preschool. I like his teacher a lot. She's great with the kids."

"Ha, that wasn't quite how I expected you to end that description. I thought for a moment you might have *designs* on this teacher."

Joan laughed softly. "No, not really. She's... I mean, if I were to go out with a woman, she'd be my type, but I can't right now. Running around after Trevor zaps all my energy as it is. I certainly don't have time to date."

Michael smiled at that. He felt a little guilty, but her tone was light. He appreciated that they could be this candid with each other, despite everything. Sometimes they still slipped into old habits, bickering like they had at the end of their relationship, Michael arguing that Joan was too selfish and Joan reminding Michael of his own shortcomings. But sometimes they were just old friends who happened to have this one strange thing in common.

"Well, anyway," Joan said. "I need to get going. Dinner's almost ready. Take care of yourself, Mike."

"You too. Keep in touch. Tell Trevor he can call me anytime. Let him send me a photo of the trucks. Or maybe we can Skype later."

"Yeah, okay. I'll text you when I work out when the best time for that will be."

"Bye, Joan. Tell Trevor I love him again."

Simon was still holding his hand when Michael put the phone down. So Michael squeezed it again. "Thank you," he said quietly.

"It eats at you, being away from Trevor."

Michael nodded. Why bother denying it?

"You could have sued for custody or to keep her from moving so far."

"What good would that do? It would basically only wrap us all up in an expensive legal battle that could have gone on for months or years, when in the end, it's really for the best that he's with Joan. She's a really good mother. And I'm... well." Michael gestured at himself.

"You're a better dad than you think."

"Doesn't matter now. Yes, I miss the hell out of him, but I can't change the situation. Him calling made me realize I haven't seen him in weeks. I'm going to try to video chat with them later. He's going to forget what I look like."

"That picture in your bedroom. That's Trevor?"

"Yeah. I took it the last time I was up there. He grows so fast. He's a little chatterbox now. He'll sit on the floor with his toys— trucks, he loves trucks—and he'll tell these nonsense stories about them, talking and rambling and making noises. It's the cutest thing you've ever seen."

That was about when Michael completely lost it. Tears stung his eyes, so he let them fall, because if he couldn't fall apart in front of his oldest friend, there was no one he could fall apart in front of.

When Simon finally pulled Michael into his arms, Michael realized that this was maybe the first time they'd really touched since Simon had come back to town. It was familiar and comfortable and exactly what Michael needed. He laid his head on Simon's shoulder and sobbed, letting all the bullshit he'd been holding onto go.

Then he sat up again, mildly embarrassed. He wiped at his eyes. "I'm sorry."

"Don't be," Simon said with a kind smile. "I know the last couple of years haven't been easy."

Michael almost laughed. "Understatement."

"Have you thought about moving upstate?"

"Yeah. I don't know. There's no work for me up there. I tried freelancing for a while, but I don't have the self-discipline for it, so I need a real job. Plus Joan doesn't want me underfoot."

"A kid should see his father more regularly than once every few months."

"Yeah, well. A kid should have both parents in a committed relationship, but we can't have everything."

Simon leaned back a little and looked at Michael thoughtfully, making Michael feel like he was under a microscope. Simon said, "You never really told me what happened. You seemed more broken up about losing Trevor than Joan."

Michael sighed. He didn't want to talk about this, although he didn't think telling Simon would hurt anything.

"You don't have to say anything if you don't want to," Simon said gently.

"It just... I don't know, exactly. I think us breaking up was a long time coming. We probably would have broken up sooner if it hadn't been for Trevor, actually. I still think she's incredible, but we were just not right for each other. I mean, the gay thing was only part of that, because I did find her attractive. But, I don't know. This is a shitty cliché thing to say, but it's true. I missed men. But I was committed to being faithful to Joan. We slept together less. And then she wanted to leave the city, and then there were a couple of months where we fought all the time, and I guess the relationship didn't have the same magic anymore. That's a shitty thing to say too. Maybe we gave up to soon, but I was still trying to hang on while she had a foot out the door, and it was all so frustrating and heartbreaking. Not a good environment for Trevor, either. So. There you have it. You can tell me you told me so."

"I won't." Simon looked toward the living room window. "You get why I was upset, right? When you first hooked up with Joan, I mean."

"Yeah, I do. And I regret that."

"Regret what you did, or regret that I was upset?"

"Some of both."

Simon nodded. "Just… you were right. You and I are never in the same place emotionally."

Michael wondered if they were now. Probably not, if Simon was planning to move out. Michael, of course, knew exactly why they were estranged, why Simon had chosen to move to Dubai, why Michael himself was a man alone in New York. If he'd had it to do over, he would have made different choices. Or maybe he wouldn't have; the things he'd done had felt right at the time. Being with Joan had felt right. Letting Simon go had felt right. He knew intellectually that things couldn't simply go back to how they'd been, but he'd hoped. He had wanted Simon to come home because he wanted to try again; he wanted to repair their friendship at minimum, but really, he wanted them to love each other the way he'd always known they were supposed to. He knew also that he had fucked up irrevocably and hurt Simon so badly that Simon had fled the country. There was likely no way to repair that.

But now Simon was holding his hand, so perhaps all was not lost.

2007

IN THE grand scheme of things, coming home to find Michael on the receiving end of a blow job from some dude was not that surprising. Hurtful, yes, but not surprising.

Simon opted to not even wait for the guy to finish. He simply turned around and strolled back out of the apartment.

He called a friend, his old college roommate, Eric, and asked if he could crash on his couch for a few days. Eric and his wife were willing to host him, so with that squared away, he went about avoiding Michael for the rest of the week.

When he finally got up the nerve to go back home, he found a contrite Michael who must have spent the week polishing the hell out of the apartment. Simon had never seen it so clean. Not even the junk from Michael's art classes was out amongst the detritus of the living room. It was Michael's way of doing penance, Simon knew.

"A mistake," Michael said.

"I thought this time was different."

"It is, but not in the way you want."

Simon had no idea what that meant. He put the shopping bag full of clothes he'd bought that week on the kitchen counter and then he put his face in his hands.

Michael approached him slowly. It wasn't until they were hugging each other tightly that Simon realized he was crying.

"Why do you do these things?" Simon asked, his voice watery.

"I don't know."

"Were you trying to hurt me or were you just being selfish?"

"I don't know. Probably some of both."

"Why, Michael? Why?" He whispered the words and clutched at Michael, wrapping bits of Michael's shirt in his fists and trying to get a handle on his emotions, which were running all over the place.

"I didn't trust us yet," Michael said quietly.

Simon knew the dude himself was not important. There was no need to explain where he had come from. Simon knew Michael could walk into any given gay bar and pick up some guy. It was Michael's special talent, it seemed. There was no need to explain, either, that Michael intended for Simon to catch him. Simon sighed and took a step backward, out of Michael's tricky embrace.

"Where did you go?" Michael asked, his tone neutral.

"I stayed with Eric and Nina."

Michael nodded. "I'm sorry, for what it's worth."

"Maybe I should move out."

"If that's what you want."

Simon lost it then. He slammed his hand on the kitchen counter. Michael jumped, which was satisfying. "That's not what I want, you asshole. What I want is you."

"I just… I can't. I'm sorry, Simon."

"But why?"

Michael walked away, stomped, really, back into the living room. He paced for a moment, and then he said, "Because I love you. I love you so much, but every time I have ever tried to make something real happen with us, you've turned me down."

"So this is retaliation." Simon followed Michael into the living room.

"No, this is me being realistic. I want for us to be together, but I'm not in a great place mentally right now, and I don't know if I trust this, if I trust you. You say you want me, but do you?"

"Of course I do! How do I prove that?"

"You can't. At least not—"

Simon smothered that thought with a kiss. Why was Michael being so stubborn? What did he mean by "not in a great place mentally"?

"You should probably move out," Michael said when the kiss ended.

"Really? Is that what you want me to do?"

Michael closed his eyes. "Maybe. Maybe if we spend a little time apart, we'll figure out what it is we really want. Maybe we just need time."

Simon thought about what Michael had said the night they'd rented that movie. They were never in the same place at the same time. "If this isn't it, when will it be our time?"

"I don't know, Simon. I don't know."

SIMON FOUND a place on the Upper East Side which, while farther from the office, was also far from Michael.

Michael was probably right. They needed time apart to figure things out. It was too hard to think clearly when they were both in the thick of things with each other. In their days apart, Simon realized that he had done the exact same thing to Michael that Michael had done to him, pushing him into a relationship before he was ready. And now they were both hurt and feeling stupid, probably. Not to be presumptive, Simon thought, but he knew Michael pretty fucking well, and knew how Michael was feeling. So they needed a little time apart. Simon signed a month-to-month lease.

Simon had never lived alone. At first, it was glorious having a whole apartment to himself, but that got old after the first week, when mostly he felt lonely and missed Michael.

So he called his old place.

"Do you think we'll ever be friends again?" he asked.

"We're still friends," Michael said. "We will always be friends."

"I'm so sorry. I miss you."

"I'm sorry too, but I'm a subway ride away."

"I know, but...." Simon wasn't sure what was left to say.

"This will be good," Michael said, the definitiveness in his voice surprising Simon. "We'll spend a little time apart—not, like, totally apart. You can still call me whenever. But we'll figure out what it is we want and then when we come back together, it will be because we're both ready for it."

"You think that's what will happen?"

"Yeah, I do. But I can't right now. I need to work through some things. I need some time and space. You do too. Okay?"

That gave Simon a little bit of hope. "Yeah, I... yeah. Okay."

This would be good, he reasoned. He'd signed the lease on the assumption that this was a temporary situation. A temporary arrangement. He and Michael would each get their shit together and figure out how to support themselves and be adults. Simon would concentrate on his job. Michael would finish school. Maybe they'd see other people, maybe they wouldn't, but then when the planets aligned, they'd be together and it would be amazing.

"Love you," Simon said.

"I know, Simon. I know. I love you too. Always and forever. Never forget that."

MICHAEL HAD never seen a more beautiful woman.

She had dark red hair that was casually pulled away from her face and tied in a sloppy bun. She had a face like an inverted triangle, but with a soft chin and a dusting of freckles across her nose. She was on the thin side, but definitely not frail, with faint muscle definition on her arms and decent-sized breasts. Michael hadn't spent much time looking at breasts, but these seemed pretty nice, and holy shit, what the hell was wrong with him?

"Oh, hey, Joan!"

That was Michael's friend Stephen, a casual friend, more of a drinking buddy than a confidant. But Stephen was not Simon, and coming out tonight had meant Michael was not stranded at home with his memories. Also, Stephen was clearly friends with this gorgeous woman, and he was calling her over, and then she was standing right in front of Michael.

"Well, hello," Joan said to Michael.

"Hi," he said, a bit at a loss for words.

"Don't bother," said Stephen. "This one's gay as the pope."

Joan put a hand on her cocked hip and raised an eye at Michael. "Really, now."

"Sorry," Michael said.

"Nothing to be sorry about. I just got over a dreadful relationship. That's why I called Stephen. I thought my time would be better spent hanging out with my gay friends than trying to get another one of those boyfriend things."

That made Michael relax enough to laugh. "Yeah, I hear that. The same thing is kind of true for me. Except here I am in a gay bar, and that seems like the wrong move, in retrospect."

Joan grinned. "Buy me a drink," she said.

That was the beginning of the end.

Michael and Joan drank and talked and scared off Stephen and generally got along like gangbusters. She was funny and sarcastic and basically exactly what Michael needed right then.

"So what do you do?" Michael asked late in the evening.

"Would you judge me if I told you I'm finding myself?"

Michael laughed. "You seem to be sitting on a bar stool in a gay bar. Spoiler alert."

Joan laughed too. "Well. Officially, I'm pursuing a career in arts and urban planning. Right now, I work for a nonprofit that develops public spaces, like parks and playgrounds and stuff. We get communities to help contribute art to the spaces, so everyone is invested in keeping them in good shape."

"Sounds rewarding."

"It is. I love it. But it pays peanuts." Joan took a sip of her fruity cocktail. "No, not even real peanuts. Styrofoam packing peanuts, the kind that are useless and get everywhere and stick to your furniture. So I have a job, but I'm living off a trust fund." She shrugged sheepishly.

"Hey, that's cool. You ever need a graphic designer, let me know."

"Yeah?" She reached over and put a hand on his forearm. Her touch was soft and warm.

"Yeah. I'm still finishing my degree, but—"

"Dude, I'm totally holding you to that." She sighed. "Of course, I may have to get a real job soon. I haven't quite mastered the art of handling my money responsibly. But, you know, life's short. What the hell is the point if you don't live it out loud?"

Michael smiled at her, though it was hard not to think of that long ago conversation with Simon, a man who still wanted to experience everything life had to offer. Michael supposed he'd always been drawn to people like that. It was a quality he admired. And, hell, even if he had moved halfway across the country to be with Simon, that didn't mean he couldn't also embrace this city, experience everything.

He found himself flirting with her. It was a skill he'd mastered as the center of a lot of feminine attention in high school, but he still enjoyed the harmless fun in flirting with a beautiful woman sometimes. Joan had fine features and freckles on her nose. She had a long neck and creamy skin. The dress she had on revealed some pretty delectable décolletage, if you went for that sort of thing. It was... wow, it was sexy the way her body curved. So different from anyone he'd ever been with. Michael found his hands itched to touch her, to see if her skin was as soft as it looked, to feel her body against his, but he kept his hands in his lap or on the bar.

What the hell had come over him?

Toward the end of the night, Michael started to feel enough affinity with Joan to confess his greatest problem. Or he was getting drunk. Either way, he said, "My best friend and I were living together, but it got complicated and he moved out."

"By 'got complicated,' you mean you had sex." She pulled her lovely red hair out of its bun and shook it out before tying it back again. She looked at him with sparkling blue eyes.

"No. Well, yeah, we did, but the complicated bits had to do with feelings."

Joan nodded knowingly. "That's a rough one."

The full extent of Michael's intoxication hit him right then. He hadn't realized he was drunk, but all of a sudden, blood rushed through his body and his head spun.

"But, I mean, it's fine. I'm fine." Even through his own drunk bravado, when he thought he was capable of sounding more confident than he actually was, the words sounded hollow.

"Are you?" She smiled knowingly.

Gosh, she was pretty.

Michael laughed and downed the rest of his cocktail. "No." The odd situation he found himself in now was not only about Simon, though. "Like, I don't know what's gotten into me, because I think you are just the sexiest thing, but that's nuts, because I'm gay!" He laughed harder.

Joan laughed with him. "It happens." She leaned closer.

They laughed together for a few minutes before Joan said, "Say, Mikey, you ever been with a woman?"

"I came out at fourteen. What do you think?"

"You want to give it a go?"

MICHAEL WOULD have felt bad the morning after, or the morning after that, or the morning after that if he hadn't been having so much fun.

They spent most of that first weekend together and all of the second, and partly Michael was happy to take Joan up on her repeated invitations, but partly he was also avoiding Simon, who had called once to ask about a shirt he'd left behind after he'd moved out. Michael had been wearing that very shirt when Simon called, but he said, "No, I haven't seen it," and then he got off the phone, feeling frustrated and sad.

So he needed a distraction, which Joan most definitely was. She bounded out of bed one Sunday morning and said, "There's an exhibit I want to see at MoMA. You should take me."

Michael laughed. "And why would I do that?"

"Well, you are an *artiste*, are you not?"

"I'm a designer."

"Same thing. I watched you take that pen the waitress left behind last night. You doodled all over your napkin. And some of it was even good. You seem to have a preoccupation with phallic objects, but…."

Michael rolled his eyes. "Aren't all men obsessed with penises?"

"Sadly, yes," Joan said. "Even the straight ones. I dated an architect for a while who was straight as an arrow, barely ever even looked at other dudes, but, man, every building he designed was basically a giant penis."

"I am not straight as an arrow."

"True. I think you've slept with more men than I have!"

Joan hopped around the room, rummaging through her drawers and pulling out clothes. She wore only a pair of panties that had red and white stripes, reminiscent of peppermint candies. Michael sat up and leaned against her headboard, pulling the covers up to cover his naked body because he was starting to get hard again as he watched her breasts jostle. What the hell was happening to him?

"You ever been with a woman?" he asked.

"Once, when I was, like, twenty-two. God, she was hot. Crazy as fuck, but totally smoking. She had this insane tattoo of Celtic knots that started on her upper thigh and went all the way up her torso and over her shoulder and her left breast." Joan traced where the tattoo would have gone on her own body. "I could have stared at it for hours. But it was mostly a sex thing. I broke up with her when she started getting wedding bells in her eyes."

"So you always pictured yourself married to a man?"

"Not necessarily. I'd date a woman seriously if the right one came along. I just haven't met the right one. This girl I dated then, she was a livewire in the sack but a total head case otherwise. So now, instead, I'm fucking gay guys, apparently."

Michael shrugged. "I have no explanation."

Joan held a dress up to herself. "What about this one?"

It was a kelly-green-and-white-checked gingham wrap dress. It was cute but a little matronly.

"Sure," Michael said, "if we're going to Amish country. What's that red thing in your closet?"

She walked over and pulled out a red dress. It was a basic wool sheath dress with short sleeves.

"Oh, no, too corporate," said Michael. "You have anything more avant-garde? Like that black-and-white thing you wore the other night?"

She stared at her closet for a long moment before hopping and shoving the red dress back in there. "Oh, what about this Michael Kors dress?" She pulled out a black-and-tan cocktail-length number that was cute and appropriate for both the weather and the venue.

"You got a wide belt to go with that?" Michael asked.

Joan guffawed. "Are you dressing me?"

"I like fashion. I went to fucking art school. So what?"

She walked back over to the bed and gave him a sloppy kiss. "You're the best gay boyfriend ever. You help me pick out my clothes *and* you stick it in sometimes."

They both showered and dressed and then went out for breakfast at the diner on the corner of Joan's East Village block. Everyone at the diner knew Joan, although the guy who actually waited on them knew Joan by her regular order—"half and half and two sugars and an everything bagel toasted with cream cheese, right?"—and not her name. Joan said, "Today we're doing it up, my friend. I want eggs and pork products."

The guy grinned. "Sure. Here's a menu, babe." Then he dipped down and whispered, "He's cute."

Joan winked.

Michael felt like they ate their weight in eggs and sausage and pancakes, and it was good in a greasy-spoon kind of way, though walking to the subway afterward was a bit of a challenge. He felt better by the time they got to the Museum of Modern Art. There, Joan dazzled him with her knowledge of art as she led him through the various galleries and finally to the special exhibit on Dada that Joan wanted to see.

"I studied Marcel Duchamp in grad school," Joan said, staring at what appeared to be a urinal glued to a board. "I'm fascinated by the absurdity of Dada. Art doesn't always have to have meaning, right? Sometimes it just is."

Michael could concede the point; sometimes in advertising and design, one chose a color or font merely because one liked the way it looked, not because one was trying to make a particular statement. Or that was his take on it. Sure, bright colors and bold fonts were eye-catching and made the advertiser look confident in their product—and thus persuasive in their argument that you should buy it—but sometimes Pantone 2718 was just blue.

"Plus Duchamp dressed in drag for a series of photos by Man Ray," Joan was saying, "something that has always kind of fascinated me. I don't think he was, like, expressing his gender identity or whatever so much as he came up with this persona and decided that becoming his alter ego involved putting on lipstick and a fur stole. So, see? Some things just are. I bet you can understand that."

"Sure," Michael said.

"So I could always appreciate what Duchamp was doing, even if it's crazy and of questionable artistic merit. I mean, if I wanted to see an old urinal, I could sneak into the men's room at the bar down the block from my apartment."

"Which you've totally done, I bet," Michael said.

Joan shrugged.

Michael continued to be impressed by Joan's knowledge of modern and contemporary art as she offered tidbits and trivia on a lot of the pieces they looked at. Michael had taken a couple of art history classes, but hardly remembered any of it, mostly because he found a lot of contemporary art off-putting. But listening to Joan explain what she knew of the artist's motivations allowed him to see a lot of pieces, particularly a violent video installation that freaked him right out, in a new light.

After MoMA, they walked downtown, and soon found themselves standing near Rockefeller Center.

"Why didn't we get on the subway?" Michael asked, the tawdriness of one of New York's tourists meccas offering an unpleasant contrast to the buzzing in his brain from the museum.

"You ever been to the Top of the Rock?" Joan asked.

Michael frowned. "Ugh, really?"

"I'm guessing that's a no."

Michael stopped walking and looked at the plaza. There were swarms of people crowding every inch of sidewalk from where they stood on Fifth all the way to the GE building. "I've never been to the top of the Empire State Building, either, although one time Simon and I went to the top of the World Trade Center. This was back in college, obviously. We went just to do it, you know? But we'd only been in New York a few months then."

"I know it's cheesy, but the view really is very cool."

"We're doing this, aren't we?"

A half hour later, they were standing atop the observation deck at the top of 30 Rock, looking downtown at the Empire State Building. The sun was starting to set on what had been a really fun day.

"We should make this a regular thing," Michael said. "I've enjoyed myself more today than I have in a long time." A *long* time. Michael couldn't remember a day that had involved more smiles and laughter and talking happily about whatever.

Joan wrapped her arms around Michael's left arm. "Yeah. This was really fun. I don't get to geek out over art very often."

"And you were right. This view is pretty awesome."

It was spectacular, in fact. Michael could follow the patterns of streetlights as they pointed the way downtown. Times Square was the splash of light to his left. Skyscrapers, including the Empire State Building, rose up on the blocks immediately in front of him and then again from the foot of the island, with the valley in between consisting mostly of Greenwich Village, his home for almost a decade now. He looked for landmarks he knew about and let Joan point out things she saw as well. Then he retrieved his arm and put it around her.

It was strange, being able to outwardly show affection without fear of anyone saying something threatening, which had happened sometimes when Michael went out with men. But a man with his arm around a woman, having a romantic moment at the top of a tall building? Well, that was downright normal. There were a dozen other hetero couples around them doing the exact same thing.

Was it a betrayal, though? Michael had felt that way a few times over the course of their epic weekends together, worried that he'd given up on his people by sleeping with Joan, but then, why the hell should it matter who he slept with? That was the whole argument, wasn't it? It didn't matter. And if he felt himself starting to fall for a woman, well, sometimes things just were what they were, like Dada.

"This is kind of romantic," he commented.

"Kiss me," said Joan.

So Michael did and he liked it, liked the way her small body fit against him, liked the taste of her, even.

It wasn't her gender he was attracted to, it was *her*. He hadn't met anyone he connected with so well in ages. Probably there was no one in his life but Simon whose company he enjoyed so much.

Which made him realize that the guilt he felt was over Simon, not over some misguided sense of betrayal of his people generally.

But with Simon... it was too hard lately. Maybe Simon was the person Michael loved best, but lately, everything felt so emotionally fraught that Michael didn't feel like he could even have an honest conversation with him. And spending time with Joan was... easy. It was fun. It didn't have the heavy baggage his relationship with Simon had.

Joan broke away from the kiss and walked up to the edge of the observation deck. She spread her arms wide. "Look at this city. Isn't it marvelous?"

Michael walked up next to her. It seemed so vast, all that city before them, descending into darkness at the same time it woke up with light. There were moving cars and bridges and Brooklyn and the Village and lower Manhattan and the Empire State Building, and all of it was right there at Michael's fingertips.

"It's all ours for the taking, Michael." Joan dropped her arms and leaned against him.

"Yes," he said, because it felt like they could conquer all of New York from this height.

"Would you like to take an adventure with me?"

Michael readily agreed and didn't want to look back.

"DUBAI?"

"It's an excellent opportunity, Simon."

Simon shuffled around the papers on his desk while he tried to formulate a response. He very deliberately glanced at the little rainbow flag in the penholder on his desk, hoping his boss would pick up his meaning. When silence followed, Simon took a deep breath and said, "Dubai is not exactly a bastion of gay rights."

"I'm not sending you to find dates. I'm sending you because you're one of the best people I have and I think you'd do really well at this job."

"I have a life in New York."

"It's only a year." Simon's boss laid a hand on Simon's desk. "Look, if you don't take the job in Dubai, it won't affect anything here. You'll keep this job and you'll be in good standing with the company. But if you *do* take it, you'll get a 10 percent raise and the company will pay all of your living expenses next year. Didn't you tell me last week that you wanted to travel more? This is a hell of an opportunity to do that, don't you think?"

Simon was overwhelmed by the prospect of going halfway around the world, to a city he didn't know at all, although he supposed it wouldn't be the first time he'd done such a thing. He'd moved halfway across the country to live in a new city before, after all. But could he really just pick up his life in New York and move away for a year? What about his friends? What about Michael? "Can I think about it?"

"Yeah. Take a few days. Let me know by next week, though, so that I can find someone else if you opt out."

"Yes. All right."

The first thing he did after that was text Michael to see if they could meet that night, because he needed someone to talk this over with. Under the circumstances, maybe Michael wasn't the best choice, but he was the first person Simon thought of. Michael readily agreed and said he had news of his own.

Simon picked a restaurant in the Village and was, of course, the first one there. He was well into a glass of wine when Michael showed up. Michael sat and smiled without apologizing for his tardiness. Simon stared at that toothy grin and found he wasn't that angry.

"Your news is good?" Simon asked.

"Yes, I think so. Maybe. Well, I don't know. But let's talk about you first. Or order food. I'm starving."

So they ordered, and then Simon said, "My company offered me another promotion."

"Congratulations! And so soon after your last promotion! Wasn't that only a few months ago?"

Simon sat back and basked in that for a moment. Michael seemed so happy for him. "Yeah. I guess my boss has a lot of faith in me. This is kind of a big deal."

"That's awesome. I should buy you a drink. You want another glass of wine?"

"Well, maybe hold that thought. There's a catch."

"Which is?"

"If I take the promotion, they'll send me to Dubai for a year."

Michael stared for nearly a minute. "Dubai?"

"It's a city in the Middle East."

Michael rolled his eyes. "Yeah, I know where it is. I went to college too. Um. They want to send you to Dubai for a year?"

"They're giving me a week to think about it. I mean, I don't know. It's a good opportunity and they will give me a big raise, but on the other hand, I'd have to leave New York. I'd be leaving you."

Michael frowned. "Yeah. Wow. You know, we haven't really lived apart... well, ever."

"I know. That's why I wanted to talk to you." Because that was at issue here. Things were currently strained between them—though you'd never know that by how easily they were talking now—but it was true that they'd never lived farther than a fifteen-minute trip from each other. Ever. And Simon wasn't entirely sure he wanted that to change, no matter his feelings for Michael and whatever Michael did or did not reciprocate.

"What are you going to do?" Michael asked. "What do you want to do?"

Simon looked at his wine glass. He had no idea. He'd been mulling it over all afternoon and he wasn't any closer to a decision. On the one hand, it might have been too good of an opportunity to pass up.

It was a fair amount of money. If the company was paying for his expenses, he'd be able to put some money away. On the other hand, he really felt like he and Michael were on the road to something. He'd give up the opportunity if it meant he could finally be with Michael.

"I'm still thinking," Simon said.

Michael nodded. "I would hate to see you go. A whole year?"

"A whole year."

"I mean, I don't want to tell you what to do or hold you back. This sounds like an awesome opportunity, and I know you've been wanting to travel more. But I sure as fuck am gonna miss you if you go."

"Well, then, you understand why I'm struggling with the decision."

They were served entrées then, which seemed like a good time to put that aside.

Simon picked up his fork and said, "What's your news?"

"Well, I... I'm seeing someone."

Simon nearly dropped his fork. "You're...."

"I mean, it's been almost two months now, actually. I didn't want to say anything, because I still can't even really believe it myself, but it's real. I'm in love!"

Simon was tempted to immediately stand and walk out of the restaurant. His heart sank. This couldn't have been happening. Had he even heard correctly? Should Simon lean forward now so that Michael could plunge the knife directly into his heart?

He took a deep breath and tried to speak. "You're... I didn't even know you were dating people. That *we* were dating people. I mean, I guess I expected you to go out and meet people and all that, but *I* haven't because I guess I was waiting for... shit. You're in love?"

"I didn't, like, set out to meet anyone. It just kind of happened. And when we started seeing each other, I didn't really see it going anywhere. But now that we're a couple of months into it, I feel, I don't know. Really happy for the first time in a very long time."

"But I thought that we were going to... I thought you needed time and space. That you couldn't be in a relationship right now."

Michael rubbed his forehead. "I know. I know, and I'm sorry, but this... happened. I wasn't expecting it. And it's so... easy. You and me, we were never easy. But this is and it makes me happy and I want to see where it goes."

It was like someone was pounding on Simon's heart with a hammer. It was physically painful to sit there and listen to this. "I haven't been on so much as a date since I moved out of the apartment."

"Because you work all the time."

A fair point. Perhaps that was how Simon had earned this promotion so fast. He had been putting in a lot of hours, although that was largely because working took Simon's mind off Michael.

It was a shame that the steak Simon had ordered looked so delicious, because he wasn't going to be able to eat it now.

"What, um. What's his name?" Simon made himself ask.

"Well, that's the funny thing. *Her* name is Joan."

Simon did drop his fork that time. It clanged against the plate so loudly that it echoed through the restaurant. Several people turned to look at them. Simon didn't care. He was too baffled. "Wait. *Wait*. Did you just tell me you're dating—you have fallen in love with—a woman?"

"I know. It's completely crazy. I can't explain it."

Simon felt like his world had been turned upside down.

"You're in love with a woman named Joan. Aren't you gay?"

"Well, yeah. It's not like I've changed my orientation. Just this one woman blows my mind. Well, and some other things."

"You've had sex with her?"

"Indeed I have. It was kind of weird at first, but it's good now. We've—"

"No, don't tell me. I really, *really* don't want to know." Simon was having a hell of a time wrapping his head around any of this. Michael was in love. He'd effectively ended whatever romantic relationship had been developing between him and Simon. And the person he was in love with was female. What. The. Fuck?

"You should meet her," Michael said. "She's so great. I think you'd like her."

That was when Simon had a vision of what his future could be. He could stay in New York and make nice with this woman that Michael was seeing and watch them get married and start a family and fall into some kind of traditional life, and every goddamn day would take a slice out of his heart. Or he could go to Dubai and get on with his life.

As Michael prattled on giddily about Joan, Simon made his decision.

MICHAEL INSISTED on throwing a going-away party, which was how Simon found himself in the haphazardly decorated party room of a bar in the Financial District. Michael had argued that it was right near his office, so he had no excuse to avoid the party. Simon had counterargued that if Michael knew Simon didn't want a big fuss, he shouldn't have made one.

Still, it was fun in its way. People kept buying Simon drinks, so he had a good buzz going, and he was content to let everything around him float about. Michael had invited all of their mutual friends, most of Simon's friends, and the select few coworkers Simon liked enough to see at an event like this, thanks to a little help from Simon's administrative assistant. There was soft music playing, people were chatting, and it was nice all around.

And then Joan showed up.

Simon figured he should have known he'd get ambushed this way. Michael had been trying to introduce Simon and Joan constantly in the weeks leading up to Simon's departure. "You should at least meet her before you move," Michael kept arguing. Simon always begged off; he didn't want to know anything about this Joan, and he worried that if he met her and she really did turn out to be as wonderful as Michael said she was, she'd become a real person and Simon wouldn't be able to hate or resent her anymore.

But a pretty woman with red hair walked into the room, and Michael immediately beelined for her. As she was the only person there that Simon didn't know, and as Michael was now kissing her quite passionately, this must be Joan.

Simon watched as Joan pushed him away. Her body language indicated she was scolding him, but she smiled. And Michael smiled.

When was the last time Michael had smiled that way?

Well, whatever. Simon was pretty good at avoiding people. He moved around the room, inserting himself into conversations, letting people congratulate him or ask him if he was excited about Dubai. He lied and said he was, but in all honesty, he was terrified of living for a year in the Middle East. Oh, he was excited about seeing a different part of the world, but he didn't know if he could suppress his sexuality for an entire year, or if he'd get in trouble if he didn't, or if people in the Dubai office would know already and persecute him for it, or what would happen.

He was at the bar a little while later, getting water and flirting with the bartender—when would he get to flirt with a cute guy again?—when someone brushed against his side.

"I know Michael hasn't introduced us, but I imagine you know who I am," said Joan.

"I do." He tried to rationalize how rude he could be, if he could bow out of this conversation. He felt a little nauseous. Here was the woman who had taken Michael away from him, or at least the woman that Michael had chosen. Simon's heart still ached when he thought about it.

She held out a hand to shake. So Simon took it. Her hands were small; up close, she looked fine and delicate.

"It's nice to finally meet you," she said. "Michael talks about you all the time."

"We've known each other a long time."

"I know."

She ordered a whiskey sour from the bartender, who walked off to make it, effectively leaving them alone.

"Look," she said. "You probably don't think much of me. I don't think I have the whole story from Michael, but I know some of it. I kind of figured you'd decided to go to Dubai because of me."

Simon sighed. "Not only because of that."

She nodded. "I wish that circumstances were different. Michael speaks so highly of you. I'd like to think we could have been good friends."

He shook his head. "Joan, I—"

She held up her hand. "I'm not the villain in this little melodrama. I know it might be easy to think so, but Michael made a choice. You and I are just the innocent bystanders."

Simon almost laughed. That sounded so apt.

Joan went on, "I intend to make the most of the opportunity that has been given me. I don't know if anything will come of this. Mike and I, I just... I haven't felt this way for anyone in a long time, and I know that he feels the same."

"He says he loves you."

Her eyes widened in surprise. "He told you that?"

Simon nodded.

She smiled. "Well. I guess I believe him now. It's so funny, you know? I knew he was gay when I took him home the first time, but he's so hot, and I thought, hell, just this once, right? But then he never really left. And, God, we have so much fun together. He makes me laugh. I keep wanting to pinch myself, like this whole relationship is a dream I haven't woken up from yet."

Simon wondered how much she really knew about his relationship with Michael if she was telling him all this. The more she talked about Michael, the more it felt like she was pushing pins into his heart.

"I'm happy for you, then," he said.

"You're not, but it's okay." She took a deep breath. "You love him too."

"I do." No sense in lying. "And I thought he loved me, but... I guess I waited too long. I missed my chance, so you took it. Who would have thought, twentysome years of friendship and the window was that narrow. I don't think I ever really thought it would end this way. Or at all." He took a sip of his water and shook his head. "God, why am I telling you all this? Shouldn't we be sworn enemies?"

She smiled. "I have one of those faces. Happens all the time. I stand on the subway platform and people come over to tell me their problems. It's really a burden."

She made a face that was so solemn Simon laughed despite himself. She cracked and laughed with him. *All right*, he thought. *I can see why he likes her.*

"Well, Simon," Joan said as the bartender returned with her drink. "For what it's worth, I don't think your story with Mike is over. I do sincerely hope that when you return in one year, if Mike and I are still going strong, that you and I can be friends. Yeah? I'd like to be your friend, not your enemy."

"Maybe," Simon said.

"And if I can do anything for you, Simon, *anything*, please tell me, okay? I know you're upset. I want to make this right. Or as right as it can be."

She flitted off then, walked over to Michael, and looped her arm around his. Simon turned away.

He planned to avoid them for the rest of the party, but later, when he was midconversation with Eric, he spotted Michael and Joan leaning toward each other and talking excitedly about something. Michael threw his head back and laughed. Joan kept talking and giggling, and the two of them were all smiles. In fact, even when she turned away, Michael gazed at her, a goofy grin on his face.

When had Michael last looked at Simon that way? For the last few months, maybe even the last year or two, Michael had mostly looked at Simon with a pained expression. Maybe, therefore, Simon had been foolish to hope. He'd been selfish, he'd waited too long, and Michael had moved on or given up or made an emotional decision that kept Simon away. But now, Michael was laughing and smiling with Joan, and Simon couldn't remember the last time he saw joy like that on Michael's face.

Simon had made the right decision. He knew that unequivocally now. He and Michael needed time apart to regroup. Simon, perhaps, needed to find someone else to fall in love with. Because if things kept going the way they had been, Simon and Michael would only bring each other misery.

A little while later, he saw Joan putting on a scarf and a jacket, as if she were getting ready to go. Simon walked over to her. "You want to know what you can do for me?" he said.

She nodded. "Seriously. Anything."

"Keep making him happy. That's what I want. I want Michael to be happy."

She nodded. "All right. I'll do what I can."

Michael appeared then. "So are you guys getting along well or what?" he said, his voice cheery but his expression a little wary.

"Well, maybe not quite yet, but I do think we understand each other," Joan said, shooting Simon a meaningful look.

"Yeah," Simon said. "I think we do." He turned to Michael. "Thank you for doing all this. I had fun, despite myself."

Michael laughed. "I really am going to miss the hell out of you when you're gone. I can't believe this has happened to our lives. I never would have predicted it. We won't be living in the same town anymore. How can that be possible?"

"It was time, I guess," said Simon. "I didn't imagine it ending this way, either, but—"

"Who says it's over?" Michael said. "Maybe this chapter is ending, but a new one is starting. You'll go do your year in Dubai and be this amazing world traveler financial genius. And I'll be here, holding down the fort in New York so the city will be waiting for you when you come back."

Simon's eyes stung. This right here was maybe the hardest thing he'd ever done. Michael was probably right—it would be better to view this as a new chapter in his life, in the whole saga of Simon and Michael. But life was going to be hard as hell without Michael. He'd give it a year, he supposed. That really wasn't so much time in the scheme of things.

He was staring at his shoes and didn't notice that Michael had stepped forward. Then he was folded into Michael's arms, pulled into a fierce hug.

"I am going to miss you incredibly," Michael said softly.

"Me too. So much."

"I know you're going to be great, Simon. This job, this opportunity, you'll kick so much ass. I know it."

"Thanks."

Michael backed away. "Well. I should go home with Joan, but stay, okay? Have a good time. We've got the bartender booked until midnight."

Simon nodded. He made himself watch Michael and Joan walk out onto the street and hail a cab. When Michael put his hand on the small of her back before ushering her into the back of the cab, Simon whispered, "Good-bye," and tried to let Michael go.

That proved impossible. As he walked back to the bar, he thought that he'd never be able to let Michael go. He imagined he would come back to New York someday, maybe after his heart had healed. Maybe one day watching Michael and Joan together wouldn't hurt so damn much. But now, the future awaited.

CHAPTER 8

Present Day

SIMON WOKE up early on a bright sunny morning. Michael had gone to bed still upset about Trevor and their phone call the night before, and Simon had tried to support him through it, though he'd felt useless as Michael struggled.

He decided he'd go get bagels. Michael was still passed out on the sofa bed, sort of scrunched over on the side of the mattress, his body contorted in one of his odd sleep positions. Simon slipped out and walked to the bagel place they'd gone to on his first day back in the city.

There was a guy in front of him in line who was really cute and exactly Simon's type: tall, thin, dark hair, a clean-shaven pretty face. He turned slightly when he moved to grab a juice from the display on the way to the counter, and he caught Simon's eye and smiled. That was promising. Simon smiled back.

Simon didn't think much of the guy's order, vegan cream cheese on a whole-wheat bagel—life was too short for that flavorless nonsense—but he was still willing to go with it until the rough-looking guy behind the counter asked Simon for his order. He ordered a bagel for himself—an everything bagel with normal, full-fat cream cheese a centimeter thick the way God and New York delis intended—and one for Michael—poppy with strawberry cream cheese, long Michael's standard bagel order. It wasn't until after the order was placed that

Simon realized what he'd done. He'd ordered a bagel for Michael as if he were Simon's lover.

The cute vegan made eyes at Simon, who was suddenly confused and disgusted. A month ago, when he'd been in Chicago, Simon would have chatted up this guy without a second thought. But now that he was back in New York....

Michael had been so sad the night before. At Simon's gentle urging, he'd talked a lot about Trevor. Eventually Michael had called and video chatted with Trevor, and then pulled Simon over to see. Trevor had shown his toy trucks to the screen and giggled through all of it. He was a cute kid, yeah, and clearly talking to him made Michael happy. But after the call ended, Michael had descended right back into his funk. Simon had gone to bed early to give Michael space.

Simon had lain awake for hours wondering if he had it in him to forgive Michael. For six years, things had been rough between them. For six years, Simon had traveled and met other men and lived his life. Dubai had been a rough, closeted experience for him, but in London, San Francisco, Chicago, or any other place Simon had found himself, he'd given himself permission to pick up cute vegans in bagel shops because he could. And none of those relationships had given him anything nearly as fulfilling as just talking to Michael on the phone late at night.

Simon smiled at the guy again.

It occurred to him, though, that perhaps he'd betrayed Michael too. He'd left. The last few years had taken a lot out of Michael and he'd needed a friend, but Simon hadn't been willing to do more than occasionally listen to Michael on the phone.

They'd both hurt each other so much over the years, and yet here they both were, back in New York and living in the same apartment. How could that be?

Well, one explanation was that they did indeed belong together. Simon didn't believe in fate, but was it possible for two people to be so integral to each other's lives without them falling in love? Or was love not enough to mend what was broken between them? Did Simon even love Michael that way anymore? He wasn't sure.

"You live around here?" asked the cute vegan.

"For now," said Simon. "Living with a friend until I get my own place."

The guy nodded. "You new to the city?"

"No, but I've been away a long time."

The guy showed off his nearly perfect teeth. The girl at the counter handed him a receipt. He asked if he could borrow her pen. To Simon, he said, "I'm Greg. I live over on Perry Street."

"I'm Simon."

Greg wrote something on his receipt and handed it to Simon. "Well, Simon, I have to run, but if you ever want to get a cup of coffee to go with your bagel, give me a call." Simon looked down and saw that Greg had written his number on the receipt.

Greg was gone by the time Simon paid for his bagels and got a couple of cups of coffee to go. On his way out of the shop, he tossed Greg's number in the trash.

2010

THERE WAS a man leaning against a streetlight who reminded Simon a bit of Michael. This man, however, was smoking a cigarette and raising his eyebrows at Simon in a curious, come-hither way. So Simon went thither.

"Good evening," said the man. "I've seen you round these parts before."

"Yes. I've lived in the neighborhood for about a year."

The man's eyebrows rose further. "You're an American. How delightful."

Simon laughed. "Yes, I guess I am a bit of a fish out of water."

"What brings you to London?" The man took a drag on his cigarette.

"Work. I crunch numbers at a financial services company. They have their offices over on Bank Street."

"Brilliant. And you live here in Soho?"

"Yes."

The man was incredibly handsome. He had dark hair that hung over his eyes a little and a lithe body, much thinner than Michael now that Simon could see him up close. His accent didn't sound local, but was more of a country accent. In his short time in London, Simon had gotten pretty good at recognizing accents. This man had a really great one.

"I also live here in Soho," the man said. "I'm Jonny."

"Simon. Nice to meet you."

"Fancy a pint? There's a great little pub on the next block."

"All right." Then, because Simon hadn't honed his gaydar well enough to always win the "Gay or Just British" game, he said, "Would you be offended if I told you that you were really sexy?"

Jonny laughed. "How could anyone be offended by that, love? I also find you quite delectable."

Well, that was a relief. "Good. Just so we understand each other."

"Perhaps after I buy you a pint, I can show you my flat. It's just off Old Compton Street."

A few hours later, Simon was on his way into a deep, postcoital sleep when his phone rang.

Jonny sat up and looked at him. "Do you intend to get that?"

The caller ID indicated it was Michael. "I suppose I should. It's a friend from back home."

"Well, I intend to sleep."

Simon got out of bed and took the phone into the living room. He answered it at the same time he realized he was still naked. "Hello?"

"Simon, I... I need to talk to you."

It would have been weird to sit his naked ass on Jonny's gorgeous leather sofa. Simon grabbed the knit throw tossed over the back and used it to cover one of the cushions. Not much better, but Simon sensed he'd need to be sitting down for this conversation. He sat carefully on the throw-covered cushion.

"What is it?" Simon reasoned it must have been serious if Michael was making an international phone call. In the nearly three years since Simon had left New York, they had talked periodically, but mostly by e-mail. Calls were rare and expensive.

"Joan is pregnant."

Well, that cut right to the chase, didn't it?

"Christ," said Simon. That was a tough thing to hear. Simon's mind was already off to the races, imagining what could happen. Was Michael asking for advice? Would Simon now have to hear extensive details about Joan he didn't want to know about? He leaned forward and rubbed his forehead. Good thing he was sitting down, because of all the things Michael could have said, this was near the end of the list of what Simon expected.

"She's gonna, I mean *we're* going to be parents. It's insane. I can hardly believe it. But now it's impossible to deny. I mean she's showing enough that it's clear what's going on, so I felt like I had to tell you. Also, you know, I feel like of all people on this planet to be elected to fatherhood, I was clearly not the right one to be chosen, but here we are."

"Wait, she's... when is the baby due?"

"November. It's a boy, by the way."

That was less than three months away. "Wait a minute—"

"See, so we were at the doctor today, and I saw the sonogram, and it's just so *real*, you know? Like suddenly it became clear that I was about to become a parent and, I don't know, I guess I kind of freaked out. I'm still freaking out."

"Michael, stop talking. Do you mean to tell me that your girlfriend is six months pregnant and you didn't tell me sooner? Would you have told me at all if you hadn't had a crisis today?"

There was a beat of silence before Michael said, "Eventually."

"When you had a baby." Because, shit, they never saw each other now that Simon was half a world away. Michael could have never said anything at all. What should have been exciting news took on a tinge of scandal if Michael was freaking out and being secretive, and Simon didn't know how to process it. It didn't feel like good news.

Michael let out a long-suffering sigh. "I didn't know how to tell you, all right? I wanted to, but I know how you are about Joan, and I couldn't find the words. All of this is overwhelming. I'll be thirty in a few months, and this is not at all how I imagined my life. I'm about to have a child. I'm in a long-term relationship with a woman. It's... it's completely crazy. Can't you appreciate that?"

"Well, yeah, but—"

"Simon, are you coming back to bed or what?" shouted Jonny from the bedroom.

"Who was that?" Michael asked.

Simon was near tears. Just when he didn't think Michael could hurt him anymore—he'd spent a hellish year in Dubai precisely to prevent this from happening—Michael had found a way. That was, Simon knew this situation was not about him, but it did have an effect on his relationship with Michael, such as it was. He wanted to be a good friend to Michael, but this was rough. A child was such a permanent thing. Not that there was any hope where Michael and Simon's romantic prospects were concerned, but a part of Simon had still always hoped. Now he could see the whole future played out before him, one where Joan and Michael were married and raising a whole gaggle of children in some quaint little house in the suburbs with no room for Simon.

He was kind of glad he was in London and not New York right then. "If you must know, you've successfully interrupted my one-night stand with a handsome British lad."

"Oh. I'll let you go, then. Um." Michael made a few flustered sounds. "I miss the hell out of you, you know that? I wish you were here more than anything. I've had a really hard time with this and not had anyone to talk to about it except Joan, who is, of course, totally over the moon. It didn't seem real, anyway, so I couldn't really accept it. But now...."

"You could have talked to me. I wish you had told me sooner."

"I didn't know what to say. How the hell do you tell the man you thought you'd end up with that you're having a baby with somebody else?"

Simon sighed. How was he supposed to maintain a friendship with someone who didn't let him in anymore?

"I wish you could come home," Michael said.

"I'm sorry, Michael. I really am. I miss you too. But you know why I can't be there."

"I know. Can I at least call you? Not in the middle of your one-night stands, obviously. I'll get better at figuring out the time difference. But I need a friend right now."

Probably Simon was a sucker, but he said, "Yeah. Call me anytime." He would have wanted the same thing from Michael, or so he told himself. There simply hadn't been an opportunity. Simon hadn't wanted to share much of himself lately.

"Thanks," said Michael. "Go enjoy your man."

Simon hung up. He walked back into the bedroom, where Jonny was awake now and slowly masturbating. He grinned as Simon stood at the side of the bed. Jonny really was ridiculously sexy, his body long and sinuous and tattooed and made for sin. Simon could imagine losing himself in this bed, finding the distraction he needed. Without a word, he crawled onto the bed and kissed Jonny, who took him into his arms and helped him forget, at least for a little while.

JOAN WENT into labor, finally, a week after the due date.

Michael was losing his mind. It took some effort to remind himself that this was not about him, this moment. It was about Joan and their baby and this crazy adventure they'd embarked on together.

Joan was a saint. She'd looked beautiful for months, though they'd been bickering almost nonstop for the last few weeks. So the gravity of the situation, of what they were doing, hit Michael slowly. They were about to bring a new person into the world, one that they'd made together. The circumstances were so odd that Michael still had a hard time wrapping his head around their situation, even though it was clear from Joan's distress that *something* was happening. Hell, they hadn't even agreed on a name, and it wasn't like they hadn't had plenty of time to decide, what with Joan's due date coming and going the week before.

And now they were in the hospital, where Michael felt like he was trapped in some kind of funhouse mirror. This was one of the most surreal things he had ever experienced, and it was all wrong, and he had no idea how to stop it.

An hour sped by, but the next dragged on. Time became elastic, stretching and compressing. And, okay, Michael was going a little nuts waiting, but he could acknowledge that his problems were minor in the grand scheme of things. He wasn't the one trussed up on a hospital bed, red and sweating and in obvious pain.

He wanted to do whatever he could to ease Joan's suffering, though in action, this mostly involved a lot of futile conversations with the nurses and letting Joan squeeze his hand when she had contractions, and nothing he did felt like he was making much of a difference.

This wasn't about him, and he knew that, but he felt as responsible for this situation as he might have if he'd run Joan over with a car.

He sat beside her in the hospital room and she squeezed his hand so hard he thought she might break his fingers, and he knew beyond a doubt that they'd passed the point of no return. He was going to be a father that very day.

After one brutal contraction, she slumped on the bed and looked at him. "Tell me a story," she said.

"Uh, okay."

"I want you to distract me. You were always good at telling me stories. Tell me something about when you were a boy. Some cute thing you did."

Michael thought about that for a moment. He took her hand and ran his fingers over it. Her skin was clammy, but it also seemed to glow. "Did I ever tell you about the magazine Simon and I produced?"

Joan sat up in bed a little. "No."

"When we were, I don't know, ten, maybe? We got a hold of a bunch of those *Tiger Beat* magazines from one of the girls in our class. Simon kept paging through one and he made this face like he'd never seen anything so depraved." Michael copied the face, widening his eyes and twisting his mouth in horror. He wanted to laugh just thinking about it; it had been seriously funny at the time. "Anyway, I thought we could make a million dollars by making our own magazine. The girls sure liked these, right? And, let's face it, I kind of did too. So did Simon, although he didn't tell me that until much later. As it turns out, he had an intense crush on Rob Lowe. Never breathed a word about it to anyone, though."

Joan smiled and shifted on the bed as if she were uncomfortable.

"We made kind of a scrapbook. We cut up a bunch of magazines and wrote super cheesy captions for each of the photos. We made up celebrity gossip and paired up celebrities into couples. Well, I made the graphics. Simon did most of the writing. At one point, he put two male actors on a page together and wrote the caption, 'Sweetheart Heartthrobs,' or something like that. Can you believe it?"

"Simon did this? Not you?"

"I know, right?" Michael squeezed Joan's hand. "This girl came over and said that two boys couldn't date each other, and Simon sat there and said, 'Why not?' with a totally straight face." Michael shook his head. "God, he must have known, even then. I still wonder why it took him so long to tell me."

"That he's gay, you mean?"

"Yeah."

Joan squeezed Michael's hand back. "Maybe he wasn't ready."

Michael could have told her a lot about not being ready. The irony did not escape him that Simon had put off sharing a piece of himself with Michael that must have terrified him, that must have impeded on his neat, orderly universe. And now Simon was bouncing around the beds of all manner of English gents while Michael was in this hospital room, in a life far more traditional and expected. How could this have happened? Michael had spent all of his teen years proving to the world that he was different, and now here he was, with a woman, about to have a baby. The piercings and hair dye and weird clothes were long gone. Instead, he was currently wearing hospital scrubs, and he hadn't shaved in a couple of days, and he probably looked just like every other harried, heterosexual father who marched through the obstetrics ward of Beth Israel.

"Did that help?" Michael asked.

Joan smiled faintly. "A bit, yeah. I can picture the two of you expressing yourselves through art."

"Well, if by art, you mean magazine clippings and cheap markers, sure. We were expressing something, all right."

She laughed, but her laughter was cut off abruptly by a cough and another contraction. Michael tried to coach her through it. Each time she breathed out or whimpered with pain, he was reminded again that the inevitable could no longer be postponed.

He couldn't have said how or when it had happened, if a condom had broken without him realizing it or if it was some fluke, but Joan had come to him one day with a plastic stick in her hand and they'd cried about it for days. Sometimes they cried with joy, sometimes with fear or worry, and they'd had a few conversations about what to do. He was impressed that they'd handled it so maturely, to the point where when Joan said, "I want to keep it," that seemed like the right thing to do.

Time warped again and sped up once the doctor showed up and said, "Okay, now it's time to push," and suddenly Joan was moaning and hunching forward, and then the doctor was saying, "It's a boy!" as the baby started to wail.

Really, it wasn't until twenty minutes later, when a drowsy Joan handed the baby to a nurse and the nurse said, "Would you like to hold your son?" that Michael's life changed irrevocably.

There was this tiny humanoid thing in his arms. He had a tuft of dark hair on his head and a wrinkly face and the tiniest fingers peeking out from the folds of his blanket. He had big blue eyes that looked up at Michael expectantly, as if to say, "Well, now what?" Then he sighed and promptly fell asleep.

It was hard to see traces of himself or Joan in the boy. That tuft of hair was the same color as Michael's, but that could have been a coincidence. Mostly, he looked like a baby. But it didn't matter. He was soft and warm and he wriggled in Michael's arms as if he were trying to get comfortable there.

Michael instantly loved this tiny boy, more than he'd ever loved anything.

He wished Simon were there. He wanted to show Simon this person he and Joan had made, wanted to be able to talk about the overwhelming tide of emotion, wanted to explain to someone that loving his son felt like a miracle. He wanted to talk to Simon about what he would do now, how he would raise this boy, what he'd accomplish as a father. He felt hopeful, suddenly, like all of this might work out after all, and he wanted to tell Simon that. He wanted Simon to celebrate this big life event with him, the way they had celebrated all previous big life events with each other.

Of course, these were conversations he should have been having with Joan, whom he still loved, though their relationship had been strained of late. He was rationalizing the distance between them as hormones or Joan's discomfort in the last weeks of her pregnancy, but deep down, he knew better. Maybe having to raise a baby together would make a difference in their relationship, would bring them closer together, but Michael knew it was just as likely to tear them apart. He knew also that their relationship had been in trouble since before they even knew this baby was on the way. Michael wanted to talk to Simon about that, too, to get advice, to say something innocuous, to make him smile, but he had no idea what to even say to reach out across that void that was their relationship now.

Michael sat in a big chair with ugly upholstery, his infant son sleeping in his arms, and he felt a profound emptiness. He was alone, except for this tiny human with him.

"You and me, kid," he said. "We're going to have something special. And I will always love you. Always. No matter what. Okay?"

One of the nurses interrupted his moment, said, "Aw," and she offered to take the boy from him.

"Let me hold him a while longer," Michael said.

CHAPTER 9

2012

MICHAEL KNEW what Joan was up to, but he followed her around the apartment anyway and watched as she plucked her various belongings from among his and put them in a box. She hadn't said, "I'm leaving," but Michael had known it was over for weeks.

They never went out anymore, which Michael understood was because they were over thirty and had a kid, but part of him missed his old life. Joan must have too. They couldn't be spontaneous anymore. No more trips to MoMA or the Met just because they had a morning free, no exploring the hidden corners of the city because Joan had a friend who tended bar at an old-fashioned speakeasy in the East Village, no fancy clothes or expensive dinners anymore. All of their money lately went to feeding and clothing Trevor. It was putting a strain on everything, and the stress and lack of sleep made Michael irritable, and he knew he'd been picking unnecessary fights with Joan a lot lately, but he just felt so adrift. What had once been fun and sweet now tasted bitter, and though Michael had a family, he felt lonely.

Trevor sat at the foot of the bed, kicking his feet. He reached out with his little hands, so Michael picked him up. He held his son in his arms as he watched his girlfriend pack up her things to leave him.

He ran his hand over Trevor's head and said, "Where will you go?"

"I bought a place upstate. About thirty miles west of Woodstock. Up in the Catskills."

She'd *bought* a place? How long had she been planning to leave? "Oh. That's far."

"You're a goddamn genius, Michael."

Michael put a hand over Trevor's ear. "You don't have to be sarcastic."

"I can't take the city. I'm done with all the noise and chaos. And you know that you and I aren't really working anymore. If we ever did."

"But how can you just pick up your whole life and move it so far away?"

Joan huffed out a breath. She pulled out one of the drawers in their secondhand dresser and started pulling her clothes out of it and tossing them at the suitcase she'd propped up on the bed. "Well, let's see. I've been out of work for three months with few prospects aside from the consulting gig I get tossed every now and then. The economy in this city blows unless you're a banker, and I don't think that situation is getting better anytime soon. And going back to work might not even be worth it, because I'd have to pay for child care while I'm there." She grunted with the effort of scooping the remainder of the shirts in the drawer and throwing them at the suitcase. "The cost of living is too fucking high. It's too loud. There are too many people. It was fun when I was younger, but I'm tired of it now."

"I don't get a say, then?"

"No. Come on, Mike, you know it's been rough between us for a long time. When was the last time we even had sex?"

Michael covered Trevor's ears again. "Geez." Though it had been... a while, hadn't it? When had they stopped sleeping together? Michael couldn't remember, which was worrisome.

"Remember when this was just... fun?" she asked. She stopped what she was doing and looked toward the window, as if she wanted to escape through it. "When did it stop being fun?"

"About the same time we became parents, I think," Michael said. Realizing this was the end and it was not negotiable—which he'd been aware of but hadn't really *known* until this moment—Michael could admit that there'd been tension and strain between them for a long time.

He considered protesting, begging her to stay, but he knew her mind was made up and he wasn't sure that was what would be best for any of them.

And thus ended Michael's romantic relationship with Joan. Easiest breakup ever. Except....

"What about Trevor?"

"He's coming with me."

Michael had known that would be her answer, but he said, "No." He held Trevor tighter. Trevor squealed in protest and whined, "Daddy," so Michael let up on the pressure a little. He pet Trevor's head again and said, "You can't just take him. He's my son too."

Joan shot him a scathing look. Ah, there was the anger he'd been expecting. "Be real, Michael. What, do you want custody? You can barely take care of yourself, and you think you can take care of a toddler?"

"I'm doing fine so far."

"Because I'm here. Besides, the city is no place for a kid. That's why I picked the Catskills. He's better off in a less urban environment."

Michael wasn't sure he agreed with that. He'd taught classes in this city; if Trevor got into the right schools when he was old enough, he'd be fine. "We can't, like, work out some kind of deal? I mean, you want to leave me, I get that. Things haven't been so great with us for a while. We're unhappy, the damage seems irreparable. I miss...." He laughed bitterly. He missed sex, but it wasn't just that. "I really did think I could... but I'm...." Michael didn't want to rehash their previous conversations, so he settled for petting Trevor's head again. Trevor leaned his cheek on Michael's shoulder.

"You're a fag, Mike. For whatever reason, you fell in love with me, but your true nature was bound to reassert itself eventually. Of course, instead of doing the sensible thing and cheating on me, you've been sitting around in celibate frustration for months."

"I haven't."

"Don't tell me you don't want to fuck the Patterson kid on the first floor."

"Well." He certainly did. Their downstairs neighbors had a twenty-two-year-old son who was bunking with them. The kid was tall and blond and gorgeous. Too young for Michael, of course, but that hadn't stopped him from looking.

Joan rolled her eyes. "Look, I'm not saying you can't see Trevor, but I'm moving and you're staying here."

"I could move."

"Honey, your whole life is in this city. This is your home."

"Yeah, but for Trevor—"

"Stop."

"Joan, please." But he could see that all decisions had been made. Joan was leaving him and taking Trevor, and yeah, he could sue for custody or he could move upstate with them and get a job wherever they moved. But he doubted he had a very employable skill set outside of the city. And he doubted he could take care of a child on his own. Joan was basically right on that account. She knew him better than he knew himself sometimes.

"I'm sorry things had to be this way," Joan said. "I was hoping we could make this work too, but I can't do this anymore."

Michael wanted Simon there. He wanted to ask Simon's advice. Simon would know exactly what Michael should do. But that was kind of Joan's point, wasn't it? Michael was so dependent on other people that he couldn't even make decisions for himself.

"So it's decided and there's no changing it," Michael said.

"Yes. Now give me my son."

SIMON WAS tracing patterns in Max's chest hair when his cell phone rang. Max was far more interesting than the phone, so Simon chose to ignore it. He lifted the sheet and looked at Max's cock, already growing even though they'd had really athletic sex a half hour before. He smiled and nibbled on one of Max's nipples.

Then the house phone rang.

Max ran a hand over Simon's shoulder and said, "Someone clearly wants to talk to you, babe."

"They can leave a message."

"Mmm."

The machine picked up the call and Michael's voice echoed around the room. "Simon! Simon, I really need you. Pick up the phone."

"Better get it," said Max.

Simon hauled himself into a sitting position and reached for the phone. "What?" he barked.

"Christ. No need to be hostile."

"I'm busy right now. What is it?"

"Joan left me."

Simon had never expected for three little words to send him into such a tailspin. He was suddenly dizzy. "She... what?"

"She took Trevor and she moved to the fucking Catskills, and I'm pretty sure my life is over. I mean, I could learn to live without Joan, I'd been sort of preparing myself for that, but Trevor is gone."

Everything receded into the background except the blunt fact that Michael was single. Hadn't Joan been the catalyst for Simon leaving New York? In the simplest of terms, Simon had once been in love with Michael, and then Michael had fallen in love with a woman. It flashed through Simon's mind that if Joan were gone, everything could go back to the way it had been.

If Simon were honest with himself, though, he would be able to recall that Joan was a symptom, not the disease.

"Simon? You there?"

"I'm here. So she... she left you."

"Which I totally get. We'd been having problems. And she was totally right about the Patterson kid."

"What?"

"Oh, new neighbors. They have a twenty-two-year-old son, boomerang kid or something, and he's so fucking hot. He's got this sweet little ass and...."

Of course, Simon thought. And there it was. Had Michael ever learned anything? "I'm really sorry about Joan and Trevor. That's... that just sucks, that Trevor's gone. Are you getting partial custody or anything?"

"Ah, well. No. I mean, Joan was kind of right. I'm not a very good father."

That was patently untrue and Simon was irritated with Joan for making Michael think that. Simon had seen Michael in action a few times, most recently when Simon had stopped in New York for a few days on his way from London to San Francisco and had visited Michael's little family. Michael clearly loved his son and doted on the boy.

"Will you visit him at least?" Simon asked.

"Oh, of course. Maybe that will be my incentive to finally get a car."

Simon leaned back against his headboard. He spared a glance at Max before he rubbed his eyes. "Sounds like you've got it all figured out," he said to Michael. "Why is this an emergency?"

"I'm upset about Trevor. But also, I thought you should know. I mean, I know you hate Joan—"

"I don't hate Joan."

"She left me, Simon. You could hate her a little."

Simon laughed despite himself. "Fine, whatever."

"But anyway, I know you don't like her much. She left me and I thought you should know. So here I am, all alone in New York."

"You're hardly alone."

"Well."

"You're gay again, I assume."

That got a raised eyebrow from Max, who looked way more amused than he should have been by these antics.

"I was always gay. But this one time…."

Simon thought sometimes that he should have been more understanding, that he should have been more supportive of his best friend falling in love. But the truth was that it still broke his heart every damn day that things between himself and Michael had gone the way they had. They'd had something really special once, but they couldn't make a romantic relationship work. Although, apparently Michael could with a woman—that had stung. Michael couldn't be with Simon, but he could be with a woman?

A woman who had just left him. So maybe Michael hadn't made anything work after all.

"I'm really sorry," Simon said. "I'm sorry things turned out this way. Certainly Trevor deserves better."

"Well, yeah. I could have told you that." Michael sighed, which came through the phone as a hiss.

Michael's tone was self-deprecating, but Simon had only meant that Trevor deserved both parents, not to be yanked away from his father and taken upstate.

"So when are you coming home?" Michael asked.

"What? I'm not. I have a good job in California."

"You can't stay away forever, you know. And I thought now that Joan's gone—"

Was that the real reason Michael was calling? "She's not the only reason I left New York."

There was a very long pause before Michael said, "Right. I know."

But Simon wondered if Michael did know. Did Michael know that seeing him every day had just clobbered Simon, that having Michael be so close but not be his was the worst kind of torture, that irreparable damage had been done to their relationship the moment Michael had said, "I love you," and Simon had believed it. That years of watching Michael self-destruct and make strange decisions had started killing Simon just as much as it had been killing Michael.

"I can't come home," Simon reiterated. "I'm… I'm not ready."

"Someday, though?"

"Maybe. I'm not making any promises."

He got off the phone and looked down at Max, who grinned.

"Sorry, old friend," Simon said.

"Yeah, I got that." Max propped himself up on his elbows. "Is this the old friend you used to fuck?"

Simon bristled, not liking how that sentence distilled the whole saga of Michael down to a few vulgar words, but he said, "Yeah."

Max nodded knowingly. "Leave it be. I can make you forget."

"Please do."

Present Day

WHILE HE was lying awake the morning after he'd broken down about Trevor in front of Simon, Michael heard Simon leave and wondered idly where he'd run off to. Probably he was fleeing the ugly, weepy mess that Michael had become the night before.

He got out of bed and went about folding the mattress back up. He walked into the kitchen to see about making a pot of coffee but realized he was out of filters. He threw on jeans and a clean shirt and was about to head out to the drug store on the corner when Simon came back.

"I got bagels," Simon said, holding up one of the two bags he held in his hand. The other he placed on the counter.

Michael thought he smelled... *could that be...* he opened the second bag. It did indeed contain two cups of coffee. One had a weird swiggle written in marker on the lid.

"Marked one is yours," Simon said, pulling plates out of the cabinet. "Cream and two sugars, right?"

"Yup," Michael said, oddly giddy that Simon knew his coffee order. When Simon passed him a poppy seed bagel with pink cream cheese, Michael sighed happily. "Dude. You seriously get me."

"I lived with you for three years."

"Yeah, eons ago. You *remembered.*"

Simon shrugged.

Since Michael's apartment was not anywhere near big enough to fit anything as fancy as a dining table, they sat side by side on the sofa and ate off the coffee table. It was a low, rectangular table that Simon had purchased from some fancy-pants furniture store in SoHo back when they lived together. Did Simon remember that?

Michael was still feeling a little wounded from the night before, embarrassed about the fact that he'd cried in front of Simon. Simon went about eating his bagel and sipping his coffee as if nothing were different.

"You sleep okay?" Simon asked.

"As well as ever. You?"

"I slept fine."

Michael wanted to bridge the awkward gap between them. He wanted to resume their conversation from the night before. He wanted to be honest for a change. He figured he'd start small. "Thank you."

"You're welcome. These really are good bagels. Other cities never figured out how to make bagels correctly."

"It's the city water," Michael said. "But I'm not only thanking you for the bagels. Thank you for, I don't know. Thank you for listening last night. Thank you for understanding how hard things have been for me."

Simon nodded slowly and put his bagel down. "You're welcome."

Michael couldn't figure out how to say what he wanted to say. "It's so much water under the bridge, and it's probably dangerous to even bring it up, but can we talk a little about what happened before you left?"

Simon's face clouded over, but he didn't yell or storm out, so that was something. "Why do you want to?"

"I never told you everything. I feel like… I think that if we're going to move on, we have to be honest. I mean, for the last few weeks, we've been coexisting and being polite, but it's very much at arm's length. I can't continue to live that way. Can you?"

Simon shook his head. "No." He turned away and sipped his coffee, but then he put the cup down and looked back. "You really should get coasters if you're going to put drinks on this table."

Michael let out a little gurgle of laughter. "Don't ever change, Simon."

"What did you want to tell me?"

"I need you to know that the reasons things didn't work out, it wasn't you. You said all these wonderful things to me and I wanted to believe them, but I was in a really bad place." Michael scooted away from Simon but resisted the temptation to curl up in a ball. He couldn't think of a time he'd ever felt so raw. But if they were talking civilly, it might be good to get everything out there. "I was going through a lot of shit I wasn't telling you about. Around the time I met Joan, I mean."

"Why didn't you tell me?"

"You weren't around much, for one thing. But I was ashamed. Things went really wrong with one of the guys I was seeing, and when I resorted to calling my parents to vent about it a little, they made me think it was my fault, and maybe it was, kind of. I couldn't have you think less of me."

"I wouldn't have."

"Eh, I don't know if that's true, but it doesn't matter now. Suffice to say, you finally said to me what I had most been wanting to hear for as long as I could remember, but I freaked right out, and I'm sorry about that. I really thought that if I could have a little time to screw my head on straight, then I could be a good partner for you."

Simon kicked off his shoes. He pulled one of his feet up onto the cushion and hugged his leg. "But you met Joan."

"I feel like such a shit for what I put you through." Michael sighed. "My feelings about Joan are complicated, but I know that what I did hurt you. I knew it at the time too. I don't think I will ever be able to apologize enough. I know why you left New York. I would have done the same in your shoes."

"Then why did you do it?" Simon leaned forward and rested his chin on his knee. Michael couldn't read his emotions at all. Everything about Simon was casual and neutral. He took a long breath and said, "I got that place uptown on a month-to-month basis thinking that you were working through whatever you were working through and that you'd invite me home when you worked it out. I was finally ready to be in a real relationship with you. I thought that was what you wanted. Then you tell me you're in love with Joan."

Michael groaned. "I know. I *know*. I am so sorry. I was wrong. Not about Joan. I loved her. Part of me still loves her. But I was wrong for how I behaved toward you. And I wanted you so badly, but everything in my head was scrambled, and then Joan came along and it was all so easy with her. There was no angst or drama then. There was no pain. We were just together. But with you, I had so much history." He poked at his coffee cup, picking it up and putting it down. "I know I hurt you and I will never forgive myself for that."

"Why, Michael?"

It was a valid question. "I don't know. I never expected any of what happened to go the way it did. Joan and I were having fun together. But you and me? We could barely talk to each other in those days."

"That's true," Simon said, raising his eyebrows and letting out a breath.

"It sounds lame to say that I didn't mean for any of it to happen, but I didn't. I didn't set out to, like, betray you. I did genuinely want to try to figure myself out. But I… got distracted."

Simon nodded at that. "I think sometimes that maybe I should have gone out with you in college like you wanted. That we could have avoided all this."

"No. I understand why you didn't." Michael rubbed his face with his hands. "And now we're like strangers, moving through this apartment like roommates who barely tolerate each other instead of old friends. I bet you can't wait to move out."

"It *is* awkward." Simon looked forward, to the window that faced the street. His face still betrayed no emotion, but it was clear he was thinking something through. "I think it's because things are weird and undefined. We can't just pick up where we left off, because where we left off was not a good place. I want to be your friend, but it's hard. I feel so much when I look at you." As if to emphasize his point, Simon looked up and met Michael's eyes. His gaze was intense. Michael imagined he could see all of Simon's emotions parading across his face: fear and anger, yes, but maybe hope. Of course, the reality was that the rest of Simon's face remained neutral.

"I know," Michael said.

"So where do we stand with each other?"

"That I don't know. Are you seeing anyone now?"

"No. I was dating a guy in Chicago, but we broke up before I moved back here. He was... shallow. Hot and really smart but not really capable of an emotion stronger than disliking asparagus."

Michael let out a surprised laugh. "Yeah. I haven't dated much. At all, really, since Joan left. A one-nighter here or there, but that's it." Michael turned to face Simon more directly. "So we're both single. That's something."

"You want to give us a go again."

"Yes, although honestly, right this moment? I don't know what I want. Here's what I know. For the last thirty years, you have been the number one most important person in my life. Even that night when I asked you out and you broke my heart in the middle of Washington Square Park. Even when you were gallivanting across Europe. Even when I was with Joan. The night Trevor was born? All I could think about was that I wished you had been there." Michael let out a sigh. "You know what else I know? We were always really good in bed together, even when we were both virgins groping in the dark. And I have been in love with you since I was about sixteen. I know these things."

Simon turned to face Michael, and there it was, finally: tangible emotion, anguish written all over his face. Simon's eyebrows knit together, and Michael could see past the reflection off the lenses of Simon's glasses that his eyes were a little damp. "I think sometimes it would have been easier if I'd always been on the same page as you. I was never as certain as you were. I didn't know a goddamn thing at sixteen. I barely knew I was gay, even."

"You didn't want to go to prom with me."

"I wasn't sure my feelings went beyond friendship. Back then, they didn't."

"But that changed."

"And when I finally fell for you, you weren't able to be with me."

Michael nodded. "And now? Now, Simon?"

"I don't—"

"The other thing I know is that the past is the past and we can't change it, but we can make our lives different going forward. I know that I hurt you. But you've hurt me too. I think we can get past it. Although, here I am, pouring my heart out, and you're just sitting there."

"Michael."

Michael reached over and ran his hand over Simon's shoulder. Everything about Simon was so familiar: the depth of his voice, the curve of his shoulder, the way his hair was combed just so, with not a strand out of place. The glasses were different from the ones he'd worn before he moved to Dubai, he had faint crow's feet at his eyes that hadn't been there before, but he was still so very Simon. Michael didn't mind Simon's outward stoicism, because he knew things were churning inside him. The poker face faltered just enough for Michael to see that Simon was wrestling with something significant.

"I didn't come back here for this," Simon said.

"I know."

"But I...."

Simon kissed Michael. It was soft and tentative at first, but when Michael pressed forward, Simon did the same, and soon they were clutching each other, tangling their tongues with each other's, and Michael moaned softly into Simon's mouth.

He was still in love. The shape and form of that love had changed over the years, from a sixteen-year-old's naïve conviction to a pained longing to a comfortable familiarity, but through it all was the knowledge that Simon was the man he felt most at home with, Simon was the man he understood and cherished and valued above all things, and Simon felt all of it for Michael in return. Michael wasn't sure how he knew that, but he did, and when Simon put his arms around Michael's shoulders, Michael felt surer of it than ever. Simon was *home*.

"You and me," Michael said when he pulled away. "We belong together."

Simon closed his eyes. "Yes. I know."

He kissed Michael again, long and lazy this time, as if he were resigned to his fate. Simon started to move his hands over Michael's body, but though Michael was hard and aroused, that wasn't what he wanted yet.

"Wait," Michael said. "Let's... let's do this differently than we did before. Let's get it right this time."

Simon leaned back. "What do you mean?"

"Every time we got together in the past, it was kind of an accident. It blew up in our faces. So what if we actually gave it some thought? Put some effort into it? We both have a lot to make up for and forgive too. This can't be like every other time."

Simon narrowed his eyes, but then he nodded. "All right. So instead of jumping into bed, maybe... maybe I take you on a date first."

"Yeah, maybe. I mean, we haven't seen much of each other in six years. Maybe we should slow everything down. Throw in some romance. Try something we never have before."

"All right."

"We've never gone out on a date together. At least not when we both knew it was a date."

Simon tilted his head. "Huh. I guess you're right."

Michael was suddenly bursting with ideas. "Oh! I know exactly what I want to do. Let me meet you after work tomorrow night. At your office. I'll meet you in the lobby. Then be prepared for me to romance your socks off."

Simon laughed. "That sounds a little dirty."

"I assure you, my intentions are pure, but if I do indeed succeed in knocking off your socks, things are negotiable."

"I'm not wearing socks now," Simon pointed out.

"Patience, Simon. There's a lot more to romance than sex."

Simon smiled. "All right. Tomorrow night. In the meantime, we should finish these bagels." He picked what remained of his up again. "This right here is what I missed about New York."

"Bagels?"

"Bagels with enough cream cheese to stop your heart. Hot dogs from Gray's Papaya. Yellow cabs. Washington Square Park. You. All of it."

"Welcome home, Simon."

CHAPTER 10

Present Day

THE DAY had been somewhat hectic, and Simon fretted all afternoon that he wouldn't finish what he had to get done by the time Michael showed up for their date. But then when Michael called to say, "I'm downstairs," Simon was somewhat satisfied with what he'd accomplished that day.

As he rode the elevator down to the lobby, Simon took a few deep breaths to let the workday go. He turned his fretting toward the date instead. He wondered if this was even a good idea. Maybe he'd forgiven Michael too easily. Maybe the damage they'd caused to each other was irreparable. Maybe allowing himself to hope was a mistake. Could he really let go of six years of pain—pain he'd been clutching to his chest like a badge of honor?

When he got downstairs, Michael was wearing a wide grin and a well-cut suit. Michael looked really good in a suit, it did not escape Simon's notice. He was handsome in the cutoff sweats and ratty T-shirts he wore around the apartment, and he was attractive in the button-down shirts and gray trousers he seemed to favor for work, but he was drop-dead sexy in a suit.

"You're dressed up," said Simon.

Michael tilted his head and ran a hand down his tie. "You like?"

Simon nodded.

"I just figured, you know, you wear suits to work every day. I thought I should be dressed as nicely as you."

Simon looked down at his own suit, a blue one he'd bought recently. His shirt was a little wrinkled from being worn all day and the pants also would have benefitted from an encounter with an iron, but he supposed he looked all right.

"I didn't know you owned a suit," Simon said as he followed Michael out of the building.

"I suppose I am full of surprises." Michael turned right as they headed out. "I got us a reservation at a restaurant in TriBeCa. The chef is kind of famous, I guess. He won one of those reality cooking competition shows on TV. It's a little bit of a tourist trap, but my assistant said the food is really good."

"You have an assistant who goes out to high-end restaurants?"

"Some of us are also capable of holding down good jobs." Michael chuckled. "I mean, I'm pretty sure Janelle has only been there because her parents paid the last time they came to visit. I don't pay her *that* well. Anyway, this place is probably a fifteen-minute walk from here. We can take the subway if you want, or get a cab—"

"No, let's walk. It's a nice night."

Michael turned to him and smiled. He was beaming practically. It was a little strange.

"I almost got you flowers," Michael said, "but then I couldn't figure out what we'd do with them during dinner. Plus, I don't know, do guys like flowers?"

"I like flowers."

"Good, okay. I'm filing that away for later. I like flowers too, for the record. I usually keep some around the apartment, but I've been so busy lately that they kept dying on me before I could remember to water them, and that made me sad."

He buzzed like a Chihuahua, patented Michael enthusiasm radiating off of him. That used to annoy Simon, back in the days when they voluntarily saw each other daily, but now Simon enjoyed it. He'd missed it. Michael had been so sad since Simon had come back to New York, but there was no evidence of that now, and Simon was determined to enjoy this, whatever it was. Still, Michael was going to hurt someone if he kept moving that way. Simon reached over and grabbed Michael's arm to pull him out of the way of a family of tourists. Michael looked at him and smiled. Simon slid his hand down Michael's arm and then threaded his fingers with Michael's. Michael's smile broadened.

"Nothing to see here, folks," Michael said with a laugh. "Just two dudes in suits, holding hands."

They did get the hairy eyeball from an older man, but Simon found he didn't care, and mostly people moved past them without reacting.

The restaurant was pretty swanky. Also very crowded. The hostess escorted Simon and Michael to a quiet corner table, which felt a little isolated, but in a good way since they could hear each other talk. Michael smiled as he looked at the menu, an expression that made Simon think he had a secret, but Simon decided not to question anything. He put aside all of his unease, his questions, his fear, his pain. He was going to enjoy this date.

And he did enjoy it. The food was good. The company was better. Michael never lost his giddy enthusiasm, regaling Simon with tales from work, with things he'd seen in the city since the last time Simon had visited, with cute stories about Trevor. Simon chimed in to tell stories about his time in other cities.

"I'd love to go to San Francisco someday," Michael said.

"I'll take you. My apartment was right in the Castro in this gorgeous old building. The commute was hell, but totally worth it. I made friends with the downstairs neighbors, an older gay couple who had been there for thirty years. Really nice guys. They'd probably put us up if you didn't want to stay in a hotel."

Michael laughed. "Look at you, planning our vacation!"

The word "our" pinged something in Simon. He was such a mess inside, trying to figure out if this was what he really wanted, if only he could drop all of his sadness and frustration regarding Michael. Really, this was what Simon needed, what he'd come back to New York for. Living in limbo would only cause them both further pain, so the options were to embrace Michael or to cut him off entirely. Simon couldn't see any other solution. Embracing Michael, embracing their relationship, seemed like the better option. It was worth at least giving it a shot.

"We're really doing this now, aren't we?" Simon asked.

Michael reached across the table and took his hand. "Yes."

It was interesting to see how happy Michael seemed now, how different this was from the quiet, morose man Simon had been living with for the past few weeks. That was the strangest thing about moving back to New York: Michael had seemed not at all himself. Simon couldn't remember ever seeing him so withdrawn. But over the past twenty-four hours, Simon had watched Michael come back to himself. *This* was the Michael Simon remembered, the one he thought about late at night sometimes, the one he'd missed with his very soul while he'd been away.

He squeezed Michael's hand.

He supposed this Michael had actually been gone for a long time. Since long before Simon had left New York.

It hit Simon suddenly, like a slap on the back or a light bulb flashing on over his head, that he'd always been tremendously selfish where Michael was concerned, taking from the relationship what he needed but never giving Michael what he needed in return. That was the problem, wasn't it? All Michael had ever asked for was for Simon to love him, but Simon had always held back, issued demands, made his love conditional. Simon was always looking for the next big adventure and hated being reminded of life back home in Iowa, of his mother's quiet disapproval, of his father's outright disavowal, of his own invisibility. And Michael was as much a symbol of his old life as he was of his new one.

No son of mine will be gay! Simon's father had said when Simon had finally come out to him. Then, *You've been fucking that Michael kid all along, haven't you?* Simon had denied it. He'd hated the lie. He'd hated pretending there was nothing between him and Michael when, really, there was everything.

And through all of it, he had never once given Michael what Michael had wanted, and then he'd balked when Michael had told him plainly he couldn't give any more. That's what had happened when Simon had moved out of their apartment. Why hadn't he seen that?

Why hadn't he seen how Michael had been suffering? Why hadn't he noticed when that light had gone out behind Michael's eyes?

"God," Simon said. "I am such a selfish asshole."

Michael's smile faltered. "You're a what now?"

"You have been bending over backward to apologize since I got here, but I'm the one who should apologize. I'm so sorry, Michael."

Because Simon had put that smile on Michael's face. This was what Michael wanted. He didn't want adventure. He didn't want the life lived out loud that Simon had craved when he'd first moved to New York. Michael had gotten a lot of that out of his system in high school.

No, Simon knew that what Michael wanted was love. He wanted a quiet life at home with a man who loved him, and maybe a family eventually. What he had instead were fractures. He had a son he loved dearly but rarely saw. He had a dozen failed relationships. And he had thirty years of memories of Simon being a selfish asshole and loving him anyway.

"I'm done trying to find the next experience," Simon said. "I don't want it anymore, not the way I used to. When we were younger, I wanted to make the most of every moment, I wanted to see and think and feel everything. I wanted to learn, I wanted to have sex, I wanted to see the world. I've done those things now. I've done more than I ever thought I would, and although a lot of it has been awesome, it wasn't satisfying in the way I thought it would be. Do you know why?"

Michael leaned forward. "Tell me."

"Because I did a lot of it without you. That was what I didn't see, that was what I didn't understand. You loved me and you needed me, all those years ago, and you told me that plain as day and I didn't hear it, I didn't get what you were telling me. And I guess I kind of took for granted that you'd always be there when I finished doing whatever it is I thought I had to do, so when I was finally ready to have something with you, it had to be on my terms. When it couldn't be, I was heartbroken, but I see now why it didn't work. I was selfish and I took your unwavering faith that you and I were meant to be for granted and I didn't treat you the way you deserved to be treated."

Maybe nobody in Michael's life ever had. Because Michael had always been light and love and happiness, but something had crushed that, perhaps years of him wanting but never receiving. Or maybe Joan had given him some of what Simon hadn't been able to, and that was how Michael had fallen in love with her so easily. Simon had opened the door to his own heartache, had invited Joan in to stomp on his heart, had crushed both him and Michael in the process.

"That ends now," Simon said with conviction. "From this moment forward, I will do everything I can to treat you the way you deserve to be treated. If you need something, ask and I'll give it. If you want me, I'm all yours. I promise, okay? I want to love you the way I should have all those years ago, and I fucked everything up, but no longer. I want to get it right this time."

Michael wiped his eyes in a way that Simon supposed was supposed to be surreptitious, but he also smiled. "Simon. Oh, Simon."

"I love you too, you know," Simon said. "I think I have forever. I was too stupid to know what to do with that."

"I think maybe the planets have aligned," Michael said.

"What?"

"Goddammit, Simon. I love you so much. Finish eating your food so I can order dessert, because the cake in that case has been staring at me all night, but I'll get it to go because I need you to take me home as soon as possible."

"I... all right."

"You are stupid sometimes, Simon, but not for the reasons you think."

But when Simon asked about that, Michael refused to elaborate.

PROBABLY MICHAEL should have seen the bigger picture, but his first thought upon entering the apartment was that he'd get to sleep in his own bed tonight instead of on the uncomfortable sofa bed again.

His *second* thought was of Simon, standing in the kitchen, fiddling with his tie.

Michael walked past Simon and put his slice of cake in the refrigerator. Simon still stood there, eyeing him pensively.

"So," Simon said.

"Don't get awkward on me now, baby," Michael said. He grabbed Simon's tie and pulled it, using it as a leash to guide Simon to the bedroom. "You just told me at dinner you'd do what I wanted, what I needed. All I have to do is ask, right? Well, consider this me asking, no, *commanding* that you make love to me tonight. Because I've wanted you since I picked you up at Penn Station however many weeks ago, and having you in my space ever since has been torture."

Simon stood there for a moment, his mouth agape, his expression unreadable, looking so very Simon. He tilted his head as if he were mentally balancing his checkbook. "I want to, Michael. I do."

"But?"

Simon took off his jacket and draped it over a chair. "No but. I'm just… this feels momentous. I got stalled for a moment. I don't want to fuck it up this time."

"It's not possible."

"Um, hello, it's totally possible." Simon loosened his tie. "I've only ever fucked it up where we're concerned."

"That's not true." Michael shrugged out of his own jacket. "I've certainly contributed plenty. I've made mistakes too. That's why this is going to work this time. We're both remorseful, but we both know what mistakes we made before, so we won't repeat them." He took off his tie. He unbuttoned the top button of his shirt. "Besides, this part of it, we never screwed this up. The sexy parts, those were always great with us."

Simon slipped his belt out of its buckle. Then he paused and looked up at Michael. "This is what you want?"

"Yes. Is it what you want?"

"Yes. Definitely."

"Then what's the problem?"

Simon sighed and shucked his pants. He draped those on top of the same chair. So proper and neat, Simon was. Michael grinned. He took off his shirt and tossed it on the floor. Then he took off his pants and tossed them elsewhere. He peeled off each sock and threw it over his shoulder without regard for where it might fall.

Simon stood there with his shirt still on but open to show the undershirt he had on beneath. He was wearing black briefs, which were neat in a very Simon way. His expression was puzzled for a moment.

Then he started laughing.

Simon lost control quickly, giggling softly at first but then devolving into some kind of belly laugh, until he was bent over with it. Michael went to his side and put his hands on Simon's shoulders. He pushed Simon back up. "What the hell is so funny?"

"You. Me. Us. I don't know. You're wearing Superman briefs."

Michael looked down. He'd forgotten he'd put those on. "So?"

"So it's funny. So is this whole situation. Come on. Laugh with me."

Michael looked at Simon and at himself and saw that they did look a little silly, half out of their clothes. He looked at Simon's suit draped neatly over the chair and his own clothes strewn about. He looked at Simon, wiping his eyes as he laughed, a huge smile on his face.

That was how this always was supposed to be. The two of them had always made each other laugh, made each other smile. Now they were again. This was how it should have been.

Michael kissed Simon, who responded right away by putting his arms around Michael, and they stood there in the middle of the bedroom, suddenly clutching at each other. Everything stopped being funny abruptly. They pressed against each other, thrust their hips forward. Simon's cock pressed against Michael's hip and slowly grew. Arousal and electricity zipped through Michael at the realization that they could still do this, that they still had passion for each other, that indeed, Simon would make love to him just as he'd asked.

They helped each other out of the rest of their clothes and lay together on the bed. Simon kissed Michael and pulled him into his arms, and they curled together in bed for a few minutes, writhing and pressing their bodies together. Simon gasped when Michael dipped his head to nibble at Simon's neck, to lick his Adam's apple. Simon's body was familiar and beautiful, and his scent brought back a million memories of them doing just this. Sex could mean anything, he thought, it could be an expression of love or a temporary escape or a way to pass the time on a lazy afternoon. But between him and Simon, sex was something else entirely. It was two souls who had known each other for a long time coming together, twisting together, fitting together the way they were always meant to. Being in Simon's arms, being tangled with him, feeling Simon's hot body against his—that was home. That was right. That was perfect.

And Michael knew this body beneath his hands. He knew Simon liked having his nipples played with, so Michael nibbled at them, pulling cries and moans from Simon. He knew that Simon had particularly sensitive spots at his neck and near his armpits, that he loved it when a lover stroked a hand over his stomach, up his sides. Michael did all of those things. He knew Simon preferred to top, and Michael intended to let him.

Simon likewise knew that Michael liked a little roughness, liked getting his hair pulled, liked when Simon bit his skin. Simon did those things too, and soon they were kissing and thrusting and moaning, all hard arousal and sweat and tangled-together bodies. It had been so long that there was a difference this time that Michael couldn't quite put his finger on, but it was like a homecoming too.

"I want you inside me," Michael said to Simon.

Simon nodded. Michael reached for the bedside table and got what he needed. Wordlessly, they prepared each other, Simon stretching Michael and Michael rolling a condom on Simon. Michael's pulse raced with anticipation as he did it. He'd done this dozens of times with Simon, but this felt like the first time. It had never stopped being exciting. He hoped it never would.

Within moments, they were joined, Michael on top straddling Simon, Simon's face twisted up with pleasure. Michael bent forward as he moved up and down on Simon, letting Simon slide in and out of him as he controlled the pace. He nipped at Simon's lips. Simon moaned and put his arms around Michael.

"I love you so much," Simon said. "So fucking much." He kissed Michael fiercely. "I was a fool to wait this long."

"No," Michael said. "It had to be this way."

Michael moved above Simon, bringing them both as much pleasure as he could. Simon stroked Michael's cock with one hand and ran his other through Michael's hair.

"You're...." Simon grunted and sighed. "You're the most beautiful person I know."

"Hush," Michael said, suddenly embarrassed by the compliment.

He put his fingers to Simon's lips. Simon kissed those fingers. He surged his hips up, pushing harder into Michael, forcing their bodies together, creating a union of sorts between them.

"It's always been you, Simon," Michael said. "Always been you."

Simon trailed his fingers down Michael's spine, leaving tingles in his wake, and grabbed Michael's ass and pulled the cheeks apart. His pace got a little frantic as he thrust into Michael, and Michael knew the end was nigh for Simon.

Simon kept a hand on Michael's ass to control the pace as he wrapped his other hand around Michael's cock. He stroked hard and fast, exactly how Michael liked it. "Come for me," Simon said. "Come, Michael."

"Yes," Michael said, leaning forward, moving his hips so that Simon's cock was hitting him just right as Simon's hand was stroking at a rate that made pleasure flow through his whole body.

"Do you love me, Michael?"

"Yes. Always."

"I'm gonna come inside you. I want you to come on me. Come all over me. Come everywhere. Come apart."

"*Yes*," Michael hissed as it all hit him at once. The orgasm started somewhere in the center of his body and flowed outward until everything was pleasure and Simon. He hunched forward, said, "Yes," one more time, and then he came hard, shooting over Simon's hand, over Simon's chest, painting him, marking him.

Simon threw his head back and murmured, "Oh, Michael, yes," and then he was coming. Michael could feel Simon vibrating beneath him.

After that, things got a little blurry. Simon cleaned them both up and kissed Michael sweetly. Michael may have cried as Simon held him, but Simon may have too. They lay together until they were both sleepy, and Michael knew something was different now. Maybe the planets had aligned, but he felt like he could trust things to work out this time, that Simon really would stick around. He certainly had no intention of pushing Simon away. This time they'd get it right.

He fell asleep with that as his last thought.

CHAPTER 11

2000

THE SPEAKERS weren't turned quite loud enough for the live jazz band to filter out the other sound in the little club on Leroy Street. Simon was working on an assignment, trying to surreptitiously take notes on the band so that he could write a paper on modern jazz for his arts appreciation class, but Michael kept talking.

"Pretty sure they haven't updated the decor in here since about 1978," he said loudly. "And, really, who besides pretentious assholes even listens to jazz anymore?"

"I do," Simon said. "Shut up."

Michael let out a breath, the fringe of hair on his forehead floating up with it. Simon knew he was bored, but there wasn't much to be done about that. Besides, it was Michael's fault for insisting he wanted to come to this club. It was famous, Michael had argued when Simon protested—anticipating this very situation—and therefore experiencing it firsthand was part of that whole experience-New-York-to-the-fullest plan Simon had enacted.

Simon was tempted to tell Michael to leave and had opened his mouth to make that very suggestion when Reed came in. Simon supposed that would deflect some attention from this situation; Michael was not exactly a member of Reed's fan club.

Reed slid onto the chair next to Simon and put an arm around Simon's shoulders. He kissed Simon's temple. Simon allowed himself to be cuddled briefly, though he was pretty uncomfortable with excessive PDA.

Michael made gagging noises.

"I've heard this band coming on at nine is really good," Reed said, picking up the little table tent that listed that night's entertainment. "My dad said they've been playing shows in New York since he was our age."

"Is this place stuck in some kind of time capsule?" Michael asked.

Reed took his arm back and leaned back in his chair. He smirked at Michael. Reed didn't like Michael much, either. It didn't take an engineering major to work out why, but Simon usually opted to ignore their animosity.

Simon sighed and tried leaning away from Reed and Michael glaring at each other so that he could hear the music.

After a few minutes, Reed said, "There's something very grown-up about listening to jazz."

Michael scoffed.

"No, I'm serious. Like, teenagers listen to bubblegum pop or angry rock music. Adults listen to, I don't know, the mainstream top forty and opera and jazz."

The expression on Michael's face—one eyebrow raised, his nose scrunched up—indicated deep skepticism at this theory.

"Fine, whatever," Reed said. He put his arm back around Simon and literally pulled him back into the conversation. "It wouldn't hurt us all to think about adult life. College isn't forever. After college there are, you know, committed relationships and jobs and all that."

"Is that what this is?" Simon asked, gesturing between himself and Reed. "A committed relationship?"

Reed grinned. "Sure. I mean, here we are, in a jazz club that has been here in the Village since the late fifties, right? And you and me have been together for a few months now. And you are going to get that business degree in two years and go on to the rule the world."

Simon laughed. "Sure."

"And, hell, maybe ten, fifteen years from now, we'll be able to go to your big corporate functions together."

"Oh, please," said Michael. "You really think corporate America is ready for a gay CEO? You think Simon will be allowed to bring his 'life partner' to fancy dinners?" Michael made finger quotes when he said "life partner"; Simon knew Michael hated the phrase.

"It could happen," said Reed. "This is a new millennium. The possibilities are endless."

Michael rolled his eyes.

"Will you both shut up?" Simon said. "I have to take notes so I can write this damn paper."

Present Day

SIMON'S BOSS came by his office late one evening, catching Simon somewhat off guard. He'd been daydreaming about Michael, he realized, especially about what he'd do to Michael once he got home. His thoughts were not exactly appropriate for work.

But, alas, here was Roger Woods, a London transplant who was now running Simon's department. Simon's path had crossed with his a few times in his London years, and he liked the man well enough. Roger leaned in the doorway and said, "We're having a dinner next week to celebrate how well we did last quarter. You're invited, of course, since your work in Chicago contributed significantly."

"Wow. Thank you, sir. I look forward to it."

Roger shifted on his feet and glanced uneasily at the little rainbow flag in Simon's penholder. "We're, ah, inviting spouses also. So Willis's wife will be there, as will Abernathy's. And mine, of course."

Simon hated situations like this. Bad enough that he was the youngest person with his job title and tenure at the company, but he was the only one who wasn't married. It sometimes made for awkward situations—he was, in particular, tired of hearing, "You just haven't found the right girl yet," from well-meaning wives—but in the past, there was nothing he could do about it because he never would have brought one of the guys he had dated the last few years to corporate events.

But now he actually had someone at home that he was serious about.

"Would it be all right if I brought my boyfriend?" Simon asked.

Roger's eyes went wide in surprise. "You're already seeing someone? You've only been in New York, what, six weeks?"

Simon sighed. "Well, actually, it's an old flame. We've rekindled things since I've been back in New York. But it's pretty serious now, and I thought that, if every other partner is bringing his wife, I should be able to bring Michael. We aren't married—yet—but we're as good as, I think." He exaggerated—he was not nearly as confident in the relationship as he tried to sound—but suddenly he wanted this, he wanted to be able to bring a date to one of these stupid corporate events. Part of it was a stick-it-to-the-man mentality, sure, but he also couldn't help but think that having Michael there with him would be really fun.

Roger rubbed his chin. "Well, that's... I'm not really sure. That is, in the past, I might have made some allowances, but he *could* legally be your spouse, and we normally don't let partners bring their girlfriends. So...."

Simon chewed on the inside of his cheek for a moment before he realized what he was doing. Christ. He'd go home and propose to Michael that night—he wasn't sure of Michael's stance on marriage, actually, but he was probably in favor given his general tendency toward liking things familiar and domestic—if it would make a difference. Although he wasn't sure of his own stance on marriage, exactly, and he and Michael had certainly never talked about it, so....

Wait, what the hell was he thinking? Was he really willing to plunge into a serious relationship just to stick to his principles?

One thing at a time. "Extenuating circumstances," Simon said. "I've only been back in New York for a short time, as you have pointed out."

Roger frowned. "I'll talk it over with Abernathy. I just don't want anything to be awkward at the dinner."

Of course. One couldn't have any awkwardness at the fancy dinner thrown by the conservative bank.

"If not this, then one day when I am married, I'm going to want to bring my husband to corporate functions," Simon said. "I mean, don't put yourself out adding an extra chair to the table this time if you don't want to, but it's something the company might want to get used to. I realize I'm the only gay executive here, but since no one in this office has ever given me any flak for it, I thought this would be all right."

"Let me talk it over with Abernathy. I'll let you know in a few days."

It was effectively a "no." That took the wind out of Simon's sails.

He slunk back home a couple of hours later, feeling tired and frustrated. He found Michael camped out on the sofa, wearing ratty sweats and watching a basketball game on TV. Simon put his things away, shrugged out of his clothes, and put on pajama pants and one of Michael's T-shirts, a habit he'd developed recently. He liked Michael's T-shirts because they were softer and didn't have the same crisp newness as the clothes Simon had had to buy while the rest of his stuff was still in storage. Also, Michael's shirts smelled like Michael, which always helped comfort Simon.

He walked into the living room, sat on the sofa, and leaned his head on Michael's shoulder. Michael put an arm around him. "Tough day?"

"There's a work dinner next week to which all spouses are invited, so I asked if I could bring you, but my boss has to think about it."

"Really? You think of me as a spouse?"

"You're certainly the closest thing I have to one."

Michael laughed. "Okay. That doesn't sound like a strong endorsement."

"My boss pointed out that there was no legal reason why we couldn't be married. Not in New York, at any rate."

Michael froze. "I... oh, yeah."

Simon sat up. "Maybe we should take this one issue at a time. We promised we wouldn't rush things, right?" Simon took a deep breath. "If my boss says it's fine, do you want to come with me to a company dinner next week? It'll probably be kind of boring and corporate and involve a lot of back-patting, but they always pick excellent restaurants for these things, so at least the food will be good. Although, you will be the only male spouse, since every one of my colleagues who would be invited to such a thing is a straight, white man."

"That's… okay. Do you want me there?"

"Yes. I wouldn't be asking if I didn't."

Michael smiled. "That is true. Okay, then. I'll go. Assuming the conservative overlords at your company allow it." He reached over and ran a hand down Simon's cheek. "All men? Really?"

"Straight, white men. I'm their token minority."

Michael guffawed. "You're basically the safest choice in that regard."

"Or I was until I asked to bring a date to a company function."

"Progress has to start somewhere."

Simon reached over to play with the ends of Michael's hair. "Have you thought about marriage? I mean, in the abstract. Just, like, out of curiosity."

Michael looked away briefly, and then he turned back and put a hand on Simon's knee. "When I was, I don't know, sixteen or so? This cousin of my mother's, Maureen, announced that she and her girlfriend were having a commitment ceremony. And even though my mother swore she was totally cool with Maureen marrying a woman, and even though I had already told my parents *I* was gay, my mother decided that a commitment ceremony between two women was no place for a child."

"I remember that." Simon had remembered how pissed Michael had been to not be able to go.

"At the time, I thought that I wanted to have a commitment ceremony like that. My mom ended up going and she took pictures. She showed them to me when she got home. It was kind of a hippy ceremony, with both brides in caftans and a lot of incense and candles and things, but it was beautiful in its way too. I mean, obviously, I thought, if I ever do something like that, my groom would have to dress really well. No bullshit flowy shirts or anything. Maybe a nice seersucker suit. I'd wear blue and you'd wear green, maybe."

"Me?"

"Yeah, of course you. Who else did you think I would have planned to commit to when I was sixteen?"

Simon nodded to concede the point.

"Anyway, when some of the states started legalizing same-sex marriage, I thought, well, that's what I'll do when the time comes. I'll go to New England. Or, hell, then I could have gone back home to Iowa. And then it happened here. Oh, I can get legally married right here in New York? God, I wept that night when it passed the legislature. I walked over to Stonewall with all the people celebrating. It changed everything, or it felt that way at the time. Did I call you?"

"You did. I was still in London and it was, like, four in the morning because you hadn't figured out the time difference yet. Not that you ever really did."

"Well, you know." Michael sighed. "When Joan told me she was pregnant, I asked her if she thought we should get married. I reasoned that a kid should have both parents in a committed relationship, and we'd been together a couple of years by then, so might as well, right? I can't tell you how relieved I was when she turned me down."

"You didn't want to marry her?"

"No, I really didn't. Something nagged at me about it. Well, honestly, I think our decision to stay together for Trevor's sake really only postponed the inevitable. We probably would have broken up sooner if he hadn't come into the world."

Simon put his head back on Michael's shoulder. "You sure do give long-winded answers to simple questions."

"It's not that simple." Michael put his arm back around Simon. "You asked how I felt about marriage. And the truth is that part of me always wanted to get married. I used to think about it when I was a teenager, picturing what my future would be like. But it's only been in the last couple of years that marriage for people like us became more than a symbolic act."

"What made you want to get married?"

"Oh, you know. I wanted the whole kit and caboodle. You at my side and a couple of adopted kids, maybe. My own little family. But nothing turned out that way."

Simon wanted to point out that Michael could still have that, but with Trevor upstate, maybe that wasn't exactly true.

"How do *you* feel about marriage?" Michael asked.

"I don't know. I got so used to thinking it was something that was off-limits to me that I'm not sure what to do with it now that it isn't. Plus there's a part of me that feels like marriage is some kind of consolation prize." Simon put an arm around Michael's torso and squeezed a little. "If I were going to marry anyone, though, it would be you."

"Good to know."

SIMON'S BOSS ultimately came down on the side of not allowing Michael to come to the dinner. Simon had expected that but was still disappointed. Michael seemed to take it in stride, although he said, "Who wants to have dinner with a bunch of stuffy bankers?" a little defensively.

Simon made it up to him the next week by taking him out to an absurdly expensive restaurant.

"I don't know what half of these things are," Michael said as he looked at the menu. "You don't have to throw your money around to impress me, you know. I would have been just as happy at a fast-food restaurant."

"I know, but... I guess this is my way of doing romance. I'm wining and dining you."

Michael smiled. "Yeah? Well, all right, then. How do you pronounce this word?" He pointed at the menu.

"Confit?"

"Okay. Now what does it mean?"

So maybe the dinner was a little over the top. The food was excellent, but perhaps Michael had a point. They didn't have to impress each other on these dates they'd been having regularly; the real goal was to spend time together and get to know each other again. They probably could have done that just as well at the much more reasonably priced little Thai place near the apartment. That restaurant at least had the fruity cocktails Michael seemed to prefer over wine.

Still, they had a pleasant meal. Michael made the waiter explain most of the menu to him, which Simon found amusing. About halfway through the meal, Michael glanced back toward where the waiter had retreated and said, "So, the waiter. Gay or just British?"

"Both," said Simon.

"Are you sure?"

"I lived in London for three years. I got good at this game. Trust me."

"Hmm. I guess you would have needed to."

Toward the end of the meal, the waiter brought them a plate of petit fours "on the house," though Simon suspected that was part of the routine to make you think you'd gotten a good value from the restaurant. The waiter said, "Do you mind if I ask? Is this a business thing or...."

"Date," Michael said with conviction.

"Oh, good," the waiter said with a chuckle. "I saw the suits and thought you might be Wall Street blokes. I mean no offense, but you look like a banker."

"I am a banker," Simon said.

"Oh, well, that's good, then. Anyway, I kept thinking, 'I wonder if the banker knows the other bloke is flirting with him,' but I suppose you do. I am glad to hear it."

Simon laughed despite himself. That seemed like a perfect summation of his relationship with Michael.

"Anyway, between us, be careful walking home tonight. A kid got beat up outside the gay bar around the corner last week. He's okay, but they hit him hard enough to send him to the hospital."

"Thanks for the warning," said Simon as the waiter walked away.

He found the news upsetting, but when he looked up, Michael was clearly trying to hold in a laugh.

"What?" asked Simon.

"You are such a square. 'I *am* a banker.'"

"You don't find what he just told us disturbing?"

"What, about the kid who got beat up? Of course I do. That's awful. And now I'm disappointed because I probably shouldn't hold your hand on the walk home."

"You do realize that we are two men in our midthirties who probably have no business holding hands in public anyway?"

"So? That doesn't mean I don't want to. Why, is that too childish for you?"

Simon found himself smiling. "No, actually, I think it's kind of sweet."

"Really?"

"Yeah. Explain to me why we didn't do this dating thing ten years ago?"

"Because you're a stubborn, selfish asshole?"

"Ah, there's the reason."

Michael laughed. "Less so these days, I'm happy to report. I'm glad your trip around the world helped you see the light."

"I suppose it did." Or being here in New York with Michael had made a strong case for it. Simon took a deep breath and gazed at Michael and realized he felt truly happy for the first time in a long time. Maybe all the angst, drama, and heartache were worth it just for this moment, when it was just him and Michael and they were happy. He reached across the table and took Michael's hand. "I love you."

Michael's grin was beatific. "I love you too. Are you going to eat that last little cake?"

CHAPTER 12

Present Day

THEY MADE love that night, hot and sweaty and satisfying love, and then passed out naked in each other's arms. Simon marveled again at how stupid he'd been to keep saying no to this. He'd wanted adventures, experiences, but he'd discounted being in love with one's best friend as being the greatest experience of all. How wrong he'd been.

Of course, if things had gone differently with Michael way back when, Simon wouldn't have gone to Dubai or London or San Francisco, so there was that too. Nor would he have probably learned from his past mistakes and made this relationship now with Michael work as well as it seemed to be working.

Simon lay awake early the next morning, thinking about that, watching the way Michael's chest rose and fell as he slept. Had he ever been this content? Even when he'd seen and done some amazing things, even when he'd had outrageous sex, even when he triumphed at work, all of it had seemed to be missing something and none of it compared to the feeling of simply being with Michael.

It didn't make much sense to wallow in regret now. His energy was better spent making Michael happy and building a future that involved each other just like this.

Just like this, he thought sleepily.

Just like….

Suddenly, Michael's phone rang.

Michael stirred, rolled onto his back, and sat up. "Christ," he muttered as he blindly reached for the night table. He successfully located his phone, looked at the caller ID, frowned, and answered it. "Uh, hello? Uh-huh. She's... wait, she's what? Are you fucking serious?" Michael was definitely awake now. He threw the covers off himself and faced away from Simon, moving his legs so that his feet rested on the floor. Simon watched Michael's back tense as he talked to whoever was on the phone. "When did this happen?" Pause. "Why didn't you call me yesterday? Oh, holy Christ. What about Trevor?"

This was bad. Simon didn't need to know what was happening to tell by the way Michael's body was starting to contort in stress and pain to know that something truly horrible had happened. Simon tried to put the clues together based on Michael's end of the conversation, but he couldn't figure out anything except that it must have involved Joan.

"I... no, I can come up today," Michael was saying. "I don't know how yet, or what I'm going to do about work, but I'll figure it out. God, Joanie. Why didn't she say anything? Ugh, no, that's so much fucking bullshit. I'm sorry, I don't mean to curse, I'm just... I'm shocked. But... when is the funeral? Uh-huh. Okay. Has anyone called her parents? Oh, duh, of course. Who am I? I'm only the chopped-liver ex. Okay. Look, I want... make sure Trevor is okay. I'll come up for him if nothing else. Can I talk to him? No, no, let him sleep. I'll... yeah, I think we can, I think. Um. Look, let me figure some things out. We'll talk when I get there, all right? Yes. Thank you, Kelly. You are a godsend."

Michael hung up the phone and put it on the night table. He leaned forward and put his face in his hands.

"Michael, what is it?"

He sat up, startled, and looked back at Simon as if he didn't expect anyone to be there. Then his face crumbled. "Joan is dead."

The surprise was like a punch in the face. "Oh, Jesus. How? When?"

"Cancer. Turned out she had some kind of lymphoma but didn't breathe a word of it to anyone until it was too late. She died yesterday afternoon."

Simon scooted across the bed and put his arms around Michael, who turned toward him and hooked his arms around Simon's. He started to weep.

Simon tried to comfort him, stroking his hair and holding him tightly. Softly, he asked, "Where's Trevor?"

"With Kelly, the nanny. I trust her to take good care of him, but, Jesus, he just lost his mother and he's too young to understand it." Michael clung to Simon. "I have to go to him. I'll have to call out sick or something. But he needs me."

Simon thought perhaps Michael needed Trevor as much as Trevor would need Michael, but he didn't say anything, only continued to hold Michael.

"What am I going to do?" Michael asked.

It didn't take Simon long to formulate a plan. "I'll call my boss, okay? I'll take a few days off."

Michael sniffed. "I'm not sure going to the funeral of your boyfriend's ex-girlfriend will qualify you for bereavement leave."

"Probably not, but I rarely take vacation. I've only been in the New York office for about two months, but I've been with the company for long enough. They know I'm not the sort of person who would take off on a whim. I'll probably have to run by the office to pick up some things before we leave town, but I'm not too busy right now, so it shouldn't be a big deal."

"You'll go with me? Really?"

"Why do you doubt me?"

Michael sat up a bit and wiped his eyes. "I don't doubt you. But I am not used to having a boyfriend type around for when things go belly up."

"So here's what we'll do. We'll call our offices. We'll rent a car. How long a drive is it?"

"About two hours, give or take. Probably closer to two and a half. The house is in the middle of nowhere."

"Okay. That's not bad. If we get going soon, we can be there by early afternoon."

Michael rubbed his eyes. "I don't believe it. She seemed fine the last time I saw her." He shook his head. "She's mentioned health problems the last couple of times we talked but wouldn't elaborate. And she was being weird about video chatting and me coming up to visit. I thought she was being selfish with Trevor, but maybe she didn't want me to see how sick she was."

"Maybe."

"Is Trevor even going to recognize me? I haven't seen him for almost five months now."

"He knows your voice. You talk to him on the phone every week. He sees you in the video chat."

Michael leaned his head on Simon's shoulder. "Joan had a falling out with her parents when she was nineteen or twenty and rarely talks to them. She doesn't have any siblings. So I'm Trevor's only family, really. It's up to me to take care of him now. I can't believe it."

"And me. I'll help you," Simon said.

"Will you?"

"Of course."

Michael pressed his face into Simon's shoulder. And Simon began to doubt.

THEY DIDN'T get on the road until almost eleven. Simon got snagged when he went into the office and took almost an hour to get back, and then Michael's usual car rental place didn't have anything available so they had to call around until they found someplace willing to rent them a vehicle. Michael fretted about the cost, but Simon kept saying not to worry about it.

Michael knew Simon was loaded now, but he tried not to think about it. It wounded his pride a little to let Simon pay for everything, but he was willing to put that aside in this emergency situation. Although, now that he thought about it, Simon staying in Michael's tiny apartment when he could afford to move somewhere bigger was kind of a puzzle. Unless Simon genuinely wanted to stay.

That, at least, cheered Michael up a little.

Nothing else about this situation did.

Simon was driving because Michael was still too out of sorts to think straight. He could not believe Joan was gone, just like that. Why hadn't she told him she was sick?

"When is the funeral?" Simon asked.

"Saturday." That was in two days. Michael had spent part of the morning calling around, getting as much information as possible. Joan's neighbors, a gay couple named Burt and Tony, seemed to be the people up there to whom she was closest, and they were handling the arrangements. Tony was a probate lawyer, so he was dealing with her estate. Michael and Joan had sat down and made a will the week after Trevor had been born, specifying that if something happened to one of them, the other would become the custodial parent. Michael hadn't even really thought about it since the papers were signed. Had Joan updated her will? She must have, if Tony knew about it. "I have to meet with the lawyer neighbor tomorrow afternoon."

"Maybe she left some money for Trevor."

"Yeah, maybe. Also, there's going to be a wake tomorrow night."

Simon reached over and took Michael's hand. "I know this is tough all around. You need anything, you tell me, okay?"

Simon was handling all of this awfully well, and Michael was grateful, but he kept waiting for the other shoe to drop, for Simon to freak out and run away again. As far as Michael knew, Simon had never especially wanted children, but now Michael was going to have to take care of one. He'd also spent part of that morning trying to work out how to make space in the apartment for Trevor and all of his things. The place was really a bachelor pad, without much room for toys or even for Trevor's bed. Hell, there was barely room for Simon.

Michael became increasingly nervous the closer they got to Joan's house. He had to gather himself enough to direct Simon once they passed through Woodstock. He had to pay attention because the roads were narrow through the heavily wooded areas and all kind of looked the same. It gave Michael something to concentrate on, but by the time they pulled into the driveway, he was shaking.

He felt unprepared. Trying to pack that morning had been part of the delay as well, since he had to find funeral-appropriate clothes, and Simon had to gently point out that he was pairing navy pants with a black blazer. Also, all of his ties were bright colors, which seemed like not the right thing to wear to a funeral. Simon had loaned him a gray tie, so that was okay, but Michael nearly had a breakdown because of how inept he felt.

But now they were here. Kelly's car was parked in the dirt driveway—next to the old clunker Joan drove around—which meant she was likely inside with Trevor. He'd called her an hour before and she'd promised to be there, but Michael kept worrying that Kelly or one of Joan's friends might have absconded with Trevor.

"Are you all right?" Simon asked.

"No."

Simon nodded. He leaned across the car and gave Michael an awkward hug. "I'm here if you need me."

"Thank you. I do need you."

"Let's get out of the car."

Michael opened the car door and took a deep breath. They were a long way from home, the skyscrapers and low brick buildings of the Village replaced with trees as far as the eye could see. Simon came around and offered a hand, so Michael took it. He noticed that the air smelled different here than in the city. It was brighter, cleaner, but emotionally charged somehow.

They walked to the door and rang the doorbell.

Kelly answered. Her eyes were red. She immediately hugged Michael. "Oh, thank goodness you're here," she said.

"Where's Trevor?"

She wiped her eyes. "Oh, he's right—"

"Daddy!"

Trevor's little legs propelled him toward Michael, so Michael knelt and caught him. He hugged Trevor tightly. Oh, it was good to finally hold him. He didn't want to let go.

Behind him, Michael heard, "I'm Simon."

"Kelly. It's nice to finally meet you."

Michael felt a little bad for not introducing them, but he couldn't seem to let go of Trevor.

Trevor put his little arms around Michael's neck. "Daddy. Something bad happened to Mommy."

"I know."

"Kelly says I can't ever see Mommy again. That she went away. Where did she go, Daddy?"

This was the part Michael had been dreading.

Behind him, Kelly said, "So are you guys staying here or…."

"Not sure. Is there even a hotel nearby?"

"Closest one is about thirty miles east. You're probably better off staying here. If sleeping in Joan's room is weird for you, the living room sofa folds out into a couch. I've been sleeping in the guest room so that Trevor can stay here and have his room."

"All right. We'll do that, then."

Michael closed his eyes. He'd rehearsed this with Simon on the drive up, anticipating Trevor's question, but it still sounded strange when he said, "Mommy got very, very sick."

"Did she leave because she doesn't love me anymore?"

"Oh, no, sweetie. No. Never. Mommy could never stop loving you."

"Then why did she go away?"

"Sometimes that's what happens when people get very sick. She hurt a lot. Now she's up in heaven where she doesn't hurt anymore."

Trevor started to get a little sniffly. "I want her back."

Michael wasn't exactly dry-eyed either. "I know. Me too."

"I want her right now," Trevor said.

Then he was inconsolable. He cried and screamed and threw his arms around. Michael could sympathize. "Shh, Trevor, it's going to be all right."

"He didn't sleep well last night, so he's extra tired," Kelly said.

"What should I do?" Michael asked.

Kelly dropped down next to him. "Trevor? Shh, baby, calm down."

That didn't get them very far. Trevor screamed harder.

"Can we give him some toys or something?" Michael asked, thinking a distraction might help.

"Yeah, maybe. Take him into the living room. That's where his trucks are."

Michael stood up. "Trev, you want to play trucks with me? Spend time with your daddy for a little while."

Trevor stopped screaming, but he was still crying pretty hard. Still, he gave Michael a sniffly nod.

Michael reached down and offered his hand. Trevor took it and allowed Michael to take him into the living room. A few trucks had been left on the coffee table, and there was a toy box off to the side of the room. Michael sat near the toy box and opened it. He took out a few trucks and put them on the floor.

Trevor sat next to him. He sniffed and rubbed his eyes. "Daddy, I have a new truck. It's blue."

"Show me."

About ten minutes later, Simon came into the room carrying the suitcase they'd packed. By then, Trevor had calmed down, although he wasn't playing so much as inventorying his trucks for Michael.

"I assume you want to stay here," Simon said.

"Yeah, I think it would be best to stay with Trevor."

"Kelly offered us the guest room, but I told her not to bother moving her things. Apparently this couch folds out."

"Yeah. That's the couch from my old apartment with Joan. I slept on it a lot toward the end of our relationship. Not the most comfortable bed I've ever slept on, but it will do for a few days." Michael looked up at Simon, who was putting the suitcase on the floor in the corner. "Come here and talk to Trevor."

"Okay."

Simon stood stiffly above them for a moment. Michael knew Simon didn't have much experience with kids. Michael didn't, either, aside from Trevor. But Simon sat next to them and crossed his legs.

"Trevor, this is Simon. You remember him from the computer chats?"

Trevor looked Simon up and down. The two of them seemed to take the measure of each other for a moment. Trevor said, "Hi."

"Hi."

"Do you like trucks?" Trevor asked.

"Yes."

"Okay. You can play with the green one."

Simon gamely accepted the green truck and drove it around on the floor. Michael also struggled with how to explain who Simon was to Trevor. "Daddy's friend" seemed insufficient. But he'd have to come up with an explanation if Trevor came to live with them in the city.

Which was what would have to happen. Michael was still trying to wrap his head around all of this, but he knew some decisions were going to have to be made quickly. Moving Trevor into his place would be an adjustment, to put it mildly. Would that finally make Simon bolt? Was there even space? What would Michael do about day care?

While Michael worried about all of this, something truly amazing happened: Simon actually played with Trevor.

That in itself shouldn't have been surprising, but Michael had never known Simon to do anything that might have embarrassed himself, such as making little motor sounds in the back of his throat as he drove his car around Trevor. Trevor was delighted, letting out a snotty giggle. He smiled and looked up at Simon with reverence.

For the first time since the phone call that morning, Michael thought maybe all of this would be okay.

CHAPTER 13

MICHAEL DECIDED to invite the neighbors over for dinner, which meant that somehow they had to come up with something to feed everybody. Kelly figured they could make something with whatever was in the kitchen, so she and Simon teamed up to cook. Simon's cooking skills were rudimentary at best, but he could chop vegetables. Kelly said they had all of the ingredients for a pretty kickass veggie lasagna, so he got to work chopping carrots and onions.

It was good to have something to do besides worry about Michael, who was now sitting with Trevor on the couch, watching a movie. Simon supposed he couldn't blame Michael for losing his mind; this was a lot of change to deal with in less than twelve hours.

They hadn't explicitly talked about it, but it seemed clear now that they would be bringing Trevor home with them after the funeral. They'd probably also have to do some work to pack up and sell Joan's house. Realistically, Simon didn't know how much time he could spend away from the office. He'd taken his laptop and a stack of paper up here with him, but cell phone reception was spotty this far into the woods, which could make getting in touch with his clients tricky. Besides, Roger hated when his employees worked outside of the office.

He'd worry about that on Monday, though. Right now, he would be here for Michael.

He put a sharp knife through an onion and thought about how much his own life had changed in the last two months. He'd dreaded moving back to New York, dreaded living with Michael again, but somehow everything had come together. It was hard to deny that things between them were better than they'd ever been.

Except here was Trevor.

He'd never wanted children. Whether that was because he genuinely didn't want them or because he'd always assumed he couldn't have them, well, those were sentiments he couldn't sort through anymore, but children had certainly never been on his agenda. He liked his life the way it was and didn't want to change it to make room for a child. He worked too many hours, he enjoyed his freedom, he didn't want to make the sorts of changes and sacrifices children required. Except he had made changes and sacrifices by merely consenting to be Michael's significant other. Those sacrifices were mostly trivial, though. They were things he didn't miss—crazy nights out, casual sex, the ability to spend all his free time however he wanted.

What Simon somehow hadn't factored into his new life as being part of a couple was that being with Michael meant being with a father. When Trevor was up here in the Catskills and Michael was down in the city, that fact didn't seem so significant. Yes, Simon knew that being away from Trevor affected Michael deeply, that perhaps Simon would be required to make trips up here to visit, but to actually be responsible for a little boy was something that frankly terrified Simon. Because that was what would happen if he stayed with Michael: he'd have to co-parent Trevor.

He had more faith in Michael to be a good father than Michael had in himself, so there was that, at least. Simon had very little faith in himself to be a good father. It wasn't like he'd had a great father to emulate; they'd hardly spoken to each other in years, in fact, since Simon's father had no interest in having a gay son. Simon's parents had divorced when Simon was nine, so he hadn't had many great years with his father, either, since most of that time was spent watching his parents trying to drive each other away with passive aggression. Simon's mother was supportive to a point, but she was self-involved and lately hadn't seemed much interested in Simon's life. Michael's parents were more like model parents, or so Simon had always thought, though he recognized that Michael's relationship with them was strained these days. Michael had said his mother in particular, who had been initially thrilled that Michael had settled down with a woman, was not so happy that he'd fathered a child out of wedlock and then shortly thereafter broken up with his parents' last hopes for having a son who maybe wasn't so different after all.

But Simon knew better than anyone that one had to make his own way in this world, so it had never occurred to him to really analyze the issues of fatherhood, because he'd long since given up on having a good relationship with his own. But now that he was faced with the prospect of parenting a child, it terrified him.

He couldn't tell Michael that, not under the circumstances. So he chopped vegetables.

He liked Trevor. The kid was completely adorable, with round cheeks and chubby limbs and a lot of brown hair on his head. He was a little small for his age, Kelly said, but neither Michael nor Joan had been exceptionally tall, so maybe that was normal. Once they'd distracted him from Joan's absence, he had talked a lot. Mostly he talked about trucks, but in there that afternoon had also been something about a cartoon character that Michael seemed to know all about and then a long treatise about a concert or something he'd gone to with Joan and the neighbors.

Then when Michael had gotten up to take a phone call, Trevor had been silent for a moment and then said, "Can Daddy stay?"

"I think you'll be spending a lot more time with your daddy from now on."

Trevor smiled. "Can we go to the zoo? I like the monkeys."

"Sure."

"Can you come too?" Trevor said, his eyes big and hopeful.

And how could Simon have kept up his stoic exterior against that kind of assault?

Kelly instructed Simon on how to layer the noodles, cheese, and vegetables. They were sliding the pan into the oven when Burt and Tony arrived. Michael brought them to the back of the house, Trevor toddling in behind them. Michael picked Trevor up as he introduced the neighbors. Simon shook their hands in turn. They were the sort of older gay couple—Simon had their ages pegged as early fifties—who had started to look like each other. Both had graying hair cut short and they were both wearing plaid shirts. The main difference was that Burt had glasses and a beard, whereas Tony had a neatly trimmed goatee.

"Did you know Joan?" Tony asked Simon.

"Not well," Simon said. "We only met a few times. I've been traveling for work the last six years. I've only been back on the East Coast for a couple of months."

Tony squinted like he was trying to figure out exactly what was going on here.

Michael hitched Trevor up on his hip and then put a hand on Simon's shoulder. "Simon and I are together now."

"Yes, you're the friend Joan mentioned," Burt said, grimacing. His tone didn't exactly convey approval.

Michael frowned but didn't respond. Instead he hugged Trevor a little more tightly.

Simon felt like he was missing something important, but this wasn't the time or place to ask about it.

He spent part of dinner trying to figure out the dynamics between everyone. Tony seemed pretty happy to talk to everyone, and Simon liked him. Burt was surlier and didn't seem to think much of Michael, but Simon reasoned that if Burt was close to Joan, perhaps Michael hadn't always been painted in the best light. The whole situation still confused Simon somewhat—leaving aside the paradox of a gay man falling in love with a woman, it had never been clear to Simon exactly why Michael and Joan had broken up, beyond Michael's repeated explanation that they'd had problems. Was it that Michael really was gay and couldn't be a devoted partner to Joan for that reason? Had Michael done something to push Joan away? Likely it was a combination of things.

Or, as Simon was starting to suspect, had Michael's feelings for Simon somehow gotten in the way of that relationship? It was hard to regret that too much, since it had led to Michael and Simon finally coming together the way Simon now understood they should have, but he still felt a little responsible for the pain caused by parents splitting up.

But there would be no more bouncing back and forth between houses for Trevor. There'd be no summers spent at Dad's but school years up here in the Catskills. Trevor no longer had a mother; he just had Michael, and therefore he had Simon.

Absolutely terrifying.

"I got a hold of Joan's mother this afternoon," Burt said. "They're flying out first thing in the morning, but probably not staying longer than necessary."

"Unless," Tony said, "they make a move for custody of Trevor."

Michael balked. "They can't do that, can they?"

"I'm still sorting through the legal stuff," Tony said, "but it looks like Joan made a provision that if something happened to her and something happened to you, Trevor would go to her parents."

"But nothing happened to me. I'm right here. And I'm his father. Joan and her parents barely had a relationship. When Joan and I made our wills, it was understood that if something happened to her, Trevor should go with me."

"Where are we going, Daddy?"

"To the city," Michael said, his attention still on Tony.

Trevor reached over and tugged on Michael's sleeve. "Daddy? Can we go to the zoo?"

Michael turned and looked at Trevor. There was a very long beat of silence before Michael said, "Okay."

Trevor nodded, satisfied, and went back to eating. More of his food was going on his fingers than into his mouth, but only Kelly and Simon seemed to be paying attention to him.

Watching them seated next to each other, Simon could actually see the resemblance between Michael and Trevor. Simon had once wondered idly if Michael was even Trevor's father, but it was hard to deny that Trevor had a few of Michael's features, hidden though they were by baby fat. There was something similar in the face shape, in the precise shade of light brown of his eyes, in the pout of his lips.

But even if Michael weren't Trevor's biological father, even if Joan had cheated—which, at the end of the day, Simon seriously doubted was the case—Michael certainly loved that boy fiercely.

"Would Joan's parents have a claim?" Simon asked.

"Not really. That wouldn't necessarily stop them from trying." Tony took a sip of his iced tea. "Maybe nothing will come of it and Joan's parents really don't want anything to do with her life, but I wanted to prepare you for the possibility. Things like this happen. Worst-case scenario, you'd have to fight it out in court."

"Do you represent this kind of thing?" asked Simon. "Or could you refer us to someone if Joan's parents do try to get custody?"

Simon saw Michael turn toward him in his peripheral vision.

"I know someone," said Tony. "I'll refer you to him if it comes to that."

"Thank you."

Simon looked at Michael, whose face was twisted up with some emotion. Simon reached under the table and grasped Michael's hand.

"How long have you been together?" asked Burt.

"Our whole lives," said Michael. "Look, we were kind of on the outs when I first hooked up with Joan, and I swear I was faithful to her until she dumped me and moved up here, but it's always been me and Simon. He's not just, like, the flavor of the month." Michael rubbed his forehead. "I am as busted up about Joan as you are, probably more. I love her too, and it's complicated, okay? And I love Trevor and I intend to figure out how to be a good father to him, and that's all you need to know."

Burt sat back in his chair, looking a little surprised. Simon guessed that Burt hadn't expected Michael to stand up for himself. "All right. I'm sorry," Burt said.

"Thank you," said Michael.

Dinner wound down a little while after that, mostly because Trevor started getting cranky. Tony confirmed his meeting with Michael the next day, and then Simon saw them out while Michael helped Kelly clean up.

At the door, Burt said, "Maybe I overreacted. I apologize if I was rude."

"It's okay," Simon said. "Under the circumstances, I understand."

"Joan didn't exactly think highly of you," Tony said.

"Joan hardly knew me," Simon pointed out.

"I know, but I think in her head, she thought you were the villain in this opera," said Tony.

Funny how that had happened. Hadn't Joan explained to Simon before he left for Dubai that she was not the villain? Simon knew he wasn't any more than she had been. Interesting what six years and a lot of bitterness could do.

"The fact that Michael's a homo probably should have been the clue that it wasn't going to end happily ever after," said Burt.

"I believe him when he says he loved her," Simon said. "It's a different kind of love, maybe."

"You're not what I expected," said Burt.

"I suppose that's good," said Simon. "I want to do right by Michael. And he loves Trevor more than I think even Joan knew. It killed him to be so far away."

"She kept him away." When Burt cleared his throat and looked at Tony pointedly, Tony said, "She did! She didn't want to share custody. And she thought Michael was unstable."

"At one point in his life, he was," Simon said. He couldn't really vouch for Michael's stability when Joan left him, but that was more because he wasn't in close enough touch at the time. "He's got his ducks in a row now, though."

"I'm glad to hear it," said Tony. "I did always kind of root for the kid. You're really together now?"

"For as long as he'll have me."

Tony nodded. "Trevor needs a solid family. If you and Michael can provide that, then I've got no problem with either of you."

"We'll do our best."

"Okay, then. We should get home. Good night, Simon."

WHILE HE helped Kelly clean up after dinner, Michael put Simon in charge of Trevor. The plan had been for them to sit and watch a little television, and then once the dishes were done, Michael would get Trevor into bed. He could tell the change in routine was confusing the hell out of Trevor, so that would be one of the first things they'd work on when they got back home. Routines were good for small children; it helped them know what to expect, how to behave.

Kelly was explaining about that as they did the dishes; it was based on a book she'd read recently. Michael nodded and made a lot of mental notes. Then he said, "You have really gone above and beyond. I don't know how to come close to thanking you, Kel," Michael said.

"I want to help. I cared about her too. And I want what's best for Trevor. He adores you, you know."

"Does he?"

"He talks about you all the time."

Partly that was gratifying, but partly it made Michael feel guilty. "I shouldn't have stayed away so long."

"Not much you can do about that now. I like Simon, by the way."

"Oh, good. I'm glad. He can come off a little distant sometimes, but once you get to know him—"

"He's great. It's clear he cares about you very much."

Michael smiled. "I was going to give you a bonus anyway. No need to butter me up."

Kelly threw a towel at him, and Michael laughed.

Once the dishes were done, Michael walked into the living room, where he found Simon sitting with Trevor in his lap. They seemed to be having a very intense conversation. Michael watched for a moment, because it was clear that Simon was so intent on Trevor that he didn't even notice Michael. After a moment, Michael was able to glean that Trevor was explaining SpongeBob SquarePants, who was presently on the TV.

Michael laughed and Simon looked up. "I suppose I'll have to study," Simon said. "Will there be a quiz later?"

Trevor's face scrunched up in confusion.

"Hey, Trev, I think it's bedtime," Michael said.

Trevor pulled a classic four-year-old maneuver of protesting loudly that he didn't want to go to bed—"I want to stay up with Simon!" he cried—in a way that indicated the poor kid was exhausted. Michael picked him up and carried him upstairs. There was a lot of squirming and crying and wrestling as Michael managed to get Trevor into pajamas and into his bed. Simon appeared at the doorway just as Michael was turning down the sheets.

"You want to help me tuck him in?" Michael asked.

"Okay," said Simon.

Simon approached the bed. Trevor was still pretty cranky, but he seemed to be calming down. He yawned.

"Now, if you need anything," Michael said, "Simon and I will be sleeping in the living room, and Kelly is right next door."

Trevor nodded as he yawned again. "Simon?" he asked.

"What?"

"Will you be my friend?"

Michael looked up at Simon, whose eyes gave him away. He blinked a few times and said, "Yes. I'd love to be your friend."

"Good." Trevor yawned again and settled against his pillow. "I'm not tired, Daddy."

"I know, but there's going to be a lot to do tomorrow, so you need your rest. But I'll still be here, okay?"

"Okay."

Trevor closed his eyes. Michael sat there until he was sure Trevor was asleep.

"I'm exhausted too," he said to Simon as they walked back downstairs.

"It's been an intense day. I pulled the bed out of the sofa when you first went upstairs. Kelly found some sheets for it."

"Okay."

They went downstairs and together they made the bed. They took turns changing in the downstairs bathroom and then settled into the bed together.

"Thank you, Simon," Michael said, meaning it. He settled against Simon's chest, putting an arm around him. "I could not have gotten through today without you. And when you said 'us' tonight to Tony, when you asked if he'd help *us* if Joan's parents tried to take Trevor, that meant a lot. The 'us,' I mean. Is that corny?"

"No."

"Mmm. I love you."

"I love you too. Can I ask you something?"

Michael gleaned from Simon's tone that it was a pretty serious question, and Michael wasn't sure if he'd be able to deal with that right now, but he said, "Okay."

"Was I a factor in your breakup with Joan?"

Michael sighed. He didn't especially want to talk about that just now, but he understood why Simon was asking. He was surprised it took so long for him to do so. "Not directly. I mean, honestly? The fact that I am not so much into the lady parts was the largest factor."

"But you said you were faithful to her. That you were attracted to her."

"I was. But it was kind of a fluke too. It wasn't like it is with you. With Joan, it was, I don't know—like a new pair of shoes. It was shiny and different and exciting. Once that wore off, we weren't left with much." Michael took a deep breath and hugged Simon tighter. "That's a terrible thing to say. What I meant was that I was attracted to her as a person. Being with her made me feel... alive. Excited about things for the first time in a while. We had a lot of fun together."

"It was easy."

It was odd hearing his own words reflected back that way. "Yeah, it was for a while. Then it wasn't." Michael pulled away and rolled onto his stomach. He looked at Simon. Their gazes met. "I loved her. I really did. But we had problems that couldn't be overcome, and there was too much weight piled on top of something that was already not so well constructed once we had Trevor. Toward the end, it felt like that love was crumbling beneath our feet like the rotting foundation of an old building." Michal laughed softly. "Wow, I killed that metaphor, huh?"

Simon reached up and smoothed Michael's hair out of his face.

Michael realized he still hadn't answered the question, so he said, "Joan didn't want to live in the city anymore, but I couldn't move for a lot of reasons, and we were at an impasse. So there was that. When it was ending, she accused me of being in love with you and I didn't deny it, so there was that too. But that's not a surprise, is it?"

"No. I guess not."

"Don't feel guilty. I made my bed there. I made some choices that I might not make if I had it to do over. But maybe...." Michael closed his eyes because he wanted what he was about to say to be true and couldn't stand to see Simon's face if it wasn't. "Maybe it all happened for a reason. That sounds hokey, but maybe things had to play out the way they did to bring us together. And, you know, every time I've looked at Trevor today, I can't get over how special that kid is. He's a part of me, both literally and figuratively. Hard to be mad at Fate for that."

"He is great."

"He is." Michael let out a breath and curled up next to Simon again. "I always expected that one day, things would fall into place and we'd all live happily ever after, but the truth is that life is messy. That perfect life I pictured for myself when I was a teenager can never be. And that's probably for the best, or we'd never learn anything."

"I suppose that's true," said Simon. He ran a hand down Michael's back. "Let's get some rest. Tomorrow's going to suck."

"I know it," said Michael.

CHAPTER 14

WHEN SIMON woke up the next morning, he had the sense that someone was watching him.

He sat up and saw that Trevor was standing at the side of the bed.

"Hi," Simon said.

"Hi!" said Trevor. He shoved his thumb in his mouth for a moment. "Can I get in bed with you? My room is too scary."

It seemed like a flimsy excuse, but Simon consented, lifting Trevor up and into the bed between himself and Michael. The movement made Michael stir. He rolled toward Simon and then woke up suddenly.

"Hi, Daddy," Trevor said.

"Hi, Trevor. What are you doing here?"

"My room was too scary."

"Okay. Well, make yourself comfortable."

Michael put one of the throw pillows from the sofa between the two regular pillows and then gestured for Trevor to lie down. Trevor did, curling his little body into a ball. The movement was kind of endearing; Trevor arranged himself the same way Michael often slept.

Father and son fell back to sleep almost immediately.

Simon stayed in bed for a while, but it was clear after about twenty minutes that he would not be falling back to sleep. He got up and wandered into the kitchen. Looking around, it occurred to him that a growing boy had different food needs than two grown-ups did, especially two men who ate out a lot. The cabinets were stuffed with the sort of snack food Trevor could probably easily hold in his little fingers: cereal, crackers, macaroni. There was fresh milk in the fridge that bore the label of a local farm. There were also a couple of prescription bottles in the fridge, a sign maybe that Joan hadn't expected to be gone so soon.

Simon was content with cereal for breakfast, and he figured he could manage that much without burning the house down, so he went about fixing himself a bowl. As he took the box out of the cabinet, a tiny voice behind him said, "Simon?"

"Hi, Trevor. Are you hungry?"

He shook his head. "I need Bunny."

"What's Bunny?"

"He's purple and he has long ears. He's in my room. But it's scary up there."

"Okay. Do you want me to get Bunny?"

Trevor nodded.

So Simon walked to the staircase. Trevor trailed behind him. He reached back his hand, which Trevor took, and then they walked upstairs together.

Trevor's room was a riot of color, as Simon could now see with the sun streaming through the windows. The walls were painted bright blue. There was a poster of a red truck tacked up to one wall. There were a couple of brightly colored plastic toy boxes on the floor as well as a bright red dresser. The bed had a wooden frame that had been painted kelly green. And right there in the middle of the unmade bed was a plush purple bunny. Trevor retrieved it and hugged it tightly.

"Simon?" Trevor said around his thumb.

"What?"

"Are you and Daddy husbands?"

Oh, boy. Explaining things was another thing that Simon was likely going to have to get used to. "Not exactly."

"Tony and Burt are husbands," said Trevor. "They had a wedding in the backyard and became husbands. Me and Mommy went. I wore a bow tie!"

"That's great!" said Simon.

But then Trevor seemed to realize what he'd said. His lower lip started to tremble. "Mommy's not coming back."

"No. I'm so sorry, Trevor. If I could bring her back, I would."

"Daddy said she went to heaven. Is that true?"

Simon was a little surprised that Michael, who had never expressed even a passing interest in religion, would have said something like that, but he supposed that was the easiest explanation. "Yes."

"Is it nice in heaven?"

"Yes. Very nice. Your mommy is comfortable there."

"She's not sick anymore?"

"No."

"She coughs all the time. And she sleeps a lot. That's how I know she's sick."

"She's better now, okay?"

"I miss her. I want to see her."

Simon braced himself for the waterworks, but they didn't quite happen. Trevor sniffed and rubbed his eyes, but there was no tantrum like the day before. Simon knelt down on the floor next to Trevor and put a hand on his shoulder. "You will probably always miss her. That's okay. I know she loves you. Even if you can't see her, she loves you and she's looking out for you. Okay?"

Trevor shrugged. Death was a terrible thing for a four-year-old to have to deal with, especially the death of his mother. God, what a situation.

In an effort to distract Trevor, Simon said, "Can I see your bow tie?"

Trevor nodded. "It's in my closet."

They went back downstairs a little while later. Trevor dragged Bunny behind him. He climbed back into the bed with Michael, who was still dead to the world. That was one of Michael's special talents; Simon had sometimes thought he could sleep through the apocalypse. Trevor curled up next to Michael and hugged his bunny. Michael grunted in his sleep and then wrapped an arm around Trevor.

Simon's phone rang then, so he grabbed it and left the room.

The name on the caller ID said "Jeannette," and it took Simon a minute to remember who that was. He didn't remember until she said, "Hi, Mr. Newell? It's Jeanette from Hogarth and Rowe?"

That was the real estate firm Simon had tried in vain to find an apartment through.

"Yes. Hi, Jeanette," Simon said.

"I finally have some good news for you. Sort of. It's not exactly what you wanted, but there's a three-bedroom in Chelsea within your price range."

It was weird how things like this came together. Simon glanced back toward the living room, where what he supposed was his new family was asleep.

"It's a co-op building, so you'd need board approval, but I saw it myself yesterday. Prewar building, but it was gut-renovated by the owner about five years ago."

"Sounds great. You should know, though, that my circumstances have changed somewhat."

"Are you still looking?"

"Yes, definitely."

"Because this place in Chelsea is really a bargain. The only catch is that it's around the corner from a couple of gay bars."

"Why is that a problem?" Simon blurted before he really thought about what she was saying.

"Oh, well, the guy I took to see the place yesterday was uncomfortable being so close to the homosexual lifestyle."

"He should stay away from Chelsea."

Jeannette laughed. "Yeah, that's what I told him. So you don't have a problem with that?"

"Only if it's loud. I mean, the reason for the change in circumstance is, well, my boyfriend is moving in with me."

"Oh, good, okay," said Jeannette. "The owner might appreciate that. He bought the unit twenty years ago, so he's been around awhile. He and his partner have kids, so they've outgrown the place but aren't willing to sell it yet."

"Actually, a three-bedroom might be ideal. My boyfriend has a four-year-old son."

"Wow, that is a change in circumstance! Well, okay. If you're willing to pay a little more, there's also a brand-new building in the West Village that has a couple of three-bedroom units available."

"That place on Thirteenth Street?"

"That's the one."

That was two blocks from Michael's current place. "That would make the move easy, certainly," Simon muttered. "All right. I know you have to move on these things fast, but I'm in the Catskills until Sunday, at least."

"Okay. Well, the good news is that the guy in Chelsea is picky, but he might like the sound of a gay couple with a young child. I'll talk to him and see if I can get him to stall until next week. I'll call him and get back to you."

"Thanks. I appreciate that."

When he got off the phone, Simon decided to check on Michael. Michael and Trevor were now sitting up in bed, and Trevor was telling what sounded like an involved story about Bunny. The expression on Michael's face was priceless, a sort of rapt joy as he gazed at his son.

It couldn't last, could it? Michael's delirious joy at getting to spend time with Trevor would fade with time, or Michael's insecurities about his skill as a father would come into play, or something else would happen. Not that Simon had expected life going forward with Michael to be all bliss all the time, but he told himself that he couldn't get caught up in this moment because it wasn't a fair indicator of what was to come.

Sheesh, he sounded like a banker.

"Bunny likes to hop," Trevor said with grave seriousness. Then he demonstrated by making Bunny hop over Michael's legs.

This poor kid, Simon thought as he sat at the edge of the bed. If Michael had been right and Joan was a good mother, it was a crime that she'd been taken away from him. Simon knew Michael would do his best, but he was unprepared and insecure. And as for Simon, well, he hadn't asked for any of this and all of it was making him feel panicky.

But he'd hold it together for Michael.

Michael ran a hand over Trevor's head. "What else does Bunny like to do?"

"Bunny eats carrots. Not real carrots, though. Pretend carrots. And he sleeps in my bed. Simon helped me get him. My room is scary."

"Why is your room scary?" asked Michael.

Trevor looked up at Michael and his lip got a little wobbly again. He said, "Mommy kept the scary things away, but she's not here."

"You know," Michael said, "I'm pretty good at keeping away scary things. And so is Kelly. Her room is right next to yours."

Trevor nodded, but he didn't look convinced.

Simon's stomach rumbled, and he realized he still hadn't eaten. "Do you boys want some breakfast?" he asked as he stood.

"Yes!" said Trevor. He crawled to the edge of the bed and hopped off, dragging Bunny with him he ran to the kitchen.

Michael yawned and stood up. As they walked together to the kitchen, Michael said, "I gave him Bunny the last time I was here."

"It was the only animal on his bed."

"Really?"

Simon smiled and kissed Michael's forehead.

"You should be husbands," Trevor said. He was already sitting at the table, although his booster seat had been put away. In a regular chair, the table came up to his chin.

"What?" Michael said laughing.

"Mommy says that when two people love each other, they get married. When they get married they become wives or husbands. Boys are husbands and girls are wives. I wore a bow tie when Tony and Burt became husbands."

Michael looked mystified.

"That's some amazing four-year-old logic," Simon said.

"Daddy, do you love Simon?"

"Yes," said Michael. He shook his head and started opening and closing cabinets.

"Simon, do you love Daddy?"

"Yes, I do."

"So you should be husbands."

"Thanks for the advice, kiddo," Michael said. "Where's your seat?"

"In the corner."

Cereal and milk was dispensed, and once they were all seated, Trevor had changed topics to explaining that milk came from cows. Then he was quiet as he very carefully tried to eat his cereal without spilling any milk.

"I may have news," Simon said.

"Oh?" said Michael.

"My real estate broker says there's a three-bedroom place available."

Michael squinted. "You're not moving out of my place, are you?"

"No. Well, yes, I do want to move, but you'd have to come with me. Trevor too, obviously. We can't all three of us fit in your tiny place."

Michael's expression was inscrutable, but he looked tired. "Yeah, I guess you're right."

"I was thinking, too, maybe we could hire Kelly. That way there's someone to watch him during the day and it's someone familiar, to help bridge the transition."

Michael nodded slowly. "It's an idea."

"I'd be willing to pay to help her move. Or we can find her an apartment. Or she can move into your old place."

"We can talk about it."

Kelly herself appeared a few minutes later. "I could have cooked," she said.

"Nah, we managed," Michael said.

She got herself a bowl of cereal and sat with them. Simon tried to guess her age. She was a little past college, but not by much, maybe twenty-four or twenty-five. Prime age to move to the city.

Was Simon really contemplating moving his boyfriend's son's nanny to New York City? What had his life become?

LATER THAT afternoon, Michael left a napping Trevor with Simon and Kelly and walked over to Tony and Burt's house for his appointment.

To say it had been a strange thirty-six hours was an understatement. Michael's whole life had changed in an instant, but part of him was convinced that the change was for good. When he'd woken up that morning to find Trevor curled up next to him, he'd come close to weeping with joy. And now Simon was trying to find an apartment big enough for them all to live in together.

He'd been resistant to change, it was true. After years of walking blindly into the next new thing, he'd settled into a stubborn routine once Joan left. Being able to move back into his bedroom once he and Simon started sleeping together was really minor in the scheme of things; he knew Simon was getting sick of living out of suitcases and should have been able to get his stuff out of storage. But, shit, his heart had nearly beat right out of his chest when Simon mentioned moving that morning.

And Simon had to be freaking out about all this. He was doing an admirable job of keeping it together, but Simon liked things to be just so, and toddlers brought a lot chaos with them.

But he'd deal with Simon when he had to. Right now, he still had to deal with Joan.

Tony answered the door and ushered Michael inside. They exchanged pleasantries as Michael followed Tony to his office, off the vestibule on the first floor. The house was gorgeous—a lot of polished wood and brass and antique furniture—and Michael admired it. It was clear a lot of love and work had been put into the building, unlike Joan's house, which looked a little worn around the edges.

Tony told him to have a seat, so he situated himself in a nicely upholstered chair near a huge antique desk.

"I'll cut to the chase," Tony said, pulling out a file folder. "Joan left everything to Trevor."

"Okay." That was not a surprise.

"She set up a new will when she found out she was sick, about eight months ago. The terms basically include putting any moneys into a trust for Trevor that he can have access to when he turns eighteen. Her intent was for him to use it for college, but I guess that's up to him."

Michael nodded, though he felt a little light-headed, thinking about what Trevor would be like at eighteen.

"The thing is, Joan didn't have much. She had a small life insurance policy, so that's going to pay for most of the funeral expenses. But she hasn't worked in six months, probably. She had no income and expensive medical bills that she was still struggling to pay off when she died."

"So she was in debt?"

"Yeah. I'm still crunching the numbers, but it looks like she still owes a fair amount. Not to be crass, but dying ain't cheap."

"Which means there's nothing for Trevor."

"My recommendation would be to sell the house. That's going to be a little tricky, since the deed technically passes to Trevor, but as Trevor's legal guardian, you could sell it, pay off Joan's bills, and put everything else into the trust."

Although Michael didn't want the house—New York City was home and he intended to set up a space that was his, Simon's, and Trevor's together—the prospect of selling it seemed daunting. He also didn't like the impersonality of the phrase "legal guardian." He was Trevor's father, for God's sake.

"As a favor to Joan, I can represent you through this," Tony said.

"Can you?"

"I handle cases like this all the time. For a fee."

Michael frowned. "And I'm guessing that, because you've already run a background check on Simon, you know he's not exactly poor. Except that we aren't married, as everyone keeps pointing out, so he's not obligated to share his money with me."

"Usually I take my fee out of the total estate."

Michael nodded. "Fine. We can work something out."

"I'm not trying to be a dick. I think you're a good guy, Michael, and I know Joan meant a lot to you. Burt, though… well, you know, he and Joan were really close, so…."

"I'm sure she said plenty of unflattering things about me. I get that I'm the evil ex here, but Trevor shouldn't have to suffer because of that. It's going to be rough when he moves with us to the city. Which now I guess we're definitely doing if we're selling the house."

"Was staying here an option?"

"Not really. Simon wouldn't. His job is in New York. It was just a fleeting thought I had. It's really beautiful up here. I guess I hadn't really noticed before." Michael took a deep breath. "I don't blame you for being like this with me."

"Well, when you bring a man like Simon around, I guess it becomes clear why things didn't work out with you and Joan."

Michael laughed mirthlessly. "I came out at fourteen. Joan is the one and only woman I have ever been with. She was just... one in a million. I don't think I really appreciated how much I missed having her around until I heard she died. I hate that this has happened. Simon had started poking me about trying to get custody of Trevor, but only because he knew how much I love that kid. I wouldn't have gotten very far anyway, because Joan was a good mother and I know it." He shook his head. "I don't know if you can fully appreciate how much this situation just absolutely sucks. On the one hand, I'm overjoyed that I can take Trevor home with me. On the other hand, I'm completely unprepared and have no idea how to raise a boy. Simon and I are finally on the same page and starting to build a real relationship, but then here comes this monkey wrench. Simon doesn't want kids, and he's kind of got that look in his eye like Trevor makes him want to run screaming into the hills. And I just...." Michael looked out the window briefly, but then rubbed his eyes, trying to keep the tears at bay. "Maybe the worst part is that all of this is happening because Joan is gone, a fact I still do not believe. Trevor lost his mother and can't understand why she's gone and won't be coming back."

"I don't envy the position you're in."

"But, I get how it looks. Here comes Michael, Joan's flighty ex, with his brand-new boyfriend and no idea how to take care of a kid. I'll grant you that last part is true, but the main problem with me and Joan was probably always that I'm gay and had no business being with her to begin with. But I can't change any of that, and honestly? I wouldn't." Michael meant it. Which was to say, if he had it to do over, he might have made different choices, but if this was where his mistakes had led him, in a solid relationship with Simon and with Trevor in his life, he'd take it. "And as for Simon, well, he and I have known each other since we were Trevor's age, and if it weren't for him, I'd probably still be in Iowa and none of this would have happened, so there's that too."

"I didn't realize you and Simon had known each other that long."

"Yeah, well. Long story. Sorry to unload on you. I was getting frustrated."

Tony leaned forward and steepled his fingers. He gave Michael a long look. "I honestly hope all of this works out. For Trevor's sake, if nothing else. If it makes you feel better, I've got a copy of Trevor's birth certificate with you listed as his father, and Joan did specify in her paperwork that Trevor should go with you if anything happened to her. I think the threat of a custody suit is low."

"Thank you." There was that, at least. If Michael had to fight with Joan's absentee parents for custody of Trevor, he might lose his mind. "I'll talk to Simon. I'm pretty sure that I, or we, or someone will hire you to sort out Joan's affairs. It sounds like she trusted you, so I will too."

"Thank you."

They spent some time sorting through paper, and Michael had to sign a few forms. When they finished, both men stood and shook hands.

"I appreciate that you were such a good friend to Joan," said Michael.

"Yes." Tony sighed. "She really was special. I miss her already." Tony coughed, clearly trying to cover up a display of emotion. "Well, if we're done here, I'll see you out."

At the front door, Michael said, "Can I ask a weird question?"

"Sure."

"You and Burt. How long have you been together?"

"Oh, twenty years, give or take."

"Trevor said you got married last year."

"We did, yes. When same-sex marriage was legalized in New York, we decided we should. I mean, I'm a probate lawyer. I know how tangled this nonsense can get. The sad fact is that the legal benefits of marriage mostly come into play when something horrible happens to one half of the couple."

"Yeah. Okay." Michael took a moment to process that, thinking about Simon.

"I'll see you at the wake."

Michael walked back to Joan's house, feeling sad. He found Trevor sitting between Kelly and Simon on the couch, narrating the cartoon they were watching.

Simon looked up when Michael walked into the room. Then he immediately stood, walked over to Michael, and pulled him into a hug. Michael rested his head on Simon's shoulder and hugged him back.

"Thank you," Michael said.

"Was it that awful?"

"No, actually. But there's so much to do."

Simon pulled away and nodded. "One step at a time, okay?"

"Daddy, come watch cartoons."

And that seemed like the only thing Michael should do right then.

CHAPTER 15

THOUGH THEY brought Trevor to the wake, almost as soon as they were inside the funeral home, Michael said, "I don't think he should go in there with her. It would probably just confuse him."

"Open casket, then?" asked Simon.

"Yes, that's what Burt said. I can stay out here with Trevor."

"No. I will. You go say your good-byes. That's what you're here for, isn't it?"

"Yes, I suppose so." Michael gave Simon a peck on the lips. "Thanks."

Simon took Trevor's hand. "Besides, I have a secret weapon."

"What's that?"

When Trevor was looking away, Simon reached into his pocket and pulled out a red toy truck.

Simon was a goddamn genius. Michael smiled despite the overwhelming sadness that seemed to permeate every part of the funeral home.

"Looks like there's a couch over there we can sit on. You go. I'll be here when you're done."

Michael lingered at the entrance to the room where Joan was laid out. He watched as Simon settled Trevor on the couch. Trevor squirmed and fussed, but then Simon handed him the truck, and suddenly Trevor was grinning.

There were not words for how much Michael loved them both in that moment.

He turned and walked into the room.

It was a fairly modest gathering. Tony and Burt had beat Michael and his entourage. Kelly had taken her own car as well. There were a dozen or so people Michael didn't recognize who were also milling about. And the buttoned-up couple who looked to be in their sixties was probably Joan's parents.

Michael took a deep breath and walked forward.

Joan looked like herself, but she didn't. There was an odd plastic quality to her face. Probably that was the many pounds of makeup required to make someone who had just died of an aggressive cancer look like she was not so far gone from the living. She looked peaceful, in fact, and not sickly, though Michael knew better, and the subterfuge bothered him.

Looking down at her, he mentally tried to come up with some way to say good-bye. His thoughts were mixed up and overwhelming. *I'm sorry things didn't work out. A part of me will always love you. Thank you so much for Trevor. I wish you had told me you were sick. I wish our lives hadn't turned out quite this way.*

Michael didn't realize he was crying until he felt a tear slide down his cheek.

He wiped his eyes. Tony walked over and held out a box of tissues.

"I want to apologize if I was an asshole this afternoon. I know you cared about her. I'm sorry if I implied otherwise."

"It's all right," Michael said.

"Where's Trevor?"

"Sitting in the hall with Simon. I didn't think he should come in here. He seems to understand 'Mommy's gone,' and I think seeing her like this will confuse him."

"Children are resilient. He probably won't even remember any of this in a few years."

"Maybe so, but he'll still have to grow up without his mother." Michael took one of the proffered tissues and wiped his eyes. He turned back to Joan. "I swear to you, Joan, I will do everything in my power to make sure that boy grows up in a good home. Okay? I promise to love him. Even if things with me and Simon don't work out, I will be there for Trevor no matter what. I just... I don't...." The tears became overwhelming then. Michael put a hand on the side of the casket, but couldn't keep himself from crying. "I don't want you to worry. Maybe you are, thinking I can't be a good father, but I think maybe I can be. I think I can figure out how to do it."

He realized with some surprise that he meant it.

Overcome, he sat down in one of the many chairs in the room and tried to gather himself. After a few minutes, the woman he'd guessed was Joan's mother sat down next to him.

"Joan meant a lot to you," she said.

"Yes."

"I'm Leslie Richardson. Joan's mother."

Michael nodded and took a deep breath, hoping his voice would be calm enough for this. "Yes. I'm Michael Reeves."

The name didn't seem to register with Leslie. She smiled blandly. Michael wondered how anyone could sit there like that, making small talk when her dead daughter was mere feet away. If it had been Trevor in that coffin, Michael would be losing his shit. Hell, he kind of was anyway, and he and Joan hadn't even been friends for a long time.

So he clarified, "I'm Trevor's father."

That got her attention. "Oh," she said, scooting back a little. "Er, where is Trevor?"

"With my partner, in the hallway." "Partner" sounded so much more adult, more committed, than "boyfriend." So that would do for now.

He expected Leslie to say she wanted to go talk to Trevor, but instead she crossed her arms primly over her chest. "I hope you don't take this the wrong way, but I understand my daughter was a bit of a wild child. That still gave you no excuse to—"

Michael held up his hand. "You can't say anything I haven't already thought myself. I realize Joan's life probably didn't turn out the way you planned for it to, but she was a good woman, one of the best people I've ever known, and I still can't quite believe that she's gone, even though I see her right there. Maybe you should concentrate on that for a little while. We'll never get to talk to her on the phone again. We'll never hear her laugh or sing. Her son has to grow up without her.

That Joan and I had an affair, that Trevor is a part of this world, those things are not worth lecturing me over. Trevor will have a good home with me and Simon. That's what you need to know."

Her eyebrows shot up. "Simon?"

"That's my partner." Michael wanted to be a little pissy about it, to say, "He's my *lover*," but he didn't want to anger the Richardsons more than he probably already had. He did clarify, "My, er, romantic partner."

Leslie swallowed. "But you and Joan—"

"Yes, but it's a long story."

Thankfully, she moved on to other guests, chatting with people as they wandered in. Michael took another tissue from Tony and tried to say hello to the other visitors. When the hollow politeness started getting to him, he went to check on Trevor.

What he found made his chest heave. It was one of the most amazing, beautiful sights he could have imagined. Trevor was curled up asleep against Simon, still clutching his red truck in his tiny hands, and Simon had a protective hand on his side, stroking gently.

Simon looked up. "How was it?"

"Awful," Michael admitted.

Simon looked down at Trevor and then at the empty seat on his other side. He held out his arm. "You want in on this?"

"Yes."

Michael sat. Simon looked at him appraisingly. "You've been crying?"

"An important person in my life is gone."

Simon wiped at Michael's tears with his thumb. "I'm so sorry. I wish I had gone in there with you."

"It was more important for you to be out here with him. I needed to go in there and say good-bye."

Simon kissed Michael. It was sweet and a little watery and tasted salty from Michael's tears. Then Simon pulled away and put an arm around Michael. So Michael rested his head on Simon's shoulder, curling toward him the same way Trevor did. He put a hand Simon's chest, about where his heart was. "I love you," Michael said. "I love you so fucking much it hurts sometimes."

Simon kissed the top of his head. "I love *you* so fucking much that I'm still here even though I'm freaking out on the inside."

Michael laughed softly. "What the hell are we going to do?"

"What else can we do? Take things one day at a time."

THERE HAD been a point that evening when Simon seriously questioned whether all this was what he wanted. It had been just him and Trevor sitting on a couch in a funeral parlor, although Trevor kept trying to wander off. He wouldn't stay still for a very long stretch of time; he wiggled, he slid off the couch, he walked down the hall, he had to be taken to the bathroom, he complained about being thirsty. One of the funeral directors had offered him cookies, and he ate three of them before declaring he didn't like them. Simon hadn't known what to do, didn't know how far he could take any discipline, had no idea what he could say or do to get Trevor to behave. He felt awkward and useless through a lot of it as he tried in vain to get Trevor to sit down for more than thirty seconds. He was very close to losing his marbles when Trevor had at last sat on the floor and driven his little red truck around, making growly motor sounds and seemingly content for a good ten minutes. Then he was up and down and needed water and the whole thing repeated itself.

When at long last Trevor yawned and complained of being tired, Simon persuaded him to sit on the couch. That went well enough for a few minutes. Then Trevor asked for Daddy. When Simon said, "He'll be right back," Trevor threw a knock-down, drag-out tantrum for the ages that Simon was at a complete loss to stop. Not wanting to disrupt the wake, Simon picked up the wriggling mass of boy and carried him outside, walked him around the block, and then brought him back inside, where, like a perfect angel, he finally curled up and fell asleep against Simon.

It wasn't that he expected parenthood to be this perfect, easy, enlightening experience. In fact, this was exactly what he expected of parenthood, and it was kind of awful, and it was one reason he had never especially wanted to be a parent.

He supposed he had a choice to make: Michael and Trevor and the family he wasn't sure he wanted, or back to his life without Michael.

Frankly, both were daunting.

The thing was, he knew if he left Michael this time, that was it. There would be no sweet reunion six years down the line. They'd come too far and there was too much at stake. If Simon left this time, that would be the end of their relationship and their friendship for good.

And, shit, a life without Michael was not one Simon wanted. He loved Michael deeply. It wasn't with the sort of conviction Michael had had since they were sixteen; for Simon it had grown over time rather than come on suddenly. Michael had been his friend and sidekick for as long as he could remember.

Simon really had thought there was something wrong with him for a long time because he never felt what Michael did, never felt that certainty that the two of them belonged together. He liked Michael and he liked sex, and when the two intersected, that was even better, but it hadn't been love, not back in high school or college. It seemed, though, like each year there was a new layer stacked on his feelings, like a new flavor or texture added to a dish at an upscale restaurant. It seemed like it grew and changed and developed into something that wasn't just friendship or sex or even the mere combination, but something more.

So then, one morning when he was twenty-seven years old, he'd woken up and realized that he was in love with Michael.

That hadn't changed much during their years of separation. His love for Michael ebbed and flowed. It was a tangible longing for a while, and then an ache in his chest. He'd come back to New York with a certain sense of dread, knowing he'd changed and Michael had changed and they might not be right for each other anymore. Or, worse, that it was too late.

But it hadn't been too late. It had been just the right time. The stars shook, the planets aligned, and Simon and Michael had finally, *finally* come together the way Simon understood now they were always meant to. They'd needed the time and space to figure themselves out, to become real adults, but they finally had their happy ending.

And then Joan died.

So now Simon was in Joan's house, an old converted farmhouse surrounded by trees up in the mountains, about as far from the city as one could get.

Trevor was plainly exhausted and would not go up to his room despite Michael's repeated entreaties. Michael himself was barely holding it together, caught in a haze of worry, grief, and fatigue.

It wasn't fair for Simon to base his decision on whether to stay or go on the hard times. It was probably more instructive to think of this as a test. He couldn't imagine that things could get much more turbulent than they had over the last three days.

Yikes, he really was a fucking robot.

Michael gave up and let Trevor sit on a chair in the living room while he pulled out the sofa bed. Almost as soon as it was settled, Trevor climbed on it and said, "I'm sleeping here with you."

Michael shot Simon an exasperated look.

"Let me talk to you out in the hallway," Simon said.

"Okay. Trevor, stay here for now. Take your shoes off if you're going to put your feet on the bed."

Once in the hall, Simon said, "It's okay with me if he sleeps with us, but I didn't want to say anything in front of him if you want him to sleep in his room."

"Are you sure?"

"Well, I'm mildly worried about rolling over him in my sleep, but I think we'll all manage."

"This won't be, like, a regular thing. Extenuating circumstances. Plus the poor guy is exhausted."

"Yeah. As are you."

Michael frowned and rubbed his face. "It's been a tough day."

"Michael. Can I just... I want to say something."

Michael looked up, a bit of fear in his eyes. He was still frowning. "Okay."

"It's not bad, I promise."

Michael nodded and looked down.

"You probably know that I'm struggling with all of this."

"Are you sure this isn't bad? Because if you leave me, I don't know what I'll do." Michael's voice was strained.

"No, that's not what I was going to say. I want you to know that while I am struggling with all of this, I keep returning to the fact that I absolutely cannot imagine my life without you as a major part of it."

"Oh."

"For years, we threw around 'I love you' like it was nothing, but I've come to realize how important those words are. What they really mean. And it's not lightly that I say that I love you more than any single other person on the planet and probably always will. If we're not together, part of my soul is missing. So if all this, if the good times and the bad times and Trevor and thirty years of memories are all a part of being with you, then I want all of it. I want *you*, Michael. And if I've learned anything this week, it's that we're not kidding around anymore. This is as real as it gets, right?"

"That's for sure." Michael took a deep breath. He reached over and put a hand on Simon's shoulder. "I, um. Well. You know how I feel. I don't know how to follow up a speech like that."

"We're not trying to one-up each other."

Michael smiled. "I know." He took Simon's hand. "My family has never been totally supportive. You know that, right?"

Simon wasn't sure where this was going, but he nodded.

Michael stepped back and leaned against the wall. "When you first told me you wanted to move to New York, I was a little nervous about moving away from home, but I would have followed you anywhere. My mother was livid I wanted to move so far. But, see, I was out of control, or so they told me. They wanted me close to home so that they could keep a tight leash on me. And I thought, hell, Simon wants to move to New York? Let's do it. Get me out of here. They never kicked me out or said anything overtly terrible to me, and they certainly *tried*, but I always thought that my biological family didn't quite get me. But you, Simon, you always got me. I had this vision in my head of us moving to New York and, I don't know, teaming up, creating our own family. We'd be this little unit and it didn't matter if no one else understood us, because we understood each other." Michael let out a breath. "Ha, look at me speechifying."

"It's a good speech. Keep going."

"Not much else to say. Only want to add that there was a time when it felt like we weren't quite getting each other anymore. I'm glad that's over. And, well, the little guy in there?" Michael gestured toward the living room with his head. "I don't think I knew how much I wanted him in my life until Joan moved up here with him. I should have made more of a point to see him before she died. And it kills me—I am well and truly gutted—that this is what had to happen to make me see that. But I think it's an opportunity. I can have the family I always wanted, the one who understands and accepts me for who and what I am, not for what they want me to be. And you are the key to that."

Simon reached over. He couldn't keep his hands off Michael for much longer. At first he merely touched Michael's shoulders, flicked away invisible dust, caressed, but then he pulled Michael into a tight hug. Michael hugged him back and sighed.

Then they kissed. They hadn't been alone together in days, and it had felt like they were holding each other at arm's length, exchanging cheap tokens of affection, but this was the real deal, a no-holds-barred kiss, the sort one remembered years in the future when recalling his greatest memories. It was soft and slick and hot enough to set them both on fire. Michael parted his lips and shoved his fingers into Simon's hair. Simon opened his mouth and tangled his tongue with Michael's and grabbed his ass to pull him closer. The kiss went on and on, accelerating and growing, and it was like everything was there at the meeting of their lips, every emotion and scar, every past transgression, all of it.

"I love you so fucking much," Simon said before he plunged back in for more.

"God, me too. I love you too. Always, Simon. Always."

Who knew how long they stood there kissing? Simon certainly didn't, though when he heard a crash in the kitchen, he was conscious suddenly that they weren't alone. He pulled away, though he kept his hands on Michael's waist.

"I'd make love to you right now," Michael said, "but Kelly's still fussing around in the kitchen, not to mention…." Michael leaned back and looked into the living room. "There seems to be a four-year-old asleep in our bed."

Simon took Michael's hand and walked with him into the living room. "Yeah, that's a problem."

Trevor was curled in a little ball right smack in the middle of the bed. He'd taken his shoes off, at least, but he was still wearing the white shirt, black pants, and little bow tie he'd worn to the wake. Michael chuckled softly and moved to the bed. Trevor gave a halfhearted groan when Michael started pulling off the bow tie and the shirt. Simon was reluctant to leave the room, but he took Trevor's nice clothes and then went upstairs to fetch clean pajamas.

They wrestled Trevor's dead weight into pajamas. Then Kelly bid them good night. By the time Simon and Michael had changed, Trevor had resumed his spot in the middle of the bed.

"He's kind of cute when he's sleeping," Simon said.

Michael laughed. "Yeah, well. He takes up a lot of space for someone so small."

They both got into bed and managed to maneuver Trevor between them so everyone seemed comfortable. Trevor sighed in his sleep and curled up against Michael.

Simon figured this lack of comfort was probably one of many sacrifices he'd have to make. He reached over and ran a hand down Michael's arm. Michael smiled back and grabbed his hand. He threaded his fingers with Simon's. And, cheesy though it was, there was something powerful about looking into each other's eyes for a long moment. Simon felt like they conveyed everything they needed to each other.

And he realized he'd made his decision.

He fell asleep that night with his hands and feet tangled with Michael's and Trevor's little butt pressed against his stomach and thought that maybe he could be happy as a part of this family.

CHAPTER 16

1995

THE SUMMER they were fifteen, Simon and Michael spent most afternoons at a public pool in Iowa City. Later, Michael wouldn't be able to remember which day it was, if it was July or August or what, since it was one of those lazy summers in which neither boy had anything in particular to do besides hang out and get sunburned, and all of the days blended together. But Michael did remember the moment when Simon peeled off his T-shirt near the edge of the pool and tossed it at a beach chair casually, as if this were just any day and not the day Michael's whole life changed.

Simon was too skinny, but somehow he'd developed a bit of muscle definition in his chest and arms. His perfect blond hair was tousled for a change, his shirt having upset the natural order of things as he'd pulled it over his head. Michael noticed these things, and he noticed that Simon had really pretty lips, that he had sparse hair on his chest and below his belly button. Michael noticed the bulge at the front of Simon's swim trunks and his long legs and his nicely manicured toes.

Michael wanted him.

Simon stepped to the edge of the pool, and there was an intense, furrowed-brow expression on his face. Michael imagined he was calculating if the water was deep enough for him to dive instead of just cannonballing into the pool, which was typically Michael's approach.

Or Simon was worrying about the density of kids in the pool and whether he could jump in from the edge without hitting anyone.

Meanwhile, Michael had broken out in a cold sweat everywhere as he realized that his best friend was, well, really hot.

Simon pressed his palms together and moved them above his head as if he were about to dive. Then he turned toward Michael. "What?"

"What?"

"Why are you staring at me?"

"I'm not."

"Quit it."

Simon turned back to the pool and executed a flawless, elegant dive into the water. He stayed under for thirty seconds before resurfacing near the edge of the water where Michael was standing.

Michael fell in love right then.

He sat on the edge of the pool and stuck his feet in the water.

"Are you not getting in?" Simon asked.

"Adjusting."

Simon balked. "Dude, wrong approach. The water is cold today. Better to just jump in."

Michael lifted himself up on his hands and then slid into the pool. He went under, opened his eyes, and looked at Simon's body, relaxed under the water. He reached over and pinched Simon's butt. Simon jerked away immediately.

When Michael surfaced, Simon was right there. "You're a jerk," he said.

Michael laughed. "You're a prude."

Simon let out a long-suffering sigh.

That only made Michael laugh harder. He could imagine a thousand afternoons just like this, the two of them teasing each other, spending time together, maybe even loving each other.

Simon ducked under the water again. He pinched Michael's butt. Michael jerked away, but only because the gesture made a shiver go up his spine, and he didn't want Simon to know about that. Not yet.

Simon surfaced, laughing. "How's it feel?"

"Oh, baby."

Simon shook his head. "That's gross." He splashed water at Michael.

Yes, a thousand afternoons. Just like this.

"Chase me," Simon said. Then he dove under the water.

Michael went after him.

2006

SIMON KNEW he had no business being out at 2:00 a.m., but here he was anyway, standing on Avenue A and watching the roving bands of other revelers walking around as some of the bars closed.

Michael walked up to him and said, "I'm hungry."

"I think Katz's is still open."

"Oh, my God. I would kill for a pastrami sandwich from there. Let's go."

"We have to wait for everyone else."

Michael waved at the bar they'd just walked out of dismissively. "We're the only ones who matter," he said.

"That may be true," Simon said, smiling despite himself, "but it's still rude to just leave."

"Fine. Have it your way."

How had they even gotten here? Oh, right, Michael's latest conquest worked as a publicist for some company that made novelty alcoholic beverages and had gotten them and a bunch of their friends tickets to a party at this gay bar in the East Village. The publicist had gotten ditched at some point in the night, probably around the third round of cocktails with cake-flavored vodka, which just tasted like vodka with a lot of artificial sweetener added.

The streetlights spun for a moment, and Simon realized he was a little drunker than he'd previously thought. He reached for the nearest solid object to stabilize himself against. That turned out to be a mailbox.

Michael stared at him. "Dude."

"I may have had too many."

"Aw, Simon's drunk!"

"Only a little."

"You never get drunk." Michael laughed. "Well, you'll be better soon enough. One of those sandwiches at Katz's will certainly absorb all of the alcohol in your stomach."

Simon's stomach growled as if in answer. Yeah, he could go for one of those gigantic, meaty sandwiches just then.

The rest of their friends stumbled out then. They congregated on the sidewalk, chatting for a moment before Michael announced the sojourn to Katz's. Everyone begged off and went to hail cabs or walk to the subway, leaving Michael and Simon alone again. Michael led the way toward Houston Street and Simon chased after him, laughing the whole way because suddenly everything was funny.

They stopped to wait for the light to change, and Simon needed something to lean against again. This time, he reached for Michael, putting his hands on Michael's shoulders. Up close, Michael was just so... beautiful. His dark hair was mussed and sticking out every which way. His lips looked red and, well, kissable.

Michael narrowed his eyes at Simon. "You're freaking me out."

Simon said, "Sorry," but he didn't move. Suddenly, he wanted to kiss Michael. That wasn't unprecedented, but he hadn't felt that urge in some time. They'd been pretty solidly in the friend zone for years now.

Hadn't they?

Michael was beautiful and close and he smelled so good, like sweet cocktails and sour sweat. Simon tugged on a lock of his hair and was not surprised to find it damp. The night was hot, it had been hot in that bar, and they'd danced a hell of a lot. Simon didn't even like dancing, but Michael made everything fun, so he'd danced.

Michael made everything *better*.

Something startling occurred to Simon just then.

"This may be the cheap vodka talking," Simon said, "but I love you."

Michael sighed and peeled Simon's hands off his shoulders. "Definitely the vodka talking. But I love you too."

Simon knew by Michael's dismissive tone that Michael just meant it in the token way they always said it to each other, or else he probably meant it in a brotherly way, but Simon was serious. He *loved* Michael all the way. Michael was the most important person in his life, the sexiest, the best.

But he couldn't make his mouth form the words to explain that, so instead he followed Michael across the street.

Present Day

NOT THAT funerals were ever good, but in Michael's estimation, Joan's might have been the worst ever.

The first problem was that hardly anyone came. Michael found himself wondering if there were really so few people who recognized what the world had just lost. A handful of Joan's old friends from the city had driven up and said hello to Michael, but he realized they were all essentially strangers. These people mourned the Joan they'd known five years ago, not the reclusive, quiet Joan she'd become once, unbeknownst to everyone, she started feeling ill.

Tony had found a minister in town who was willing to do the ceremony, but only if it was at the funeral home and not in a proper church. Michael didn't much mind it, but apparently this caused a fairly bitter argument with the Richardsons, who weren't so pleased a couple of gay men were handling their daughter's funeral. Mr. Richardson, in fact, shouted at Burt, within earshot of everyone, that of course a godless heathen faggot would create this mockery of a memorial. The minister almost walked out right then, but Simon, of all people, talked him back inside.

The funeral home, at least, had closed the casket at Michael's request. But then he had to explain to Leslie why he'd made the request to begin with: primarily so as not to confuse Trevor.

And Trevor was something of a loose cannon. Simon volunteered to watch him while Michael took care of things, but poor Trevor's mood swung wildly from perfectly fine one moment to screaming inconsolably the next. Michael didn't think Trevor understood what was happening, but he definitely sensed that something strange was going on. When he had the worst tantrum of all in the middle of the service, Simon carried him out.

When it was over and the processional was to start toward the cemetery, Michael found Simon and Trevor sitting on the steps in front of the funeral home. Trevor had calmed down and was listening intently to whatever Simon was saying, but he still had red eyes and a wobbly lower lip, sure signs he could lose it again at any moment.

"All these people came to say good-bye to your mommy," Simon was explaining. "They all miss her, just like you do."

"Is she here?" Trevor asked.

"No."

"Because she's in heaven and she's not sick anymore."

"Right."

"Hey, Trevor?" Michael asked.

Trevor looked up. "Hi, Daddy."

"Come here, kid."

Michael knelt on the stairs and opened his arms. Without even asking what was needed, Trevor came over and gave Michael a hug. Michael held him until he started squirming.

"Thank you," Michael said. "I needed that."

"Daddy, can we go? I'm hungry."

"We can go, but there's one more thing to do. After that, we'll have lunch at Tony and Burt's house."

Michael found the pace of the funeral procession to be unnervingly slow. Simon sat beside him in the passenger seat of the rental car, perfectly quiet and still, which was also unnerving.

"Daddy?" came a tiny voice from the backseat.

"What is it, Trevor?"

"If Mommy is gone, what will happen? Am I going to live in the house by myself?"

"No, you're going to come live with me and Simon."

"Can Kelly come too?"

Simon had finally broached that topic at breakfast that morning, offering to put her up either with them or at a hotel temporarily, and then helping her either stay at Michael's old apartment or find her own place. Kelly seemed reluctant to leave her little town, explaining that all of her family was still up here in the area, but she agreed to come on a temporary basis to see how it went. Michael was kind of hoping she'd fall in love with the city so that he wouldn't have to find another babysitter or put Trevor in day care, but that was a bridge they'd cross when they came to it.

"Yes, Kelly is coming too. At least for a little while."

Trevor kicked his feet against his seat a couple of times, but was otherwise quiet the rest of the ride to the cemetery.

The ceremony was mercifully short. Tony got Michael a chair, so he sat with a sleepy Trevor in his lap through most of it. Trevor kept tugging at the lapels of Michael's suit jacket, but he otherwise gave no indication that he knew what was going on. By the time the ceremony ended, Trevor had fallen asleep.

Simon hoisted Trevor up so Michael could stand. Trevor mumbled something and then curled against Simon, shoved his thumb in his mouth, and fell back to sleep. Michael patted Trevor's head. He was feeling drained himself and could have used a nap, but there were still a couple of hours of being sociable to get through.

The Richardsons approached then.

"This must be Trevor," Leslie whispered.

Michael nodded. When Simon shot him a quizzical look, he said, "These are Joan's parents. Ah, Mr. and Mrs. Richardson, this is Simon."

"Hello," said Simon.

Michael panicked that he hadn't properly briefed Simon on this situation. He stalled, fretting about what to do for a moment, and then put a hand on Simon's back. "Simon is my...."

"Fiancé," Simon said.

Michael almost passed out right there.

He managed to hold it together, though, and looked at the Richardsons expectantly.

"Oh," Leslie said. Her husband looked on, a blandly uninterested expression on his face. Michael was starting to see why Joan had never gotten along with these people. "And you will be raising Trevor."

"Together. Yes," Michael said, still barely able to form words. He took a deep breath. "He'll have two parents who love him, okay? I know this situation is not ideal. I miss the hell out of Joan, and I wish that Trevor could grow up with his mother. But given the circumstances, this is the best we can do. He'll be with me, his father, and Simon is a good man too. We can provide a good home where he'll never want for anything."

That came out sounding reasonably confident, but inside, Michael's head was spinning. He still wasn't even completely sure Simon was sticking around, or that between the two of them they'd always have the resources to take care of Trevor well, or even if they'd make good parents—probably not, actually—but Michael's desire to raise Trevor was a palpable thing, and he was not about to let these people who hadn't even met him before this moment take Trevor away.

Leslie smiled sadly. "She didn't even tell us about him until after he was born. I would have come to the hospital."

"I was there," Michael said. "She... she got through it. And she loved Trevor so much from the moment he was born. She was a great mother."

"I wish she'd let me see that."

She looked so sad, this woman. Joan had never talked much about her parents, only ever said that they didn't get along, so Michael didn't really know what the deal was here. Leslie seemed nice if a little narrow-minded. "I know you have some misgivings about him being raised by two men, but I promise, we will take good care of him. And if you're ever in New York...." Michael reached into his pocket, withdrew his wallet, and found a business card. "If you're ever in New York, my cell phone is on there. You can call me and come visit."

Had he really just done that? Was he inviting more anguish by allowing this to happen?

Leslie nodded and put the card in her purse. "Thank you. I appreciate that. I'd like to visit sometime."

Trevor started to fuss. Simon jostled him a little, rocked him to get him to calm down. Michael was pretty impressed by the parental instincts of a man who claimed to know nothing about children. He smiled at them.

Simon smiled back briefly and then said, "I think we should probably...." He tilted his head toward where the car was parked.

"Oh, yes," Leslie said. "Don't let me keep you."

"Will we see you at the lunch thing?" Michael asked.

"Maybe," she said in a way that basically screamed, "We don't approve of two men shacking up in a house so we probably won't." Just as well, Michael reasoned.

They made their farewells and then Michael walked with Simon and Trevor back to the car. They arrived together and exchanged a look over the top of the car before Simon ducked to put Trevor in his car seat.

Once Simon had Trevor all buckled in and propped up with Bunny in the backseat, Michael grabbed him before he could get back in the car.

"Did you say 'fiancé'?" Michael asked.

"I suppose I should have asked first," Simon said with a little bit of a smirk, "but I decided sometime last night that I want to stay and make a family with you, so we might as well make it official. I mean, you want to marry me, right?"

As if that were even a question. "More than anything."

"Good. We're engaged."

The word *engaged* made Michael's heart flutter. "You suck at proposing, by the way. That was really terrible. And at a funeral?"

"Well, I've never done it before. I haven't had much practice. Plus, that whole bended-knee thing is such a cliché."

Michael laughed and walked around the car to get in. Simon slid into the passenger seat.

"Simon?" Michael asked when they had settled into their seats.

"Hmm?"

"I love you. Don't ever change."

Simon laughed. "I love you too. You could kiss me, you know. Make it more formal."

Michael smiled and then leaned across the car and did just that.

EPILOGUE

One year later

SIMON FELT a certain measure of dismay at the smattering of brochures on the coffee table before him. "I would move to the Catskills just to avoid this nonsense," he told Michael.

Michael picked one up and frowned at it. "This school is only three blocks away. And, look, there's a photo of a kid with two dads."

"I think the one on the left goes to my gym."

"Daddy?" Trevor said, wandering out of his bedroom with a book in his hands. "Can we read this?"

"See that?" Simon said. "He likes books. Maybe he's a shoo-in for this place after all."

Michael shot Simon a dirty look and then patted the space on the couch beside him. Trevor climbed up and handed Michael the book. It was one from the box of things Michael's parents had recently sent— books and toys and a couple of cute outfits. Michael's mother had written a long letter explaining how delighted they were that Michael had finally settled down and was taking responsibility—Michael had read that bit aloud to Simon and rolled his eyes a lot, which made Simon laugh—but Michael said he appreciated the sentiment. At the time, Michael supposed aloud that if his marriage was good enough for the US government, it was good enough for his parents.

The book had a big red truck on the cover and seemed to be about different kinds of vehicles. Trevor held the book and could read most of the words, but he liked to read aloud and then point to pages and say, "Now you read this one, Daddy."

"This book doesn't have much of a plot," Simon commented.

"Hush, peanut gallery. Figure out where my genius son will be attending kindergarten."

"This one has an entrance exam." Simon wondered what on earth the school could even put on an entrance exam for kindergarten.

"We're going to become the crazy parents we make fun of, aren't we?" Michael asked.

"Daddy! Pay attention!"

"Okay, okay."

Simon chuckled as he looked at the brochure. He was starting to really like the local private school as a good place for Trevor. Certainly Michael would do well with Trevor in school at least a few hours a day.

Michael had decided to try his hand at freelancing while staying home with Trevor, which was going pretty well so far. Kelly had tried, taking care of Trevor for three whole months before homesickness and the stress of the city weighed her down too much. She had apologized profusely before handing over the keys to Michael's old apartment and moving back upstate. So Michael decided to quit his day job. He'd told Simon that this was a good opportunity to get to know his son, since he'd missed the years Trevor had lived upstate with Joan. Really, he seemed happy to work from home.

Well, work was sporadic and Simon had to help Michael stay on target sometimes, but Michael was happy with his contributions to their finances. Really, Simon had been saving for so long that he could lose his job tomorrow and still have enough money to support them all for a while, even with the big move from Michael's cramped one-bedroom in the Village to the spacious three-bedroom in Chelsea, but Michael's pride made him contribute *something*, so Simon was happy to let him.

Of course, the fact that Trevor was not yet in school put him at something at a disadvantage in the strange, competitive world of private New York City kindergartens. Most of his competition had gone to fancy preschools and were taking music lessons and whatever else. Trevor had instead spent part of the last year living in the Catskills before a shaky six-month transition to city life. Public school was an option, of course, but all of the advice they'd gotten from the other neighborhood parents indicated private school was the way to go.

Simon really was going to be one of *those* parents, wasn't he? The job in finance, the fancy apartment in Chelsea, the son in private school. And Trevor was almost legally Simon's son; the adoption paperwork wasn't quite final, but Simon's lawyer thought it was just a matter of time. It was a little weird to have a son, but Simon was enjoying parenthood for the most part, and that poor kid was starting to look more and more like Michael as he aged.

"Simon! Now you read a page."

Simon gamely leaned over Michael to read a page about fire trucks, and Trevor squealed with laugher when Michael reached over and tickled him. Trevor climbed over Michael's lap and situated himself between his two dads and opened the book again. He read a couple of pages aloud, demanding their complete attention.

The phone rang, so Michael got up to answer it. Trevor pressed himself against Simon and continued reading in his slow, deliberate, five-year-old way.

"Hi, Mom," Michael said. He wandered into the kitchen.

"Simon?" Trevor asked when the book was finished.

"What, Trevor?"

"Were you and Daddy talking about school again?"

"Yup. You'll like school. There will be more books to read and lots of other kids your age."

"Like Joey and Maura at the playground?"

"Yup, just like them."

Michael had befriended a few of the moms and another dad who brought their kids to the playground on the next block during the day. Trevor was making friends, which was a fun thing to watch; he'd had playdates and birthday parties occasionally while living with Joan, but there weren't many other kids up in Joan's town in the Catskills.

Trevor settled against Simon, who reflected that he'd grown more confident at this parenting stuff as time went on. He still sometimes had moments when he had no clue what to do, but usually Michael was around and they figured it out together. Trevor seemed happy, which was the important thing.

Trevor started flipping through the book. Sometimes he'd explain something to Simon about one of the pictures, but mostly he looked quietly. He was a smart, verbal kid, and Simon hoped that meant he'd get into one of these schools. After all, Michael kept insisting that if Trevor wanted to get into one of the city's elite high schools, he needed a solid, private-school education. So, yes, they were *those* parents. Simon laughed to himself.

"What's funny?" Trevor asked.

"I was thinking about being a daddy."

"You're Daddy's husband, so that makes you my daddy too."

"Yup."

"That's good."

"Why is that good?" Simon asked.

Trevor shrugged. "I love you."

Simon smiled and smoothed down Trevor's wild hair. "I love you too, kid."

"Do you think I will have a husband someday?" Trevor asked.

"Sure. Or a wife. Whichever you want."

"I'll have a house with only boys. We'll drive a red truck. And get a dog." Trevor hopped in his seat. "Can we get a dog?"

Simon laughed. "Where would we put a dog?"

"He can live with us," Trevor said as if this were obvious. "He could sleep in my room. Then I would take him to the dog park and he could play with other dogs."

Michael walked back in the room looking a little exasperated, which was often the case after he talked to his mother.

"Daddy, we're getting a dog!" Trevor said.

Simon shook his head vehemently, trying to convey that he had not approved of this plan.

"We don't have space for a dog," said Michael.

"We could get a little dog! Joey's mom has a little dog."

Michael frowned. "They have a corgi," Michael said to Simon. "I'll think about it, okay?"

"Okay." That seemed to satisfy Trevor, although usually when Michael said "I'll think about it," what he meant was "I'll put off making a decision until you've forgotten about this."

"My mother wants to send Trevor another box of stuff," Michael said. "I told her he had plenty of stuff, so now instead she's threatening to visit."

Despite many years of hand wringing over Michael's lifestyle, Michael's mother had turned around once Michael had announced the pending wedding. His parents had flown out for it, in fact, even though Michael and Simon had gone to City Hall, nothing elaborate. There hadn't even been a party. When Michael said, "I thought you weren't so keen on my marrying a man," she had merely pinched his cheeks and said, "It's not a man. It's Simon." Simon wasn't sure if he should be offended by that or not. Either way, Michael's mother doted on her grandson, and Trevor enjoyed being doted on, so now she was going about spoiling him in the manner only a grandmother could, despite living halfway across the country.

"We've become rather domestic, haven't we?" Simon asked Michael.

"I'm afraid so. I mean, we can get a sitter and go out tomorrow night. Find a gay bar, get a little silly."

"Nah. This is all I need."

Michael smiled and leaned over to give Simon a quick kiss. "Yeah. This right here is all I ever wanted."

KATE McMURRAY is an award-winning romance author and fan. When she's not writing, she works as a nonfiction editor, dabbles in various crafts, and is maybe a tiny bit obsessed with baseball. She is active in RWA and has served as president of Rainbow Romance Writers and on the board of RWANYC. She lives in Brooklyn, NY.

Website: http://www.katemcmurray.com

Twitter: http://www.twitter.com/katemcmwriter

Facebook: https://www.facebook.com/katemcmurraywriter

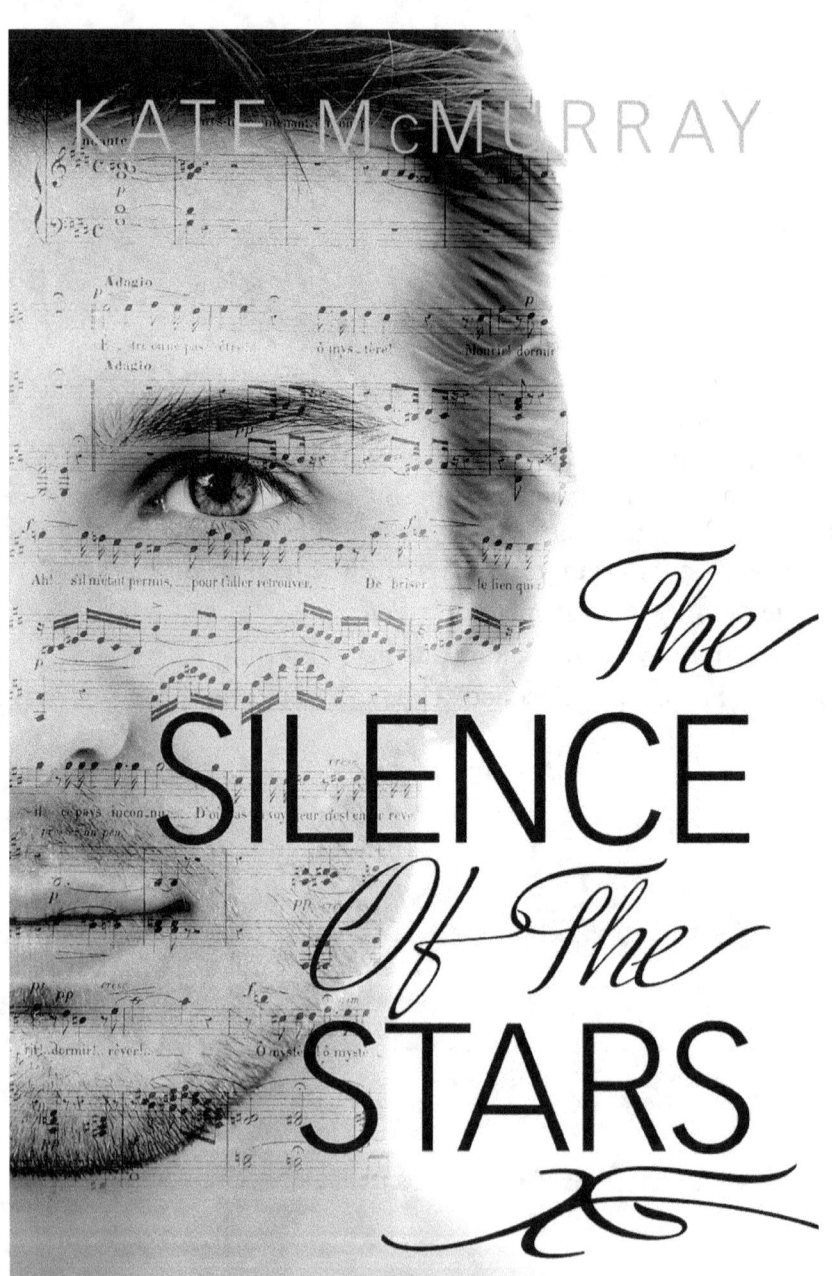

KATE McMURRAY

The SILENCE Of The STARS

KATE McMURRAY

The
STARS
That
TREMBLE

http://www.dreamspinnerpress.com

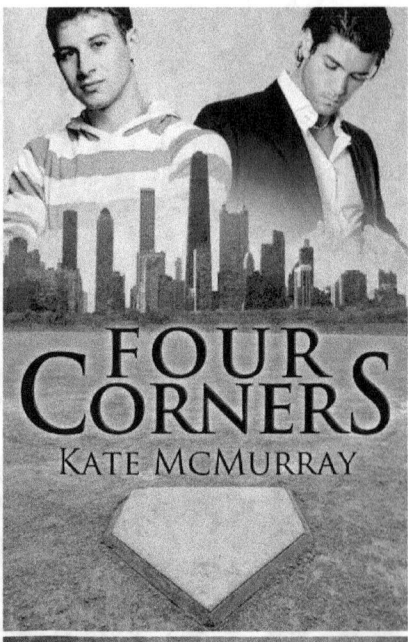
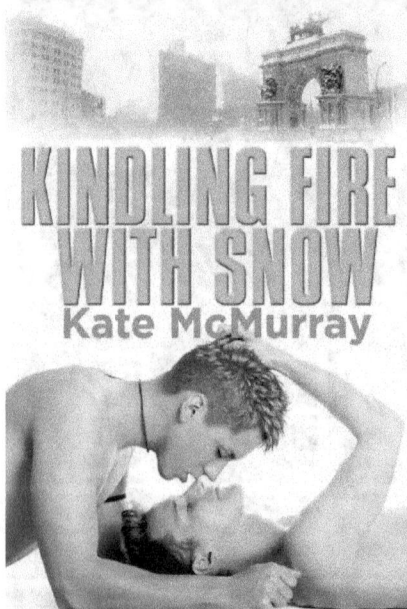
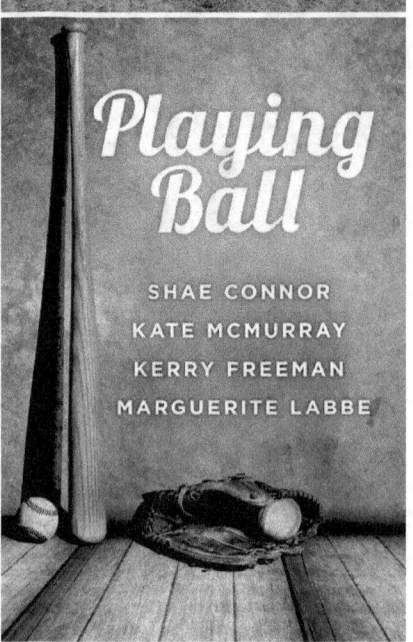

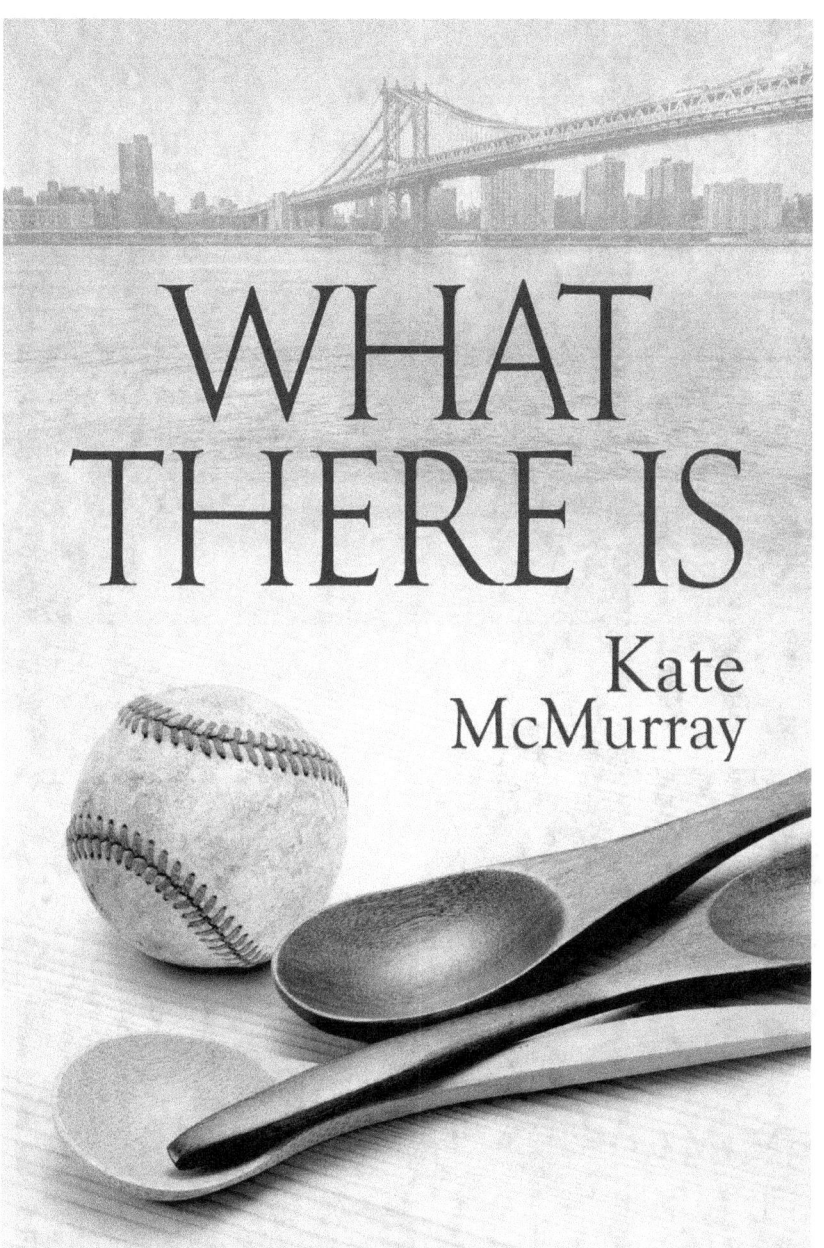

WHAT THERE IS

Kate McMurray

http://www.dreamspinnerpress.com

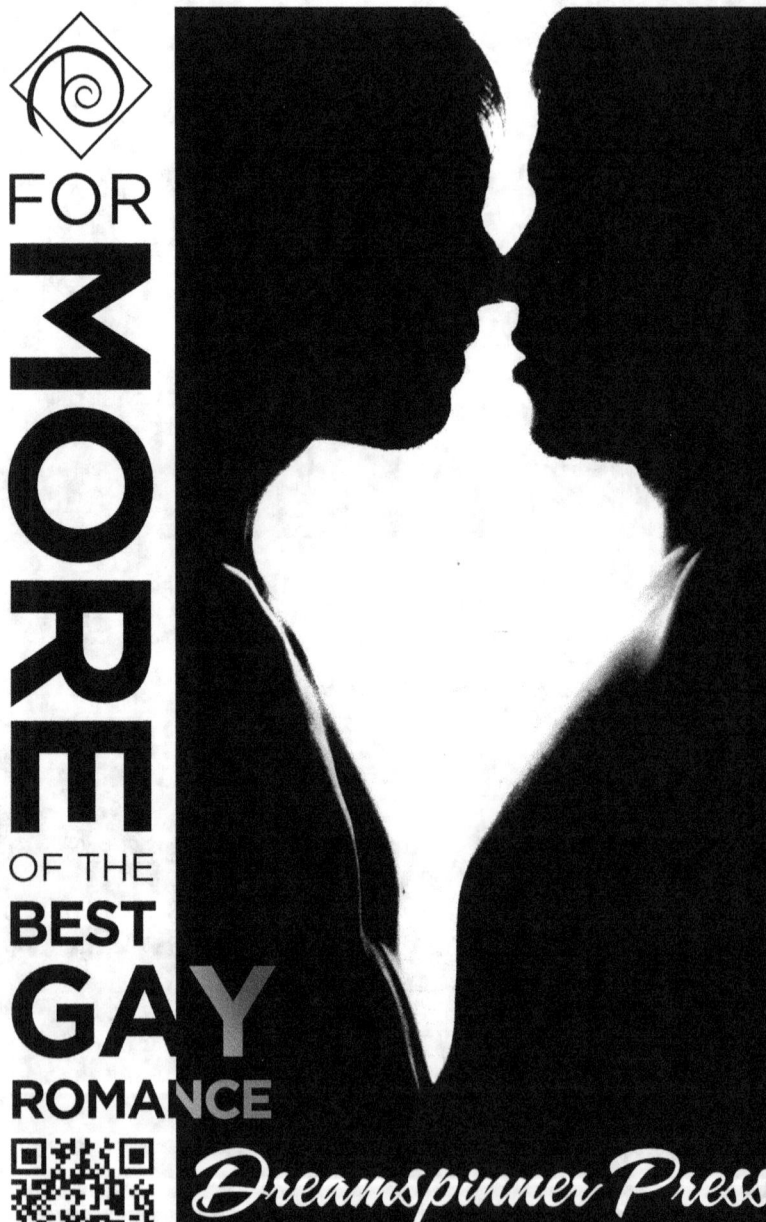

www.ingramcontent.com/pod-product-compliance
Lightning Source LLC
Chambersburg PA
CBHW070115260626
47160CB00004B/1474